A Demon in My Bed

Sarah Winters

First Publication: February 2017

Published by Sarah Warren
Cover design by Marie Wohl of Riverlife Design
Cover image from RomanceNovelCovers.com
Edited by Erin Doucette

Sarah Warren
465 University Avenue, PO Box 21021
Charlottetown, PEI, Canada C1A 9H6

www.SarahWinters.ca

DEDICATION

To Sonic the Sheepdog,
You were the best writer dog I could have ever asked for.
Through thick and thin, as long as there was cheese.
I miss you.

ACKNOWLEDGMENTS

There may only be one person sitting at the keyboard when a story is being written, but it truly does take a team to bring a manuscript from the first draft into a finished book.

Firstly, I have to thank my three biggest supporters. Erin got the task of playing editor to my wandering thoughts. Thank you for always telling me the truth, minus the sugar coating, and fielding my awkward questions at all hours of the day. Jess, my mother and beta reader, got the first edition of this tale and has been begging for the next book ever since. Thank you for the endless encouragement and for not minding when I've been buried in writing and forgotten to do the dishes yet again. Ron has been a patron of my writing since first reading my work and his stellar support has been a highly appreciated haven during this process.

A huge thank you to the awesome folks at the Latin Discussion forum for helping me get the summoning spell just right. I appreciate them not letting me look like a bumbling idiot.

Finally, I'd like to thank you the reader for taking a chance on this book. The writing of which has been a surprising journey for me and I hope its path was enjoyable for you as well.

CHAPTER 1

Verrin growled low in his throat as he paced the cell's cramped confines. His bare feet scuffed quietly over the dirt floor as his continued steps slowly wore a visible track in the already packed earth. He dragged his hands through his dark hair again in frustration until he was positive it's short length was sticking up in all directions like a fluffy porcupine.

I'm never going to live this down. Once his siblings found out about the mess he'd gotten himself into, he'd be eating crow for years to come. Hell, once his eldest brother heard, he was going to be in a world of hurt! Dantalion was always chiding his younger siblings to keep their guard up and listen to their instincts. It wouldn't take Dan long to point out how he'd walked straight into his current predicament.

With a frustrated curse, he threw himself against the cell wall, wrapping his fists around the cold metal and shaking it with all his might. The iron bars groaned in their moorings but didn't budge. Disgusted, he dropped his

1

head forward to rest against a crossbar and tried to sort through the haze of the last 24 hours.

Two days ago Merihem had called to inquire if he'd heard from their youngest sibling, Seir, recently. While it wasn't unusual for one of the brothers to lose themselves in a woman for days on end, they would always surface periodically to stay connected. Realizing no one had heard from Seir for almost a week was reason enough to cause them all a little worry.

"I'll go see him," Verrin assured Merihem over the phone. He'd been sprawled on one of the black leather sofas in his New York penthouse at the time, watching the Wednesday evening news while halfheartedly perusing a dirty magazine. The magazine, one of three titles his pain in the ass brother Pithius had subscribed him to as a Christmas gift, was full of bleached blonde women who couldn't lay on their backs without fear of mammary assisted suicide. Not really his cup of tea. "It's been a while since I've stopped by the villa."

"I will finish up here and accompany you." Merihem had offered distractedly.

"Meri?" Verrin asked, smirking at his brother's absentminded tone as he no doubt worked on whatever groundbreaking experiment had caught his attention this time. It was a miracle Merihem had pulled himself away long enough to even call. "What are you working on?"

"Oh!" Merihem got immediately more interested in the conversation, obviously thrilled anyone would want to know more about the work he dabbled with. "I recently acquired some fascinating strains of *Vibrio cholerae* and have been testing it to see if I can..."

At this point Verrin tuned his brother out. Merihem

was locked up in that grand London house of his playing with cholera. How very disturbing. Not wanting to risk his as yet undefeated immortal immune system on some warped form of bacteria his brother cooked up, he begged off Merihem's assistance. "You just stay there. I'll go by myself and call you when I find him."

"Are you sure?" Merihem asked. "I can put this aside for now."

"Yes, I'm sure. You just play with your cholera. I can manage on my own."

"All right, but do call if you need assistance."

He had just rolled his eyes, ended the call and went to pack a bag for his trip. He'd catch an early flight and be relaxing beside Seir's pool by tomorrow evening.

Verrin spent the flight to Italy enjoying the non-explosive nature of his cholera-free bowel and relishing the little indulgences that the lovely stewardesses heaped upon him. Between the flight staff and the passengers, he'd received more than one offer to join the mile high club he'd had to decline. Having squeezed his big body into one of those tiny bathrooms once before, he'd learned his lesson. The cramped quarters were not only hard to navigate for two people, but when you finally emerged the rest of the plane assumed you'd just experienced a scene from the Exorcist.

After the uneventful nine hour flight and a three hour train ride into Ravenna, he'd been happy to get into a car and drive himself the rest of the way to Seir's villa overlooking the Adriatic Sea.

The grand white facade stood out amongst the colorful flower beds that surrounded the entryway and he breathed their scent in deep as he got out of the tiny rental car. The late afternoon air was warm and sunny when he mounted the small stone semicircle that made up the villa's entrance to use the door's brass knocker.

An inkling of worry started to unfurl in his stomach as he stood there, the minutes growing long as he'd waited for the door to open. No one answered. He'd knocked again politely before banging with the side of his fist. Silence. He'd sunk into full out dread when he'd tried the handle and found it unlocked. Inside, the normally raucous household had been eerily silent. No one, not his brother nor one of the well paid servants, answered to any of his calls. Even Seir's so-called harem of adopted human sisters had been suspiciously absent.

Perhaps they're on vacation, he'd speculated hopefully as he'd walked through the uninhabited halls. It was a rare occurrence, but not unheard of for Seir to take his harem and go visit one of the other homes he owned around the world. Although Seir wouldn't have left the house unlocked and completely vacant had that been the case. There was always staff left behind to tend the place in their absence.

Nothing about this feels right.

Verrin had explored the large house, looking through doorways at the unoccupied rooms they guarded, with worry curdling in his stomach. Everything was as it should be, closets full of clothes, electronics untouched, food still in the fridge. Even the flowers gracing the dining room table were still in full bloom.

It wasn't until he had exited into the backyard and followed the garden path to the hidden oasis that he'd come across another living being.

The patio and its in-ground pool were occupied by a

host of nymphs, their ethereally beautiful bodies laying out on lounges sunbathing or swimming nude.

Verrin had frowned, knowing Seir would never have let these women anywhere near his harem's home. His brother liked to keep the debauched side of their nature away from his regular life if at all possible. He stepped forward, drawing their attention as he called out. "What are you doing here? Where's Seir?"

A dozen pairs of eyes in varying shades of new leaves and sea foam focused on him and welcoming smiles crossed pouty lips. Not one of them responded to his question, instead coming toward him smoothly, padding silently across the patio stones or rising dripping wet from the pool. The sunlight shimmered across the vine and wave markings that marked them as tree or water nymphs respectfully.

They encircled him, whispering their desires in hushed, passionate tones. Their arousal at his appearance was like a drug to his Incubus senses, blurring the line between his purpose here and what they wanted from him. Nymphs were a sensual lot by nature, their earthy ways giving them the power to seduce mere mortals in heartbeats and casting quite an appealing spell over immortals as well.

In an instant, Verrin had felt feminine hands all over him, running over every inch of flesh they could reach. They tugged at his clothes with needy draws, trying to uncover more of him. He felt warm air grace his skin as they had managed to strip him of his dress shirt and one sly wench tugged at the belt that circled his hips with eager frenzy as she sunk to her knees before him.

He tried to push past them. He really did. He held

onto his resolve even as his body begged him to stay and play with the nubile nymphs. Hell, he'd almost freed himself when a fiery beauty stepped directly into his path and smiled entrancingly up at him. The curvy redhead wore a skirt that hugged her hips and dropped straight to the flagstones, her bare breasts covered only by waves of her flaming hair.

His gut had given a disturbing churn that, in hindsight, he really should have listened to.

Verrin had watched enraptured as the redhead lifted a wine glass to her full lips and took a mouthful of the rich red liquid. The other nymphs pulled back slightly as the ruby haired female stepped up to him, melding her lush curves to his solid frame. Burying her free hand in his dark hair, she dragged his lips down to hers and kissed him. When his mouth opened, wine flooded in as she transferred her mouthful to him. He swallowed the dark bouquet down even as he felt his lips start to tingle and go numb.

The red haired nymph pulled back and the look on her face had gone from lusty to calculating. She watched him carefully as numbness spread like a plague through his limbs. As he stared into her sea green eyes they started to fade into amber with unusual sparks of gold and her whole visage blurred.

She's using a glamour! He realized, panic rising. He reached out, wanting to get his hands on the wench to question her motives when he felt his limbs weaken and his legs gave out. Verrin crashed to his knees on the sun baked patio stones, the pain that no doubt blossomed going unfelt. His eyesight blurred and Verrin realized the tart had found a way to drug him. Her distorted face grinning maniacally down at him was the last thing he remembered before the darkness devoured his senses.

His next recollection had been waking up in his current location. He'd been laying on the dirt floor of a dimly lit cell, stripped of everything but his black jeans. Broad golden bands with runic designs scrolled into them encircled his wrists. He knew instantly none of this boded well.

Verrin had spent what seemed to be hours investigating every inch of his cell and yelling into the silence. Unfortunately, the only attention he'd attracted was from a rather sizable rat who seemed to be contemplating the likelihood of making a meal out of him. No matter how he had yelled and cursed no one had shown themselves and as time passed his anger had grown into a roiling fury.

In frustration, Verrin pushed away the memory and moved from the bars. He wandered to the back of his cell and dropped down to sit against the back wall and examine the gold bands that were snug against his wrists. They made his skin tingle as he ran his fingers along the careful engravings. There was nothing good about these bands. They brought to mind manacles even though they appeared too light to be of use. The damn things must be imbued with some sort of enchantment. There was a good chance they would block his powers if he tried to use them.

A creak of old hinges had him jumping to his feet and rushing to the bars. It had felt like hours since he woke and the idea of coming face to face with his captor was one he relished. The sight of two hulking men dragging a body between them was a surprise and Verrin

7

felt his blood chill when he recognized his brother's messy light brown hair.

"Seir!" He yelled, hands gripping the bars in desperation to get to him.

Seir didn't so much as twitch as he was hauled past, feet dragging limply. His chest was bare and as they opened the cell directly across from Verrin's, the bloody red stripes crisscrossing his brother's back came into view.

The guards dumped Seir on the dirt floor face down and left, locking the barred door and walking away without giving Verrin so much as a glance.

"Seir? Seir! Answer me, dammit!" Verrin yelled, wishing he could examine his brother. His only sense of peace came from the knowledge that the other man obviously wasn't dead as they wouldn't have bothered to lock up a body.

Verrin sank to his knees and leaned his head against the bars, determined to watch for any sign of consciousness from his youngest sibling. At the earliest opportunity, he would be getting both of them out of this hell hole.

CHAPTER 2

Cassidy ran her finger along the shelf edge, her head tilted to the right to make reading the titles easier. *Got it. Got it. Don't care. Got it. Ugh, that one sucked.* She moved to the next shelf of used romance novels and continued on, searching the stacks for something that piqued her interest.

In her twenty seven years, Cassidy O'Neill had never found a used bookstore she didn't adore. Between the smell of old books and the feel of being surrounded by so many potential adventures, she could never resist. Each one beckoned to her like a hidden treasure trove just waiting to be explored. Worse, she rarely walked out empty handed.

Sad as that was for her wallet.

She picked up a novel with a sword bearing Viking posed strikingly on the cover and flipped it over to read the back before adding it to the small pile on the floor at her feet. Today was shaping up to be a slow day. She'd been here almost an hour now and only found four books. She went on tiptoe to peer over the shelf at the wall clock

9

behind the cash. She had thirteen minutes before she had to be back to her car to feed the meter. With a sigh, she gathered her pile and tucked them into the crook of her elbow, freeing her hands to dig for her wallet.

She couldn't help but snoop at the other shelves as she worked her way to the cash. As she came even with a section of antique books something caught her eye.

On the top shelf, nestled between the other leather and cloth bound titles, an ebony spine stood out among the more faded covers. A little sign beside the shelf requested customers not to handle the antique and rare books without staff assistance.

Cass glanced at the cash to see if the elderly woman who ran the store would help her but an older gentlemen had claimed the cashier's attention. She looked back up at the book. Curiosity blossomed inside her. The book called to her. Trying to look casual, she eyed the owner and her customer, determining if they would catch her handling the expensive book. If she was quick, she could probably get it down without anyone noticing.

Deciding to risk it, she stretched up and snagged the corner of the clear bag the old book was being stored in, tugging until it was free of the shelf. With another covert glance at the cash, she hugged the book to her chest and moved to put one of the big shelves between herself and the cashier. If the older woman caught her, she would no doubt be chastised for touching the expensive antiques without permission.

Once she was safely out of sight, Cass looked down at the prize she held. The worn leather cover had been dyed a deep ebony with a faint silver styling bordering the edges. There was no title on the front, just a picture of what looked like two wings – one feathered like a bird's and one more like a bat's – forming an intricate circle. She turned it over but the spine and back of the book were both blank.

A little white sticker on the bag gave its price at fifty dollars. She winced. She'd have to break out the credit card if she wanted to add this intriguing piece to her collection.

Cass eyed the bag. Her hands itched with the desire to open it and leaf through the book but that was an obvious no-no. If the cashier catching her with one of the rare books was bad, the older woman would probably pop a blood vessel if she caught Cass flipping through it like the latest Cosmo. *Hmm... so we're left with the age old question. Can you judge a book by its cover?*

Just thinking of putting the book back on the shelf and walking away made her fingers twitch.

With a helpless sigh she gave in, tucking the book with the others in the crook of her arm. She switched her debit card for her credit card and headed for the cash.

The older man was just turning away when Cass reached the counter, piling her paperbacks on the desk and slyly putting the black book at the bottom. The owner, Mrs. Bradley, had never been the warmest person but as she rang the books through she shot Cass the evil eye upon seeing the old book that she had obviously not been assisted with.

Cass feigned ignorance even as her belly squirmed like a recalcitrant four year old, cutting off any chiding by asking, "How much will that be?"

"$67.55, Miss O'Neill." The cashier replied curtly, remembering her from her many previous visits. No doubt she'd have to weather Mrs. Bradley's suspicious stare next time she stopped in.

Cass forked over her credit card, watching the bookseller ring her through and put the books in a bag. She took the proffered receipt and stuffed it into the bag before heading for the door.

Slipping the handle of her shopping bag onto her wrist, she reached for the handle of the glass door. The bell above it jingled merrily and it swung open before she ever touched it.

She stopped on the threshold, suddenly in the personal space of another individual. He was amazingly tall, so much so that his softly waved blond head was ducked to avoid the top of the door frame. She could just catch hints of his lean body through the opening in his unbuttoned great coat. His startling amethyst eyes blinked in stunned surprise for a second as he took her in and she could have sworn they flashed bright with recognition before he gathered himself and stepped aside. With a wave of one leather gloved hand, he elegantly gestured her past him as he held the door for her. "Please, after you Miss."

"Oh, thanks." Cass murmured, glancing down shyly to dig into the pocket of her coat for her gloves. Tugging them on, she smiled slightly at the man and gave him a courteous nod as she slipped carefully past him. His model worthy features didn't so much as twitch but she felt like his eyes followed her even after she was past him and out on the street.

Cass pulled her coat tight around her body and hurried down the snow covered sidewalk. She shot a look back over her shoulder to see him going into the bookstore and shrugged the strange feeling off. The icy wind whistled past her and she had to tuck a rogue strand of her long chestnut hair behind her ear to keep it out of her eyes.

Winter on Prince Edward Island was not for the weak. With frigid winds off the water and the constant threat of a nor'easter, the season was filled with more snow shoveling and ice scraping than was generally thought tolerable. Thankfully it had its fringe benefits in the form of picturesque snowy Christmases and frequent well-deserved snow days.

She was almost to the car when her Doctor Who ringtone blared from her purse. Digging through the bag, she retrieved it and hit the answer button when she saw the smiling blonde's picture on the screen. "Hey, Savvy."

"You forgot, didn't you?" The normally sunny female voice on the other end sounded mildly exasperated.

Cass racked her mind as she unlocked the car and threw her purse and shopping bag onto the passenger seat. "Forgot what?" She questioned, sliding behind the wheel and shoving her keys in the ignition distractedly.

"You do realize it's Friday, right?" Savannah's voice sighed. "I've been sitting in your driveway for twenty minutes. It's almost six and we're wasting important drooling-over-sexy-vampires time. Are you *ever* coming back or am I spending the evening with a hot Norse vampire alone?"

"Oh God, I'm so sorry!" She mentally kicked herself for not realizing what day it was. Every Friday evening they got together to discuss their week over good food and great shows. It was a long standing tradition. "It was quiet at the library and Miriam let me go a bit early. I just popped into the bookstore after work and -"

An undignified snort of laughter rang out on the

13

other end. "Ah! The evil bookstore strikes again! I swear I'm going to have to hold an intervention one of these days."

Cass chuckled and tried for an affronted tone. "I'm not *that* bad!"

"Oh yeah?" Savannah challenged, her voice disbelieving. "You stood your friend up just so you could score. Sounds an awful lot like an addict to me."

"Okay, you got me." She laughed, turning the car on and reaching to adjust the heat dials. "I'm on my way home right now. It's pizza week, right? Go ahead and order if you want. I'll be there before they deliver it. It'll be my treat."

"Damn straight it will! My time is valuable!"

Cass couldn't help but snicker at that proclamation. "Yeah. Right. I forgot you charge by the hour. See you in ten minutes." Ignoring Savvy's indignant huff Cass hung up and reversed the car out onto Queen street.

The best part of living in a small town is that traffic is almost non-existent. It took a little more than ten minutes to go across town, mostly because she got stuck behind a snow plow for a while, but thankfully the pizza hadn't arrived by the time she pulled her little red compact into her driveway beside Savannah's blue Corolla.

The big fog coloured Victorian with its swirling white trim was the best thing she had left from her beloved grandmother. Well, that and the overgrown beds of wild roses that blossomed on either side of the porch every summer. The interior had been updated as far as plumbing and electricity but still maintained most of its classic charm. She had moved into the house four years ago after her grandmother's passing and hadn't had the heart to change too much. Some paint and a few new light fixtures and knobs had given the place a quick update while leaving the old house with all its well-earned creaks and quirks. Now it was filled with an eclectic mix of Ikea furniture and her grandmother's antiques and made the perfect haven.

As she got out of her car, Savannah stepped out of her blue sedan to join her. Her petite figure was bundled into a puffy black winter coat and dark blue skinny jeans tucked into her customary high heels, this time in a seasonally appropriate winter ankle boot style. "Finally dragged yourself away from the books, huh?" Savannah smirked at her over the roof of her car, hazel eyes twinkling out from beneath her fur lined hood.

"Ha ha, very funny." Cass stuck her tongue out at her friend, rounding the car with her purse and bag. She watched Savvy grab a few grocery bags from the backseat of her car and they headed for the front door together, taking the few steps onto the porch.

"Here, let me get that." Cass unlocked the big oak door and held it open for Savannah, who came in and dumped her bags on the hardwood floor. "Jeez, did you bring enough? We still have stuff left over from last weekend." Cass dropped her purse and bag on the little hallway table before flicking on the light switch and hanging up their coats in the hall closet.

"I just brought the necessities." Savannah laughed, hopping a little as she unzipped her ankle boots and pried them off. She gathered up her bags and dragged the load into the spacious kitchen, piling them on the kitchen island. "I brought coolers, chips, chocolate, and I downloaded the fifth season of True Blood so we can binge watch all the sexy supernaturals."

"Isn't that illegal?" Cass smirked, stuffing the coolers her friend handed her in the fridge.

"Arrr, I'm a pirate. Swash, swash. Buckle, buckle." Savannah mocked unapologetically as she pulled a box of chocolate chip cookies out of a bag. "If some sexy police officer wants to break into my bedroom with handcuffs to tell me I've been naughty, I am not going to complain." Savannah grinned wickedly, breaking into a bag of sweet and salty popcorn and tossing some in her mouth.

"You're incorrigible." Cass laughed, balling up a plastic bag and tossing it at her friend. "And with your luck, it would be one of your brothers who got the call."

"Hey, no using big words! It's not fair to the rest of us. And if you are implying my brothers are sexy, that's disgusting. Truly disgusting. I don't think we can be friends anymore."

Cass was about to retort when there was a knock at the door. "Ooh, pizza's here!" She went to the door and paid for their dinner, giving the pizza guy a tip.

"Get the plates, dinner is served!" Cass called, coming back into the kitchen. She laid the large pizza across the counter and grinned. "You couldn't resist the big one, huh?"

"You know what they say, bigger is better," Savannah replied with a wink and pressed a plate into Cass's hands before turning her attention to dinner. She flipped the lip and dug into the warm meat lovers pizza. "Oh yes, now that's a gorgeous pizza. Who needs vegetables anyway?" Savvy murmured lovingly to the slice in her hand before taking a big bite. Chewing with relish, she groaned in blissful abandon. "Oh my god, this is so good!"

Cass grinned at her friend's nearly orgasmic enjoyment of dinner. "Long day?" She asked, helping herself.

"You have no idea. There's a flu going through the staff and residents so we're scrambling to cover shifts and get everything done. I swear I haven't had anything but coffee and a handful of almonds since supper last night." Savvy replied around another big bite.

"Wow. I'm pretty sure I would have wasted away if I ate like that." Cass shook her head, having no idea how her friend could survive on so little. Savvy had once referred to it as the 'nurse's diet plan' and swore it's how she kept her trim figure. She pushed the pizza box toward Savvy and grinned. "Help yourself. You obviously earned it."

Savvy grinned and grabbed a third slice, dropping it across the other two on her plate. "All right, let's get started. We have thirteen episodes to watch and time is ticking."

"Lead on!" Cassidy gestured to the living room, grabbing them a couple of bottles of strawberry daiquiri cooler from the fridge on her way.

They dropped their bounty on the coffee table and Cass tossed a couple of throw pillows out of the way as Savvy set up the TV. Settling in on the sofa the blonde snagged the remote and aimed it like a phaser at the blank screen. "Are you ready? If I remember correctly there were some seriously sexy scenes in this season."

Cass grinned and raised her bottle up. "Let's do it!"

Five episodes and six hours later they had gone through half a pizza and a bowl of butter praline ice cream each. After much complaining of being stuffed they had settled comfortably to watch the next episode. The evening had passed with them chatting about work and snickering over blush-worthy sex scenes they'd read.

Cassidy's attention was dragged from the credits of yet another episode by a soft snore. With a smile, she noticed Savannah was sleeping, sprawled out on the couch behind where Cass sat on the floor with her legs crossed under the coffee table.

Cass climbed to her feet and turned the television off before grabbing a throw blanket and covering her friend up. As quietly as she could she gathered their dishes up and put the rest of the pizza away in the fridge. Turning off most of the downstairs lights, she checked to make sure the front door was locked and grabbed her bag of new books before heading up the stairs to her room.

Her master bedroom was the one room she had given a complete overall when she took possession of the house. The daisy covered wallpaper had been replaced with cream walls and mouldings painted white. The ceilings were high enough that she managed to fit the big four poster bed she had bought in with just a smidge of room to spare. The old fireplace that hadn't seen a flame as long as she could remember had been serviced and the mantel repainted white to match the room. Her pride and joy, however, was the window alcove that looked out on the backyard that she had turned into her reading nook. Complete with window seat, throw pillows and a shelf of her favourite novels right beside it, it was the perfect place to nestled into with a good book.

Her own little piece of paradise.

Diverting her course to the bathroom, she brushed

18

her teeth and used the washroom before crossing the hall to the master bedroom. Cassidy flipped the light on as she wandered in and up-ended her bag of books onto her bed's deep purple comforter. Sitting down beside the spill of novels, she started to organize her loot. She pulled the four novels out and set them on the nightstand with the rest of her 'To Be Read' pile before she pulled the antique book towards her in anticipation.

A shot of excitement struck her when she looked at the black book, still safely sealed in its plastic bag. With gentle fingers, she pulled off the tape sealing the bag closed and slid the book out.

The black leather cover felt incredibly soft to the touch and Cassidy stroked her fingers lovingly over it. The silver designs were tooled into the leather with care and it seemed to glimmer as she traced the image with a delicate finger. With bated breath, she opened the cover and touched the first of the vellum pages within. The symbol from the cover was copied here in slightly faded dark ink.

As she flipped pages she realized there was no copyright page nor one that gave a title or author. The text appeared to be in various languages and written in multiple handwriting styles. Some lines here and there seemed to be in semi-recognizable English but others looked like Latin, Arabic, Cyrillic and some even she didn't recognize. One of the more prominent ones was a pretty scrolling script with lots of embellishment that curled across many of the pages.

Every few pages there were hand drawn illustrations, pictures of creatures the likes of which she had never dreamed of. Some of them had horns and hooves, others wings and talons. They all had something in common though. Every image had eyes that scared her, dark and knowing even though they were simply an artist's rendition in ink. She turned the pages quickly until she came to an image of a beautiful man.

He was built like a warrior, his body appearing hard and muscled, his long fingered hands were curled slightly at his sides as if he was seeking to fill them with a weapon. Cut abs and broad shoulders stood out above the line of the dark leather loincloth wrapped low around his hips. Long dark hair was pulled back into a ponytail, revealing a face of full lips and startling eyes. He looked slightly angry, as if having his likeness captured annoyed him, his features pinched with a frown as he stared out at the viewer.

Cassidy stared at the man's bold image and for some reason, a shiver of something akin to anticipation went down her spine. A man with his stunning good looks would have women panting after him everywhere he went. *Hell*, she thought, *I'd be sorely tempted to throw myself at him given half a chance!*

Not that a man like him would look twice at a girl like her.

Cassidy wasn't a fool. Vertically challenged, a little too plump and an introvert through and through. She was solidly in the girl next door category. If a guy like him actually existed he wouldn't pay her any attention, too busy with all the svelte model types to notice the bookworm in the background.

Shutting down that depressing train of thought she set the book of fantastical drawings on her pillow. There would be time for more fantastical creatures once she was settled in bed for the night.

CHAPTER 3

Verrin's eyes flicked open and he realized he must have dozed off at some point. His whole body was stiff as he straightened up from where he'd been leaning against the corner of his cell watching Seir. Shuffling toward his cell door, he watched his brother groan and curl forward to lay on his front, head buried in his arm. From where Verrin had sat he'd watched the whip marks on his brother's back slowly heal, the blood drying and the redness fading thanks to their inherited accelerated healing. Seir had yet to fully wake but at least he seemed to be coming around slowly if the grunts of pain were any indication.

It had been at least a day since the guards had unceremoniously dumped Seir in the cell opposite his. The light had slowly faded to dark and brightened again through the meager slit of a window high on the wall between the cells. No one had shown up. No food or water had been given to them and Verrin doubted whoever was holding them intended to offer them any sort of comforts.

The lack of intrusion, however, had given him plenty of time to check out his surroundings. From what he could tell of his current accommodations there were a total of six cells, all unoccupied except the two that held him and Seir. Each cell was backed by an ancient stone wall and barred on the other three sides. The bars themselves looked relatively new, their iron only slightly pitted from the humidity that seeped in from outside. An aisle divided the six cells, three on either side of the room leading to a wide entry space with a set of stairs that led to a floor above. Only faint light filtered into the cells from tiny slits carved into the top of the stone walls.

There was a soft creak of ancient metal hinges somewhere out of sight making Verrin jerk his head up in surprise. Finally! On a rush of adrenaline, he got to his feet and crossed to stand before the bars, waiting to see who came down the stairs. He figured it would probably be the guards again and could only hope it was him they were coming for. Their breed was tough but Seir wasn't up to more abuse.

As the footsteps grew closer the click of high heels on stone surprised him but then the woman who walked down the aisle between cells was not exactly your average jailer.

A frown creased his forehead as he stared at her blankly. "Empusa? What the hell?"

The smile that crossed those blood red lips was sinister. Empusa, Greek demigoddess and part of a seductively ruthless mercenary triad, brushed some of her fiery red hair over her shoulder and approached the cell slowly, staying just out of arm's reach. As she walked, the hip high slit in her long black skirt showed off her prosthetic left leg, a skillful piece of godly engineering and magic crafted from brass and tooled with mystical swirling symbols that made her stride seamless.

"Well hello, Verrin. I'm so glad you could join us." She grinned at him, amber eyes lighting on his shirtless body with appreciation.

"Don't play with me, Empusa," Verrin growled, hands fisting around the bars. "What's going on here? Why are you holding us?"

"Oh, Verrin, playing with you is exactly what I intend to do." She stepped forward until she was pressed against the cell wall opposite him, full breasts brushing him through the bars. Her lips curled into a devious smirk. "Maybe you'll be more fun than that bleeding heart brother of yours. I did so enjoy our kiss after all." She ran her tongue over her full bottom lip as if she still savoured his taste.

Things clicked and he sneered at her. "Considering you had to glamour yourself just to get that kiss you must be pretty hard up. Is that why you took Seir? Needed a good roll in the hay?" Verrin mocked, pulling back slightly to put some space between himself and that snake of a woman.

Empusa just gave him a cheshire smile. "I'd watch your tongue, Incubus. You might just lose it."

Verrin shrugged nonchalantly. "I'm just trying to figure this out. You've never had anything against us before. Why take us? Why hurt Seir? If not to fulfill some sick sexual fantasy, you must have some reason."

"True. Let's just say he is currently in possession of something I need. Unfortunately for him, I'm working

23

under time constraints and he wasn't keen to give me what I wanted promptly." Her fingers reached out to stroked his hands where they curled around the bars. "I'm hoping you'll be more considerate of my desires."

Verrin yanked his hands back and scowled. "What the hell are you talking about? What do you want?"

Empusa's smile turned sly. "I just need you to fill a vial for me."

Verrin narrowed his blue eyes. "Empusa..." He growled in frustration, not enjoying her hedging.

"It's really not that bad. All I need is a vial of your freely given blood. Sadly, Seir has not been co-operating with my demands. At present, your dear brother is slowly going mad from lust. He has refused my polite demands to give me what I require and, although I have personally offered to curb his sexual urges if he helps me, he has rejected me. I plan to hold him until either he gives in or...." She ran a fingertip across her red lips, pausing to stare at Verrin in speculation.

"Saint's blood woman! Out with it!" Verrin growled, practically throwing himself into the bars again when she started to move away toward Seir's cell.

"Or...you could take his place and I'll let him go when I have what I want from you. I'll even give him a woman to tide him over."

"Seriously?" Verrin scoffed, needling her, and pulled back from the bars. "Are you sure you're not just doing all this to get laid?"

She gritted her teeth and glared at him. "Don't be stupid. I have no problem finding a bed partner."

"You've obviously never indulged in an Incubus before," Verrin said smugly as he crossed his arms and took her in from head to toe. "We are not your average bed partner."

Empusa tipped her head back and laughed wholeheartedly, her length of flame hair shimmering around her hips. "You, little demon, are a riot! You're nothing to me but a part of my current assignment. Now, either you agree to help me or I wait until your brother is too lost to lust to hold himself back from agreeing to anything. One way or another, I'll get what I want." She turned on her heel and started out of sight of the cell. "I'll give you some time to think about it. My guards will be down here to collect one of you this evening. Choose wisely, demon."

Verrin considered yelling at her to return but decided it wasn't worth it. He had dealt with Empusa a time or two before and she could give the most patient of immortals a headache. Arguing with her was the definition of futility. He would be better off spending his time trying to figure out how to manipulate the situation to get Seir and himself out of this mess.

Preferably without giving Empusa what she wanted.

Why Empusa needed their blood so bad that she would go to the extreme of holding them captive was unknown, although the fact that she was calling this an assignment meant someone else was pulling her strings. When she mentioned needing their blood to be freely given that struck a chord with him. The soul was a fickle thing, blood forcefully taken from a body was powerless because the soul rejected the donation but blood given of a person's free will could carry with it a great deal of power and a touch of that person's soul.

As Incubi, their blood was something special. Being

25

half angel and half Djinn, their blood ran with traces of ichor, the golden blood of a true angel, as well as the magic born into the Djinn race.

He wasn't sure if she was after a piece of one of their souls or just the power inherent in their blood but he knew he couldn't leave Seir with her for long. As far as he knew Seir had disappeared about five days ago and if he hadn't bedded a woman since his capture than he would be fading fast. Without obtaining the energy of a woman's pleasure, Seir would be racked with cramping pain and the mindless lust would start picking away at his sanity.

Verrin started his pacing again, trying to think through possible situations, anything that could turn this disaster in his favour. He just needed to get his brother and get the hell out of here. If he could convince the guards he would give Empusa what she wanted they would unlock the cell so he could have a chance to take them out. With any luck, they would have the keys to the other cells so he should be able to free Seir. Then it was just a matter of getting them both out of there.

He shook off his frustration and prepared for the fight ahead of him, thinking through his plan carefully.

***

Cassidy rolled over in the warm cocoon of her bed and bumped her nose on something solid. With a muffled grumble, she opened one eye and stared at the cover of the black leather book, it's silver scroll work shimmering in the morning sunlight.

Ah damn. She hadn't meant to fall asleep with it but she had been hard-pressed to put the book away last night.

She'd laid in bed flipping pages long into the night. Most of the writing was unreadable to her but the illustrations were so finely crafted she had a hard time not imagining some ancient explorer carefully drawing the magnificent species he'd stumbled across. She desperately wished she could read the penned words, sure they were information on the minotaurs, gryphons and other assorted creatures whose images graced the pages.

She reached out and moved the antique tome to the safety of her nightstand. The digital clock glared at her over its cover, reminding her it was 9:12 am and beyond time to get up. With a yawn, she sat up and stretched hard before swinging her feet to the floor. The golden hardwood shone in the morning light as she made her way out the door and down the hallway to the bathroom.

She could hear Savvy moving around downstairs as she tried to make herself relatively presentable. With her toothbrush sticking out of her mouth, she fought a hairbrush through the tangled chestnut waves and pulled it all back into a low ponytail. Mission complete, she padded downstairs, the old steps creaking with their usual grunts and groans.

Savannah was busy yanking out mixing bowls from the cupboards by the stove when she entered the kitchen. The counter already showed the fruits of Savvy's ingredient raid with a collection of eggs, milk, flour and butter.

"Morning Cass!" Savvy greeted her cheerily as she scooted over to the coffee maker to pour a cup.

Cass parked her butt onto one of the padded stools by the kitchen island and nodded at her friend. "Morning. Sleep well?"

"With dreams of sexy vampire Norseman in my head? How could I not!" Savvy grinned and practically bounded back across the kitchen to her ingredients.

Narrowing her eyes, Cass watched her friend flit around the kitchen, preparing breakfast. The little blonde practically vibrated with energy. "How many cups of coffee have you had?" She asked suspiciously.

Savvy stopped and turned to her with a beatific smile on her face. "This is only my second." Turning back to the counter, Savvy started measuring cups of flour out. "I honestly have no idea how you function without it."

"Slower," Cass muttered, rubbing the sleep from her eyes. "I function slower."

Savvy blew her a raspberry over her shoulder and spun back to her mixing bowl, her bob of blonde tresses swaying around her jaw. "Coffee has been compared to ambrosia, the nectar of the gods, I'll have you know."

Cass snorted and leaned her elbows on the counter top. "The gods must have no taste buds because not only does that stuff taste like absolute swill, but I burn my tongue every time I try it."

"And that," Savvy whirled, gesturing at her with a wooden spoon, "Is exactly how I can drink it. My tongue is so burned I've lost all my taste buds!"

The two women burst into giggles. They'd had this same discussion multiple times when Savannah stayed over and it had become almost routine. They'd long ago realized that while blood made up the main component of Cass's body, Savvy's heart pumped pure caffeine.

"Pancakes okay with you?" Savvy inquired, stirring milk into the bowl.

"Absolutely." Cass got up and poured herself a glass

of chocolate milk before getting to the portion of breakfast that Savvy would let her help with. She pulled plates out of the cupboard and gathered utensils as she asked, "Did you want raspberry syrup or just the regular maple stuff?"

"Ooh, raspberry!" Savvy exclaimed as she poured batter onto the hot griddle. "So did you get anything good from the bookstore yesterday? You're my dealer and I need to know what you're pushing."

Cass grinned and set napkins and pancake syrup on the breakfast bar. "Got a few novels, another Viking one. I think I may have to change bookstores for a while, most of the stock was stuff I've been seeing there for ages. Might be time to try that one in Rustico. I've heard their worth the drive." She turned to root through the fridge for butter. "I did find something interesting though."

Savvy shot her a questioning look over her shoulder. "What was it? Something really naughty?"

"Nah, it's like some sort of mythology book. I can't read most of it but it's filled with hand drawn illustrations. I couldn't pass it up."

"Nifty." Savvy swiped a plate and flipped three fluffy pancakes onto it from the griddle. "Here. Eat. Then you can show me that book."

Cass took her plate to the table and Savvy followed with her own, the two of them settling at the breakfast bar with a platter stacked high with pancakes between them. After the first bite Cass let out a little moan of appreciation. The pancakes were fluffy and perfect with raspberry syrup. "Savvy, you are seriously the best cook. These are amazing!"

Savvy grinned and cut a piece of pancake off with her fork. "That's self-preservation for you. If I had expected Grif or Gray to cook we'd have all starved and Perry thought macaroni and cheese was a part of a body's daily nutritional requirements."

Cass snickered past her mouthful of raspberry drenched pancake. It wasn't hard to imagine a younger version of the normally stoic Perry serving his younger siblings home a pot of cheesy macaroni only to a chorus of tired groans. From the times she'd eaten at her friend's house as children she remembered being thankful Savvy or Perry had cooked. The twin terrors, Griffin and Grayson, had believed for years that relish made all foods better and had regularly seasoned anything they made with it. *Ugh, I will never forget the taste of peanut butter and relish sandwiches.* Not wanting to spoil her appetite she choked back her mouthful of pancake and took a swig of chocolate milk, decidedly changing the topic. "Is Perry coming home for Christmas this year?"

"Hopefully. He hasn't given us any firm dates." Savvy toyed with a hunk of pancake, spinning it in a pool of syrup until the fluffy batter was dark pink. "I really hope he can get time off. He tried last year but Christmas isn't the same when you're opening his presents for him over video chat while he's stuck on a military base somewhere."

Cass reached out and squeezed her friend's shoulder in comfort. "I'm sure he'll make it this year. You know he wouldn't miss it if he had a choice."

Savvy had just opened her mouth when the twang of a country accent and a peal of boot stompin' music rang out from the living room. "Damn, that's work. One sec." Savvy wiped her fingers quickly on her napkin and scrambled off the stool to run for her phone. She talked for a few moments as Cass finished eating and a defeated tone entered her voice. She said goodbye and hung up.

"Looks like the fun ends here." Savannah sighed, stuffing her phone in her purse as she wandered back into the kitchen. "That was work. Looks like the new guy didn't show up for his shift so they called me in."

"That sucks. Did you want me to pack something for your supper? There's still pizza." Cass asked her friend as she carried their dishes to the counter.

"If you don't mind. I have to get home to change and get over there to let the other girl off her shift. Buying something would just be another stop." Savvy headed back to the living room to gather up her belongings.

"Sure. I have dry shampoo in the bathroom upstairs if you need it." Cass offered, digging out some Tupperware.

"You're a life saver!" Savvy called as she dumped a tote bag of her stuff beside her purse and ran for the stairs.

Cass put a few slices of cold pizza from the box into a plastic container and filled up a to-go mug with coffee for her friend. Digging in the fridge she found a strawberry yogurt and an apple and tossed everything in a grocery bag. When Savvy came back in, patting her perfectly smooth blonde hair into even more perfect order, Cass held out her offering. "Here, I packed you some pizza, yogurt and an apple. This way you have no reason not to eat something."

Savvy grinned and gave her a one-armed hug as she swiped the bag of food and coffee. "Thanks, mom!" She teased, before grabbing her purse and tote and heading for the hallway to hunt down her shoes.

"Have a good day, sweetie," Cass said, assuming her best 1950's happy housewife tone.

"I will." Savvy snickered and yanked her coat from the closet. Armed with everything she needed, she gave Cass a mock salute and headed out into the morning cold.

Cassidy waited until Savvy got her car started and was pulling out into the newly plowed street before closing and locking the big oak door. Around her, the house was suddenly silent, not even the usual creak of old wood breaking the peace.

With all her original plans for the day based around Savvy's accompaniment, she was suddenly faced with a whole day to herself.

Deciding the breakfast dishes could wait, she let her inner bookworm loose and jogged up the stairs to her room. She had new books calling her name.

Over twelve hours later, Cassidy's whole body gave a jerk as her head dipped forward for the third time, rousing her from the sleepy doze that had slipped over her. With a yawn, she set her novel down on the bench seat of her alcove window and got up. The sky outside had darkened to navy velvet and the clock by her bed told her it was nearing midnight.

She had spent the day after Savannah left doing minimal housework and just enough laundry to get through the week between chapters of her new book. With a leftover pizza break for supper, her evening had been relaxing and low maintenance. There weren't even dishes to be done since she'd managed to cram everything in the dishwasher. She really couldn't have asked for a more relaxing Saturday.

Figuring she might as well go to bed if she was starting to fade anyway, she got changed into her black panties, purple tank top and black flannel pajama bottoms before getting ready for bed.

Coming back from the bathroom she turned off the overhead light and flicked on the bedside lamp. The room glowed with a soft golden light and glimmered off the antique book she had left on her nightstand that morning.

Cass slipped out of her pajama bottoms and into bed, propping her back on a pillow against the headboard before dragging the book into her lap. Flipping pages, she ran loving fingers over the image of a graceful unicorn and marveled at the detail put into the drawing of a feathered serpent. When she came to the warrior's page again she stopped, admiring the physique of the illustration's subject.

He really was the epitome of male beauty. Tall, dark and handsome, it wouldn't have surprised her to see his image gracing the cover of one of her favourite romance novels. She wished she knew the story behind this drawing but most of the text on the opposite page was in some unintelligible curling scrawl.

Cass ran her fingers over the writing, line by line. Whoever had written it had a beautiful hand for script even if the words were undecipherable. The faded dark ink didn't have a smudge or accidental inkblot anywhere. As she followed it along her eyes caught on letters she could almost read amongst the rest of the text.

"Voco te verrin et -" She paused to mentally sound out the next words before continuing. "Quaero voluptatem tui tactus."

Cass sat back and blinked at the book. She wasn't sure but it sounded like Latin. Her high school biology teacher had stressed how helpful Latin was in science and so she had tried to learn a bit back then. With her limited knowledge the line could have been anything from an ancient prayer to a list of someone's preferred pizza toppings.

She shrugged and set the book on the bedside table once more, flicking off the lamp and plunging the room into darkness. It wasn't until she had found a comfortable position and she was closing her eyes that an uncomfortable thought struck her. *Did I lock the front door?* She had been home all day so she hadn't really thought of locking it earlier. Knowing that nagging feeling would stay with her all night if she didn't go look, she groaned and rolled onto her back. Better to check it now than spend all night wondering if she'd done it or not.

With a deep sigh she flicked back her comforter and climbed out. Padding barefoot across the cool hardwood floor, she didn't bother to turn on the light or slip her pajama pants on as she left the room and jogged down the stairs. With a twist of the knob and a wiggle of the deadlock, she verified the big oak door was secure and headed back upstairs to her nice warm bed.

CHAPTER 4

Verrin was focused on Seir's body through the bars. He listened carefully to the soft sigh of his brother's even breaths and was relieved to know his sibling was doing a bit better. He had hoped his brother would wake up but no matter how many times Verrin had called his name or thrown loose stones from the cell floor at his prone form, Seir didn't stir.

He knew their time had to be almost up and he was more than ready for Empusa's guards. His fingers twitched at the slightest noise, ready for a fight. He just needed to take them out and free Seir then they could escape.

Where they would escape to he wasn't sure yet but that was a minor detail considering the circumstances.

He climbed to his feet and continued his earlier pacing. One hand rubbed irritatedly at one of the golden cuffs that encircled his wrists. He'd noticed that Seir had a matching pair and Verrin realized his guess that they must be enchanted manacles of some form was probably right. Hopefully, they wouldn't be too hard to remove once they were free.

The now familiar creaking sounded and Verrin stepped into the middle of the cell, facing the barred door. His body tensed and he growled as the first of four guards appeared. They filed down the stairs and came to stand behind the first one, blocking his view of Seir.

The four men wore a mixture of shorts, pants and t-shirts that looked like they had seen better days. With their olive skin tone and dark hair they looked human but when Verrin caught sight of their eyes he recognized the vertical slit of their pupils as belonging to snake shifters. Each man had two healing puncture marks on his neck and Verrin figured they were probably under a compulsion from a vampire.

Evidently, Empusa had one of those in her pocket as well.

"The Mistress wants your answer. Will you come willingly?" The first guard asked, his face impassive. Verrin's answer didn't matter one wit to this man. His hands were occupied, one on the hilt of the machete at his side and the other on a length of golden chain.

"I'll give her what she wants." Verrin lied, trying to assume a more resigned posture.

One of the other guards stepped forward and unlocked the cell door, holding it aside as the others came in. The one who had spoken held up the chain. "Put your hands behind your back."

Verrin did as he was told, turning and putting his hands behind his back. He waited as they closed in on him. In a few more feet they would all be in the cell with him and he would be free to attack.

He glanced over his shoulder, gauging their distance

and opening his mouth to issue some snarky remark, when the first touch of the call went through him.

A sensation like warm, sensual fingers stroked up from the base of his spine, moving up his back and circling around his hips.

Holy hell! A Summons? Now? He nearly groaned at the feel of that seeking magical touch and wasn't able to resist the wicked shudder that stirred within him.

He bit his lip to stay silent and swayed on his feet. The guards were almost to him, holding out the chain. His eyes closed as he felt the ghostly hands sink into his body. They wrapped around him, body and soul, and pulled at his very being. It was as surreal and disorienting as it was freeing.

This wasn't good. Couldn't have happened at a worse time. He needed to fight, to save his brother. He was Seir's only chance to escape. Instead, all he could think of was the soft, warm female body that he would be sinking into momentarily. She had summoned and he was powerless to ignore the call that was attuned specifically to him. His body ached, fading and dispersing. His form curled into fog, disappearing from within the cell as the guards yelled frantically. A jingle of metal as the golden cuffs hit the floor, his wrists not solid enough for them to hold onto, and he was away.

Rescue via Summons. Didn't see that coming.

***

Cassidy climbed the stairs and padded down the dark hallway while she tugged the purple hair elastic off her wrist to pull her hair into a low ponytail. She had made it two steps past the threshold of her bedroom door when her blood froze in her veins.

What the hell...?

The room was almost pitch black, with just the barest diffusion of exterior light coming through the blinds on the windows, but it was just enough to see a darker shadow against the dim shape of her bed. A hulking mass of darkness was perched on her mattress, directly over where she had just been laying moments ago.

The rustle of her sheets alerted her as the stygian shadow twisted, turning in her direction. Glowing eyes pinned her with neon blue intensity as the obscured figure adjusted to face her fully. A soft rumble filled the air as those brilliant unblinking eyes stared at her. Whatever it was watched her intensely, the illuminated gaze taking in her curvy form from head to foot.

A fine tremble had taken over her body. Her mind was terrified, running wild with all sorts of home invasion nightmares, but her body had flushed with unexpected arousal. Her heart was pounding so hard she was sure the sound must be echoing off the walls. With her fight or flight instinct so disturbingly torn, she was frozen in a state of limbo.

Her chest ached and Cass realized she'd held her breath. She forced her lungs to draw in air and slammed her lips together. She wasn't sure if a scream would break the tableau that seemed to hang between her and the blue-eyed shadow but she wasn't willing to risk it.

The glow of the shadow's eyes made it hard to focus on any other feature of the face that held them. Those eyes came incrementally closer as the figure slowly crawled toward the end of her bed, closing in on her.

A deep rumble rolled into the air, sounding almost like a satisfied purr. "I came for you, little Summoner." The voice called out of the darkness, sensual and dangerous. It slid like silk down her spine and Cass felt herself shudder – whether it was from pleasure or fear though she wouldn't say.

Her fingers twitched and Cass thanked her lucky stars her body was finally coming back under her control. She tried to be as quiet as possible, not wanting to alert whatever creature was occupying her bed, as she slid a foot backward and shifted her weight slowly. She had to put some more space between them.

The shadow kept moving, its bulk coming closer to the end of the bed. The antique bed creaked as it crawled across the stretch of mattress toward her. Those neon eyes never looked away, attention never straying from her. She felt like the prey of some big cat gearing up to pounce.

Her heart stuttered in her chest and she drew in a ragged breath.

The liquid velvet voice was a caress in itself and his words were both a threat and a sensual promise. "Now I think it's time I made you come for me."

Just as the shadow reached the end of the bed and rose to its full towering height, the spell Cassidy was under broke. Her hand slapped out blindly, finding the light switch on the wall beside the door and flicking it on.

They both groaned as bright light flooded the room.

"Argh!" Those luminous blue eyes disappeared behind shielding hands as the light revealed a huge man by her bed. He reared back until his calves bumped the edge of her mattress and he stumbled into a sitting position.

Her eyes widened as she took in the broad

shoulders, bare chest and hard abs. She couldn't resist letting her gaze travel down the thin line of dark hair that disappeared into tight black jeans and her mouth went uncomfortably dry. She went to speak but her voice died before it made more than a sad little mewling noise.

"Dammit woman, a little warning would be nice!" That dark voice growled out in irritation. His hands dropped and her breath caught. Even the grimace on his face couldn't hide the heady beauty of this man.

Hair so dark brown it was almost black, cut short on the sides and spiking into soft curls on top, begged her fingers to sift through it. Strong jaw, the dark shadow of a days growth of beard on his cheeks, lush red lips pulled into a tight line. Those startling azure eyes, looking normal in the light, blinked a few times before focusing back on her. He quirked a dark brow, obviously wondering what her reaction would be.

Cass felt that tremor worsen, an internal earthquake that made her breath come faster as she stared at the half naked man sitting on her bed. Her brain had shut down when she realized she was blushing because this amazingly gorgeous man was seeing her plump little self in naught but her skimpy underwear and a tank top.

Oh. My. God. It was all she could think of. There were so many thoughts clamouring for attention in her head. She just couldn't process it. The only thing that was clear was that a strange, half-naked man was in her room uninvited.

Without a thought, Cassidy turned on her heel and ran for the stairs.

***

Verrin stared at the empty doorway a moment before biting out a bitter curse and jumping to his feet. He gave chase, following her rapid footfalls down the hardwood of the hallway, and clamoured down the stairs behind her.

When his body had reformed he had been shocked to find himself alone in a dark, feminine bedroom. The bed beneath him had held traces of warmth and he'd known she hadn't been gone long. He'd wondered what could have distracted her from awaiting his arrival.

I summon you, Verrin, and beg for the pleasure of your touch. Her voice had stumbled over the ritual words as if she had shuddered in pleasure while trying to speak them. It had hardened his cock to imagine what she would be like underneath him.

To see her standing in the doorway, body compact and lush in all the right places, he had thanked his lucky stars. She was just the type of woman he'd have picked for himself. Seeing her dressed in nothing but a pair of little black panties and a purple tank top that comfortably sexy was a bonus. He would definitely love to hold her sweet little body to his and wasn't able to resist telling her exactly what he wanted to do to her.

Then she had turned and bolted like Cerberus himself was on her heels.

He barely caught up to her as she reached the bottom of the stairs. Verrin reached out to catch her but his fingers only brushed softly through the end of her ponytail as she turned quickly from the front door and ran for the back of the house.

Throwing herself headlong through a wide archway,

41

the woman shot into the darkened room beyond. He hounded her, skidding into the room just in time to watch her knock over a tall stool by the kitchen island and swipe something off the counter. She whirled, chest heaving with breathless pants, and squared off against him. In one hand she held her cell phone, in the other a tiny aerosol spray can. A purse lay at her feet, its contents spilling out across the tiled floor. "Don't come any closer!" She warned even as her voice wavered unsteadily.

Verrin stopped short, leaving her plenty of room. She was trembling with adrenaline and cornered on the other side of the island, warding him off with her minuscule weapon. He didn't like to see her scared, her fear filled the air like an acrid scent in his nose. Women were treasures to his kind, the essence of their very lives. One did not go stalking them through their homes scaring them senseless. Well, not unless they ask you to.

"It's all right, little one. I won't come any closer." He held his hands up in a placating gesture and tried to look harmless. Not an easy task when you're almost seven feet tall but he tried his best. He softened his tone and tried to project calm into his voice. "I'm sorry if I startled you. You weren't there when I arrived and I -"

"What do you mean *when you arrived*?" She queried, cutting him off. Her hands were white-knuckled around the little canister and she seemed ready to bolt again.

Verrin took a deep breath and shoved a hand through his hair, giving the dark strands a little tug in frustration. He cocked his head to the side to stare at her quizzically. "I arrived just after you called me. That's how it works. You call one of us and we come to you."

"Call you?" She looked confused until she shook

42

her head, ponytail swishing behind her. "I never called anyone. I don't even *know* you! How could I call you?"

She really didn't know.

Verrin relaxed, realizing what had happened. The woman had no idea she had summoned an Incubus to her bed. *Well isn't she in for a surprise.* He lowered his voice to a sensual purr and put his hands on the island's counter to lean toward her slightly. "You called my name, little one. Begged for my touch. I have no idea where you found the summons bearing my name but I felt you call me, so here I am. I promise nothing will happen until you will it." He smiled and raked his gaze down her curvy body with appreciation. "Although I do hope it's sooner rather than later."

Her face paled and her voice shook. "Get out. Get out of my house! I'll call the cops and have you arrested if you don't leave *right now!*"

Verrin smiled. She was a feisty little thing. He liked that in a woman. He stood straight and moved around the island toward her, hands raised peaceably. "It's okay, I'm not here to hurt you."

He had planned to say more. He had a whole reassuring spiel ready in his mind.

He just never got to use it.

The hand that clutched the little can rose between them and she depressed the trigger.

The little minx maced him.

CHAPTER 5

The big man gasped in pain as the aerosol spray caught him in the eyes. His hands came up to guard himself against more injury and Cass lunged for her keys on the counter before trying to dodge past him. If she could just make it to her car she could call the cops as she got the hell away from this sexy home invader.

She had almost made it past him when a thick arm swiped out and caught around her waist, pulling her inexorably into his side. She cried out and pushed at his caging arm with her fists, not wanting to relinquish either her cellphone, keys or her only weapon even as she tried to struggle free. Instead, she was dragged back against him, her breath stuttering as she choked on the offensive cloud of vanilla air freshener that surrounded him. A growl reverberated in her ear as a strong hand came out and knocked the little spray can from her hand as she brought it up for another assault.

Cass flailed, frustrated at being so easily disarmed and desperate to get away. She held her cell phone as far away from his blindly seeking hand as she could, trying to dial 911 through the jostling of their awkward wrestling match. He grasped her wrist in an almost bruising grip and dragged the hand bearing her cell phone toward him. He seized the phone and it disappeared into one of his pants pockets.

"Let me go, you bastard! What the hell do you want?" Cass cursed him, pulling at his restraining arm so hard her nails left little crescents in his skin. She rammed her elbow into his stomach and received nothing more than the barest grunt from him and a blaze of pain through her arm. *Damn him! His abs are like of steel!* His fingers bit into her hip, pulling her up his body until she stood on tiptoe.

"Just relax sweetness. You're going to hurt yourself." He chastised calmly in her ear.

She threw her head back, grazing his chin with the violent movement. *Does he seriously think I'm going to listen to anything he says?*

"Dammit!" He hissed, his grip loosening for a moment as he tried to adjust his hold on her. "Calm down! I'm not going to hurt you!"

"Calm down! Calm down? Do you seriously think telling someone to calm down ever actually calmed them down?" She retorted indignantly. "How about you try having some gorgeous lunatic sneak into your house – *into your bed* – then chase you down and see how easy it is for *you* to calm down!"

"Tell me how you really feel." The man grumbled sarcastically before pausing to think. "Wait... Gorgeous?" He asked playfully.

She felt frustration rise up in her chest in an audible

growl. It figured he would catch that slip of the tongue. Irked at herself, Cass threw her body forward with as much leverage as she could muster. All her determination went down the drain as he caught her hips in both hands and turned her until she was pinned to his broad chest. He leaned down, one arm encircling the back of her thighs and the other at her hips and casually popped her off her feet. She kicked wildly, ramming her bare toes into his knees and braced her hands on his shoulders to try and push herself away from him.

"Put me down!" She hissed, glaring at him as she thrashed.

"You think I'm gorgeous." He taunted, those eerie blue eyes glimmering with mirth.

She blinked at him and frowned. "That was nothing! I meant enormous! You heard it wrong! Now put me down you – you-" She flailed for a word foul enough to describe him.

"Gorgeous man?" He supplied, giving her a wicked smirk.

She growled at him again, an aggravated grumble breaking from her in lieu of all the curses she wanted to fling at him. *Damn the frustrating, arrogant, home-invading, cocky, gorgeous jerk all to hell!* Her body was practically vibrating with the desire to wipe that smirk off his face, although she hadn't quite decided if she'd do it with her palm or her lips.

One of his arms dropped away and she gripped his shoulders to make sure she kept her balance. Cass glanced over her shoulder to see him sweeping an arm across the kitchen island to clear a spot, dumping a few scattered items and a plastic bowl of clementines to the floor with a clatter. She opened her mouth, about to ask him what he thought he was doing, when he changed his hold on her again and set her neatly up on the island. His now free hands came up and circled her wrists, drawing her hands down until he pressed her palms onto the countertop behind her and held them there. Nudging a hip between her knees until he stood between her open thighs, he managed to effectively negate her frantic kicks.

"Well now, this is a little better." The big man purred at her. His eyes flickered down, taking her in and spending a little too long eyeing her bust in the soft purple tank. He cleared his throat roughly and pulled back, giving them both a few extra inches of breathing room. "Now I suggest we start over."

"Start over?" Cass echoed, looking up at him suspiciously. Her body trembled as her adrenaline ran out. She would never admit it but she was pretty much at the end of her rope.

"Yes, little one. You're not in any danger from me. Come on, take a deep breath and let me explain." He stared into her eyes, wordlessly pleading with her to follow his lead. She hesitated for a long moment and then grudgingly took a deep, tremulous breath making him smile warmly. "That's it. All right now, what's your name, little Summoner?"

She blinked up at him for a moment, unsure she should really tell this strange man anything personal. He was behaving as if this was all some very odd misunderstanding and, while she had really tried her hardest to kick his ass, he had refrained from injuring her in any way. Still, it was a moment before she managed to force her name out. "Cassidy."

"A good Irish name. It suits you." Her home invader smiled down at her, eyes twinkling. "I'm Verrin."

"Verrin?" She repeated, studying him. *What a strange name.* Something he'd said caught her attention. "Wait, why did you call me Summoner?"

Verrin seemed to debate how to answer that for a few moments. "First, let me ask you a question. Did you happen to read something, perhaps in a foreign language, in the last little bit?"

Cassidy stared at him hard, unsure where this was going. "Uh...yeah. What does that have to do with you being in my house?"

"More than you might think. Did this something sound a bit like this..." He leaned forward until his cheek rested against hers and whispered softly against the shell of her ear. "Loco te, Verrin, et quaero voluptatem tui tactus."

His voice ran like a river of silk through her body, causing a shiver to spread up from the base of her spine. The words she had stumbled over earlier slipped off his tongue like a lover's plea, as if he'd been born to the language.

"Those words made you my summoner. You asked me to come to you and that was exactly what I did." Verrin grinned down at her and winked. "Although, usually when I arrive my summoner is still in her bed, awaiting me with longing."

Cass blushed before she could help it. Damn him. It wasn't like she was faced with guys this hot every day. She had absolutely no idea how to handle someone so blatantly flirtatious. Definitely, time to change the subject. In desperation, she spit out the first thing that came to mind. "I thought you needed a pentagram to summon a demon."

48

Verrin sighed and pulled back slightly, freeing her hands and giving her a bit more space. "Can I just assure you that everything you've heard about us is probably wrong?"

Cass felt her eyes widen. *Is he admitting to being a demon?* Her hands slipped over his arms to circle his biceps, giving him a little push backward to try and gain even more space. "Now you're seriously scaring me."

Verrin captured one of her hands in his and held it over his heart where she could feel the steady rise and fall of his chest as he breathed. "I know you have no reason to trust me but I promise you I would never hurt you. To harm a female is the most revolted action a man could commit. I would turn on my brothers before I raised a hand to do you harm." He stared at her, azure eyes trying to will her into believing him.

Cassidy watched him, carefully taking his measure. He seemed to be telling the truth and seeing as he'd had plenty of opportunities to hurt her and hadn't, she had to at least give him that much credit. She pulled her hand back and crossed her arms, giving him a pointed stare. "Okay, say I buy into your supposedly honourable nature. That still doesn't answer the question of what you are or why you're in my house." She narrowed her eyes at him, determined to get an answer. "Your eyes glow. I saw it. That's not normal."

Verrin grinned at her perceptiveness and casually dropped the bomb. "I am a descendant of angels."

"Angels?" She stared at him in disbelief for a moment before her gaze flicked over his shoulder, casually checking for wings. "Is that why you're shirtless?" She asked curiously.

"Uh...no." He chuckled. "I'm a descendant, not an actual angel. No wings for me. My father has them but my mom wasn't an angel and I took after her."

"What was your mom if she wasn't an angel?" Cass prodded, eyes narrowed in suspicion.

"Have you ever heard of the Djinn?" He shot back, obviously amused with her reaction.

"You mean like genies?" She asked skeptically.

He nodded, a wide smile stretching those full lips.

"You're seriously telling me you're part genie and part angel?" She queried, doubt edging into her voice as she tried to appear unswayed by his interesting story.

He nodded. "My father came to Earth and fell in love with my mom. Unfortunately, the big guy didn't like the fraternization and got kind of pissed about it."

"'Big guy'?" She repeated, wondering if he could mean what she suspected.

"God." He announced bluntly.

"Wouldn't that make your father a fallen angel?" She asked, head spinning.

"Not quite. Fallen angels are angels who have crossed into the underworld." He answered with a shrug. "My father was one of the Grigori or Watchers. Basically, a couple hundred angels descended to Earth a couple of millennia ago. They weren't evil, just determined to find their own way in life. Some were looking for glory, a few for love. Unfortunately, God didn't take the defection very well."

"So you're saying there are angels wandering around the streets?" She questioned. His story was interesting – completely ludicrous – but definitely interesting and she found herself entertained. It was almost like one of her

50

books. He seemed so earnest that he made you want to believe him.

Verrin laughed. "Yeah, but you wouldn't see them. Humans don't take it well so they tend to keep themselves hidden. Plus, with all the FAA restrictions they don't fly too often. Angels and airplanes don't mix."

A hysterical giggle escaped her at that mental image and she slapped a hand to her mouth, trying to hide her amusement. It must be getting seriously late if she was starting to get giddy.

Verrin's body was suddenly in her space again, leaning forward and putting his cheek beside hers without touching as he dropped his voice to a sultry murmur. "I like that. You're sexy when you're laughing."

Her hands came up to push at his chest and he withdrew a bit, giving her the space she required to draw a breath into her lungs. She could feel the heat of her red cheeks and her gaze flitted away from his direct stare. Definitely time to return to safer topics. "So...uh... if you're half angel and half Djinn, what exactly does that make you?"

"That depends on who you ask. Technically, as the child of an earthbound angel, I'm a Nephilim. But Nephilim are the product of a human and angel mating, not a Djinn and angel. I fall into a slightly more exclusive and obscure category." He grinned wickedly and ran a hand through his messy dark hair. "Have you ever heard of Incubi?"

"Incubi? You mean the sex demons?" Cassidy ground out, suddenly hoarse. *Dear god, I summoned a sex demon? Savvy is not going to let me forget this!* Her hands came up to press against his shoulders again, trying to budge his bulk. "Let me down." She ordered flatly.

"Cassidy, darling, I'm not a monster. I would never do anything you don't want me to. I did tell you I wouldn't hurt you and I swear I meant that." Verrin stroked his hands up her arms, trying to soothe her with his touch.

Even through her sudden fear his touch affected her, causing the strangest flutter to take flight in her stomach. Ah hell, if something as simple as him stroking her arm comfortingly caused her pulse to quicken with desire what would his touch feel like if he meant to seduce her? For that matter, did she want to be seduced by an Incubus?

Cassidy shook her head, trying to clear her thoughts, and shoved his hands away. "You're a demon!"

"Technically any creature that God didn't directly have a hand in creating is a demon." He pointed out smartly.

"Are you insane?" Her voice sounded pained even to her own ears when she met his eyes. "You're saying you're a demon that feeds on sex! I've read enough to know nothing good comes from associating with demons. And I for one am *not* going to have sex with you!"

Verrin stared at her blankly for a moment, appearing taken aback, before a chuckle burst out. "Okay." He agreed easily. "So we don't have sex. No worries."

It was her turn to be stunned, transfixed by his deep masculine laughter. It was a moment before his words sunk in but when they did her fear immediately rerouted into anger. "Did you just say *okay*?" Cassidy scowled at him.

He nodded, a peaceable smile pinned on his face.

"So you're okay not having sex with me?" She

clarified skeptically.

"Absolutely." Verrin agreed, nodding.

"Don't you need sex to live?" She shot back.

"To live? No. To put a smile on my face?" He broadly grinned at her before he answered seriously. "Absolutely. I don't need it every day, just on a fairly regular basis."

Cassidy narrowed her eyes at the stunning, supposedly supernatural being that stood in front of her. Why did it even bother her that he was totally blasé about having sex with her? Why the hell did she even care?

CHAPTER 6

Seir took a breath and immediately wished he hadn't. Every lungful of air felt like it was filled with razor blades. He groaned and blinked his eyes open. His exhale sent grains of sands skittering across the dirt floor beneath his head.

Earlier he had thought he'd heard his older brother, Verrin, calling his name, but he didn't hear him anymore. Factoring in his current condition, it had probably been a hallucination.

Four days ago he'd been sitting in the garden of his villa with a few of his ladies playing an epic game of Monopoly that involved far too much cheating and cheesie throwing. His stomach had ached from laughter as Amelia and Dori, two of his adopted human sisters, argued over bank mismanagement. Amelia, as the banker, had tried to assure Dori that she was being perfectly honest with the cash when Dori had called her out. Seir had refused to admit he'd been watching the little cheat skim money from the bank to fund her hotel building enterprise the entire game. It had quickly devolved into snack food throwing that had the rest of the group taking cover.

His brothers mocked him for his ladies, laughingly referring to them as his harem, but Seir loved having them around. When his parents had learned of God's judgment on the Watchers they had decided to hide their children from God's wrath, splitting up the boys and giving each of them into the care of those they trusted. He had been given to his mother's sister to hide and when the angels killed his parents she had welcomed him into her family officially. Between her and her four young daughters, he had taken the big brother role and grew to adore it.

His aunt was long gone now, as well as two of his cousins. So many years had passed since he had laid them each to rest. He had followed the two cousins he had left as they grew up and had their own families. He'd made sure they were happy but always thought it best not to get involved, assuming they would be better off with their own people.

Instead, he had begun to collect sisters of his own choosing.

At first, he had just stumbled across them, women stuck in bad situations who could use a helping hand. Whether it had been escaping an arranged marriage or struggling to get out of poverty, Seir had stepped up to the plate to help them in any way he could. He'd married, stolen, lied and cheated to free each of them from the trouble that dogged their heels and had been rewarded for his efforts with lasting friendships.

Some of the women would stay with him their entire lives, feeling secure only with him, while others would eventually prefer to go their own way. Regardless, he would set them up the best he could and assure them he would always be there if needed. Sometimes they developed feelings beyond friendship for him but he never let himself cross that line, hating the idea of letting them down but not wanting to lose their trust should things go awry.

Instead, he would take his ingrained lusts to young widows and women who enjoyed the pleasures of the flesh. Women he could wine, dine and bed without hurt feelings or lost relationships. It's how he'd done things for nearly 1400 years.

Now whenever he felt his homes were getting too quiet, he would travel, hoping to find a new addition to his makeshift family. Each of the eleven women who now lived with him at his Italian villa had been brought into his family by sheer chance. Amelia had tried to pick his pockets on a busy London street in an effort to feed her young self. Dori had offered herself to him in exchange for cash to help pay her grandmother's medical bills. Everyone had their own dark past that he had done everything in his power to rescue them from.

He'd tried his best to recreate the feeling of family he remembered from growing up with his aunt and her daughters. In the end, the women saved him as much as he did them. He had helped them out of their circumstances and in return, they rescued him from his loneliness. They were his haven.

It was mutually beneficial in his books.

His brothers thought he was nuts to have so many women in his house and not be sexually involved with any of them. There had been many arguments over Seir's demand that his siblings leave his girls alone. They

complained it was like being at a buffet and not being able
to eat anything while Seir just couldn't wrap his head
around his brothers sleeping with his 'sisters'.

He'd give anything to be with them all now.

There was a jangle of keys and the sound of metal
grinding as a lock was turned. The rustle of cloth preceded
a rough hand grabbing his shoulder and jerking him over
onto his abused back.

Seir bit his lip, tasting blood when he refused to cry
out at the pain of the dirt floor rubbing into his abraded
back.

Two big men stood over him, staring down with
pitiless expressions. The one on the left reached down and
grabbed his wrists, both of which bore wide golden cuffs.
The other man touched a golden chain to each cuff and
the metal melded together, effectively creating manacles.
They gripped him by his upper arms and hauled him to his
feet.

Seir's head spun the moment he was vertical. He
would have fallen flat on his face if the guards hadn't been
holding him up. He watched his feet stumble and drag as
they hauled him bodily out of the cell and up a flight of
stairs.

Spots danced in front of his eyes and he groaned,
blinking to try to clear his vision. When he managed to see
clearly he saw the dirt strewn stone steps had turned into a
light gray stone floor and he lifted his head enough to see
he was now in a large room. The ceiling rose up a good
fifteen feet and the walls were smooth with painted murals
of people and animals that reminded him of some he'd
seen at a Mayan art exhibit in a museum years ago. The
room was long and sparsely furnished, just three carved

wooden chairs at one end and a bunch of long tables and low benches pushed against the walls, leaving the middle clear. A mixture of torches and electric lanterns lit the space in varying degrees. At the other end of the room, great pillars held up the ceiling, opening the room to a midnight view of a rain-soaked dark jungle and the sprawling shadow of a tiered stone temple.

Entranced by the sight, his weary mind failed to notice when four men hauled a large wooden structure in, dropping it to the floor with a thud. A large wood platform balanced a free standing X made of wooden beams stained dark with age. Solid metal rings graced each point, waiting for something to secure. A Saint Andrew's cross.

His stomach churned as he was led to the cross and, with a tap of the guard's finger, the golden chain split in half leaving a length of chain on each cuff. One guard pressed his chest into the wood and the other stretched his arms up, shackling him to the structure. They tied his ankles and then left without a word.

Seir tried to take the weight off his wrists by standing but his body shook when he tried to put too much weight on his feet. He rested as much weight as possible against the wooden structure and let his head loll, resting it against the side of one of the wooden arms. He stared out at the jungle scene in front of him, the patter of rain making his parched mouth crave a drink. His stomach had gone past grumbling and now he just felt hollow. How long had he been here? He was having trouble remembering.

The scent of a woman reached him and his body instantly hardened. Damn, he needed sex. The desire was eating away at his thoughts, distracting him from everything but the one thing his body needed more than any other in that moment.

Soft, feminine fingers touched his shoulder and trailed across the bunched muscle to the other side. He groaned, needing so much more. The press of lush breasts against his back made him moan in mixed pleasure and pain and thrash against his bonds. Those hands traveled around his abdomen and raked nails gently up his stomach, the muscles twitching beneath the touch.

"Hello, Seir. Did you miss me?" Her voice hummed in his ear and he shivered as her hair slid along his skin.

"Gods woman..." He groaned, his erection pinned painfully inside his pants. "Let me free. I need to touch you. Now."

"Tsk, tsk. One thing at a time." She chided as she slid a hand down over the fly of his jeans and gently stroked the hardness beneath. "As much as I'd love to play, we have some business to conclude first."

"Anything." He promised, hips jerking against that barely there touch.

She chuckled. "Lovely. All I need is a little of your blood and then we can get to it."

"My blood?" Seir questioned, this somehow striking him as odd. "Why would you need my blood?"

The woman growled softly and circled the cross, coming to stand before him. "Yes, Seir, your blood."

He stared at the woman and his blood chilled. Suddenly his brain kicked in. "Empusa."

"So you're not entirely gone yet." The red-headed wench sneered at him.

"Why do you need my blood? What the hell are you

up to?" Seir wanted to yell but his throat was so dry his voice was naught more than a fierce hiss.

Empusa stepped forward, her metallic prosthetic leg glimmering in the watery daylight beneath the tight black shorts she wore. "I'm not at liberty to tell you, I'm afraid. Mercenary-client confidentiality, you know. On the upside, you give me your blood and I'll give you anything you want." She purred, gliding a hand down his ribs on one side while she sighed in appreciation. "I get the blood, you get sex, everyone wins. Hell, I'll even acquire a dozen women to keep you busy until my client comes to collect. Once the client's happy, you'd be free to go. What do you say?"

"Burn in hell, bitch." Seir spat at her.

She looked away and gestured for someone to enter the room. A burly, bare-chested guard brought one of the ornate wooden chairs around and positioned it about ten feet in front of him. Empusa took up a seat facing him as the man disappeared again, crossing her long legs at the knee. "Well if you won't give it to me of your own free will, I guess I'll just have to take it from you."

With a nod at the man who no doubt stood behind him, Seir heard the whistle of air and felt the first crack of the whip against his skin, layering fresh strikes over the previously healing stripes.

He held on to the chains, refusing to cry out until he felt his blood soaking wetly into the back of his jeans. Empusa gave some sort of order and his abuser exchanged the basic whip for a crueler weapon.

When the metal barbs in the ends of the multiple tails sliced across his skin, he screamed out his agony, almost drowning out Empusa's laughter.

***

Cassidy stared up at the big man and frowned.

This gorgeous man had just admitted to being a creature that fed on sex and yet he had no desire to get sex from her. Somehow that knowledge pissed her off.

What the hell am I worried about? It's not like I want to have sex with an Incubus! She railed at herself. Unbidden her gaze raked down his bare chest to his abs and her core gave a betraying little shudder at the treasure trail that led into the waistband of his black jeans. Her face heated and she forced herself to look away. *Dammit, all to hell!*

"But we do have a slight problem," Verrin informed her slowly. His face seemed suspiciously blank for some reason and he looked to the side, refusing to meet his eyes.

Cass glanced back at him, narrowing her eyes and crossing her arms in the best mimic of skeptical disdain she could manage. "Problem?"

His gaze drifted down to her breasts briefly and those blue eyes flickered with an inner glow as he took in their fullness before he shook his head slightly as if trying to focus. "Uh, yes." He met her eyes again. "You summoned me. You spoke the ritual and brought me here. I can't leave your side until I complete what you summoned me for."

"What does that mean?"

Verrin grimaced. "You don't want to know."

"Why not?"

"Let's just call it a good guess."

Cass tried her best to glower at him, which would have been a hell of a lot easier if he wasn't over a head taller than her even when she was sitting on the counter. "Tell me." She insisted.

Verrin looked up at the ceiling as if he could find salvation there before he mumbled. "You requested an orgasm."

"*Excuse me*? I did no such thing!" Cassidy practically shrieked in disbelief.

"You did. You begged for the pleasure of my touch." Verrin sighed. "I'm sure you didn't realize it, the words you spoke were in an ancient language, but the fact is you did summon me for just that reason. I'm bound to you until I give you what you asked for."

"I am not having sex with you." She told him flatly.

"We've established that." Verrin sighed. "I think the binding should wear off. Eventually."

"How soon is eventually?" Cass questioned, not sure she liked the tone of his voice.

"A week, maybe two. Or three. I've honestly never had to wait for it to fade." Verrin answered with a sly grin.

She just bet he hadn't. With his good looks, it was hard to imagine Verrin being rejected all that often. As much as she hated to admit it, even she was tempted to agree to let him have her.

Only she was afraid that once wasn't going to be enough with him.

She took a deep breath to brace herself and let it out slowly. "So basically I'm stuck with you."

Verrin looked pained. "Sorry. I know it's not ideal."

She eyed him suspiciously. "I could call the cops and have you arrested for breaking and entering."

A chuckle broke from the gorgeous man and his eyes seemed to gain a bit of that glow they'd had upstairs.

"Yeah, just try it. We're bound. You put that much space between us and you'll be bailing me out in the morning just to have your wicked way with me in the parking lot."

Cass narrowed her eyes at him and took his measure. It hadn't escaped her that he looked identical to the man in the old book. It was entirely possible he was lying to her but what if he was telling the truth? Cassidy closed her eyes and rubbed the bridge of her nose. Her head was starting to pound and a sudden wave of exhaustion had settled over her. Maybe if she took a step back from things for a while they might be able to sort things out. "Look, I can't deal with this stuff right now. Do you promise not to murder me in my sleep?" The fact that she was asking a possible home invader if he planned on killing her and expected an honest answer was a particularly good example of how tired her brain was.

Verrin blinked. "Murdering you wasn't on my to-do list, so no."

"Good. I vote we sleep on this whole situation and try to work it out in the morning."

Verrin smiled brightly and nodded. "That's a great idea." He caught her hips up in his big hands and swept her off the counter, lowering her down his body until her feet touched the floor again.

Cassidy stared up at him, neck craned back to take him in. "Good god, you're huge!" She murmured in amazement.

Verrin's full lips curved into a slow smile and he patted the top of her head like she was a good child. "You're just a tiny thing."

She narrowed her eyes at him, trying to look disapproving even as a small part of her preened at being called petite. "How tall *are* you?"

He chuckled. "Last time I checked, six foot ten. And you're what? Five foot nothing?"

She drew herself up to her full – if meager – height. "Five foot two and an eighth."

Verrin snorted. "Gotta count every little bit huh, short stuff?"

Cassidy stuck her tongue out at him and blew a raspberry.

"All right, enough fun." Verrin dug into his back pocket for her phone and pressed it into her hand. "I'm trusting you not to call the cops on me. I promise you're completely safe with me." He clasped her shoulders and spun her around, directing her to the base of the stairs. "Time for bed."

She was nuts. That was the only viable reason why she would let a strange man stay the night in her home after he'd obviously broken in somehow. *I'm probably going to regret this in the morning if he murders me in my sleep. Wait...* Her brain stalled out on that mixed up thought and she sighed. Both her mother and grandmother had always told her to go with her instincts about people and she had never regretted doing so. Verrin, for all his overwhelming stature and unexplained appearance, didn't set off her radar. In fact, under different circumstances, she would have gone out of her way to talk to such an interesting man.

Grandma, where ever you are, don't let this go horribly awry on me. She prayed for the first time in ages.

With her apprehension eased slightly and a jaw-cracking yawn, she did as directed, climbing the stairs and heading for her room. It wasn't until she reached the

64

threshold to her room that she realized Verrin was directly behind her, intending on following her in.

"Where do you think you're going?" Cass inquired archly, turning on him.

Verrin blinked innocently. "To bed."

"Oh no, you don't! You are *not* sleeping with me." She pointed across the hall to the spare bedroom. "You can sleep in there."

For a big man, he took the look of a kicked puppy very easily. His bottom lip pouted slightly and he blinked long dark lashes slowly over those brilliant azure eyes.

Without a word, Cassidy stepped back and shut the door in his face, flipping the lock with an audible click. She turned on the light and checked her room, making sure no other surprises lurked within its confines. The antique book sat on the bedside table where she had laid it earlier and on instinct she went and grab it.

Throwing open the bedroom door again, she shoved it into Verrin's arms. "Here. You get to deal with this. If anyone else pops out of it tonight they can appear in your bed."

With that, she shut the door on his surprised face but even still his soft laughter filter through the wood. "Don't I get a kiss good night?"

CHAPTER 7

After he'd been unceremoniously ditched in the hallway, Verrin decided to check out his new accommodations. Ignoring the bedroom Cassidy had told him to use, he opted to go downstairs. He took some time to wash off as much of the vanilla air freshener as he could in the kitchen sink before scavenging through her fridge to assuage the gnawing hunger that ate at him. Two ham and cheese sandwiches and a glass of milk in hand, he'd parked himself in front of the TV in the wee hours of the morning to see what he could learn about his whereabouts.

The major problem with a summons was that it pulled you out of your everyday life and plunked you wherever the summoner happened to be. He'd had more than one instance of falling asleep in his own bed and waking up in someone else's. The whole scene was disorienting. Thankfully, in this modern age, he wasn't stuck asking his hostess where he was or having an exceedingly long walk home.

With a few clicks of the remote, the local weather

network told him he was not only in Charlottetown, Prince Edward Island on Canada's east coast but that it was a startling -22 degrees Celsius outside this early Sunday morning. Verrin cast a baleful glare at the living room's big picture window and eyed the snow drifts he could barely make out of the darkness in the backyard with disdain. Early December in Canada was not his cup of tea.

He watched the local weather report as he ate, amazed at how casually the anchor told the audience that a storm was going to drop another 20 centimeters of snow on them in just a few days. He thought of little Cassidy out there, dressed in a puffy parka and snow pants, cheeks flushed from exertion as she shoveled big heaps of fluffy snow. She'd be adorable.

With his stomach now full, he sat his empty plate and glass on the coffee table and grabbed the old book Cass had shoved at him before she locked him out of her room. It was bound in soft leather and almost two inches thick. As he started to flip through he realized he was holding an old Mythos.

It had been centuries since he'd seen one of the handcrafted encyclopedias of mythical beings and whoever had made this one had gone through a lot of trouble. Stories, tales, and facts on a startling number of creatures had been collected in the volume, each with a hand-drawn picture and as much detail on the subject as the author could come across. Some of the text seemed to have been copied from other texts and some appeared to have been the author's own assumptions.

Coming across his own likeness had been kind of surprising. He figured she had found the summoning spell within its pages but hadn't expected to come across a drawing of himself to go with it. Having no idea when the artist had gotten close to him was a little eerie.

The writer had also made some false assumptions. The text described the act of fornicating with an Incubus as 'an unwilling woman being ravaged by his barbed member'. He was glad Cass couldn't read the old languages or she'd have run screaming from him when he'd first appeared.

Scratch that. She *had* run from him. But if she thought his dick was some sort of torture implement, he was pretty sure air freshener wouldn't have been her go to weapon when she'd reached the kitchen. Butcher knife anyone?

Verrin groaned to himself and sat the book aside, deciding to take a closer look at it later. He grinned to himself as he wondered what she'd reward him with if he translated some of the old text for her.

Getting up, he wandered around the living room, going first to the window to stare out at the snow filling the fenced in backyard. Some of the snow piles had leafy protrusions he assumed would be bushes and plants in the spring and a little shed in the back had a patio set and covered barbecue nestled up to the side of it for protection. Her yard wasn't huge but obviously a place she enjoyed during the warmer months.

The pictures decorating the mantel of the fireplace on the opposite wall drew him next and he couldn't help but smile as he saw Cass's smiling face in many of them. He picked up one of a younger Cassidy standing in graduation robes between a proud looking older man and a teary eyed but beaming woman. She looked young and ready for anything standing between her happy parents

68

and he realized she really took after her folks with her dark hair and eyes but that smile was all her own. He set the frame down and gazed at the rest. Cass and a blonde woman dressed in white T-shirts bearing the Canadian flag, red maple leaves painted on their cheeks. Cass standing behind a seated older woman, arms wrapped around her in a hug amongst flowering rose bushes. Cass as a little girl, hair in braids and wearing a pink swimsuit as she played with a blonde girl and three slightly older boys at the beach.

A dozen frames littered the mantel, all colours and sizes, showing snapshots out of this one human woman's life. It made him long for pictures of his own.

While he saw his brothers frequently he had almost forgotten what his parents looked like. He'd been only eleven when they'd died and after so long it was hard to remember. A picture of his mother's smile or his father playing with them would have gone a long way.

With his heart in his throat, he turned away, needing to distract himself.

He poked through the downstairs for a while until he came to one of the many bookshelves that occupied the walls of her home like silent sentinels against boredom. He casually read titles until he came to the realization that his little summoner was thoroughly obsessed with the paranormal. Books about vampires, werewolves, aliens and fae lined the shelves. Pulling a volume free he noticed that several pages were carefully dog-eared. He had spotted the mason jar of bookmarks on her coffee table earlier, their little tassels and ribbons just waiting to be put to use, so he figured the dog ears must be some sort of system she had.

He flipped to one and read a bit, a smile curving his

lips. The scene described a woman being pinned down by her ardent demon lover and kissed until she screamed his name. Only the first of those kisses had been on her lips.

Mmm... I think I'm going to like this woman. She had a hankering for the magic in life and a passionate side he heartily approved of. Now if he could just get her to trust him enough to show it.

He knew the binding wasn't going to let him get very far from her side until he had completed the necessary task, but seeing as Cassidy wasn't comfortable with that, it could be a while. He could either drag her with him to rescue Seir – which was an unnerving idea – or work on getting past her defenses so he could complete the summoning and leave her here in safety.

Opting for the latter, he had borrowed the cordless phone he found charging in her living room to call his brother, Pithius. Thius, as they all called him, was the only one of his brothers he knew was currently in North America and should be the easiest to get a hold of. He called his Laguna Beach house first, hoping to catch him. If Thius wasn't home he was going to owe Cass a fair bit in long distance bills by the time he tracked another of his brothers down.

Thankfully he'd gotten him on the first try.

Thius had laughed at him hysterically when he'd been forced to admit the reason he couldn't help find Seir immediately. "Seriously? The great Verrin got shot down by a woman? She must be quite the feisty little thing. I can't wait to meet her! Maybe she'll like me more."

Verrin growled, not liking the idea of Cass around his strikingly handsome blond brother. "Just find Seir. He wasn't looking so good when I last saw him. Bring a woman with you, Empusa isn't letting him have one."

He didn't have to see Thius's face to know the other man was wincing. A couple days without a woman started to make them twitchy. More than that and they started to lose it. First, your focus would go and you'd react to any woman. Then you'd start to lose the ability to restrain yourself from taking the nearest female body. It was a scary situation and one they all did their best to avoid. Getting Seir out of there before he did something he'd regret was their top priority.

"How long has he been there?" Thius asked, his voice sounding worried even over the phone.

"At least five days now. Maybe more."

"Shit." Thius ground out. "All right. I'll contact Meri and we'll hunt down Leon. He was headed out to his cabin the last time I was talking to him."

Verrin smirked. "Stop that. If Dantalion hears you call him Leon he'll kick your ass and Seir doesn't have time for you two to go round."

"Whatever. He'd have to catch me first." Thius snorted. "All right, bang your chick and get your ass out of there. We're going to need as much help as we can get."

"I'll get right on that." Verrin had hung up with a sense of relief, confident his brothers would handle things in his absence.

A glance at the microwave told him it was nearing eight in the morning and he was getting hungry again. Perhaps he could lure a little orgasmic charity out of Cass with a good breakfast. That tactic always worked on him anyway.

Verrin hummed a little song as he got cooking, setting up bacon to fry and pulling eggs and butter out of the fridge. After last night's debacle, he wanted to prove to his hostess that he could be a civilized male and figured a full Sunday morning breakfast was a step in the right direction. He hoped to deliver it to her in bed but doubted she'd appreciate the intrusion. The toaster popped and he pulled the slices out to butter them before setting them on a plate to the side.

Pulling the bacon out of the pan, he dumped it in a bowl and wondered when the woman in question would wake up. He couldn't blame Cassidy for being leery of him. As far as she was concerned he appeared randomly in her house in the middle of the night and proceeded to chase her down. It certainly wasn't his smoothest introduction ever but he had no way of knowing she hadn't summoned him purposefully.

Considering his traumatizing entrance into her life, Cassidy would probably be happy to know that this predicament wasn't going to last too long.

A knock at the front door brought his head up and he paused before dumping the scrambled egg mix in the pan. Setting the bowl aside, he flicked the burner off and went to stand before the front door. The knock came again and he looked up the stairs, hoping Cassidy would hear it and come down.

No such luck.

He took a deep breath and flipped the deadbolt, opening the door a foot. "Hello?"

A blonde woman who looked somehow familiar stood there, rummaging in the huge shoulder bag she used as a purse. "Hey, I just - " She looked up and her eyes widened, mouth dropping into a perfect O. "Who are you?" She asked warily, letting a smartphone with a sparkling silver case fall back into her purse.

Verrin smiled politely. "I'm Verrin. Cassidy is still sleeping. Can I help you?"

The blonde arched an eyebrow at him and looked skeptical. "You can help me by explaining why a strange man is in my best friends house, answering her door. Because when I left yesterday, she didn't have a male guest and if she'd gotten a boyfriend, I would have been the first person to know."

Verrin glanced over his shoulder at the stairs. Still no sign of Cassidy. Damn it. "Why don't you come in?"

The blonde narrowed her eyes and pulled her phone from her purse again. She poked at the screen before holding it up so he could see, showing off the numbers she had already punched in on the screen. "See that? You do anything weird or I find anything hinky in there and I'm calling 911. Then you can explain to the nice men in blue what you're doing in my friend's house."

Verrin held up his hands in a placating gesture. *What is with these women?* They came out all guns blazing and not even his significant amount of charm seemed to deter them. "Okay, calm down. Come on in and look around all you like. I was just making breakfast." He stepped back and let the door swing wide open.

The woman he now recognized as Cass's friend from the photos breezed past him, going from room to room, peeking in and checking for signs of disturbance. Verrin didn't step away from the door, wanting to leave her an open escape route. When she circled back to the hall, obviously finding no trace of theft or violence, she stood at the bottom of the stairs and looked him over carefully.

"So Cassidy is upstairs?"

"Yes, she's sleeping. She had a late night." Verrin explained.

The blonde snorted indelicately as she eyed his bare chest. "I just bet she did." She dropped her bag on the hall table and shook her phone at him. "Okay, here's what we're going to do. We're going to go into the kitchen, you are going to continue cooking because that bacon smells amazing and I am going to make coffee. The phone will remain pre-dialled until such time as I see my girl. Deal?"

Verrin nodded. "That's fine. You're welcome to go check on her if you like. She's in her room."

The woman smiled wickedly at him. "Yeah, if she was with you last night, there's a good chance she's going to need all the sleep she can get and won't appreciate me interrupting. I'd rather take my chances with the sexy home invader than face her wrath."

***

Cassidy rubbed her face into the pillow, trying to find a comfortable spot in her sleep dazed state. When that failed to lull her back to sleep, she rolled over in bed and stared at the ceiling in tired disgust. The sun streamed through the slats of her bedroom blinds and caught in the lazily drifting dust motes. Her bed was warm and she had no desire to leave it anytime soon. Reaching out, her fingers fumbled across the night stand, hunting for her cell phone. She dragged it into bed and saw a low battery warning and three missed text notifications.

Savvy: Hey! I'm heading over. My neighbour was

threatening to drop by after church again
and I need to hide out for a while.

Savvy: Answer this message!

Savvy: You have been keeping secrets, naughty
girl. This is unacceptable. I need all the
details. Get your butt down here or I may
just steal him for myself. :)

Cassidy blinked at her phone in confusion before it
clicked.

Oh God. Verrin!

How had she forgotten there was a strange man in
her house? Worse than that, how had she forgotten he
wasn't a man but supposedly some sort of supernatural
stud whose mere presence was orgasm inducing?

She threw the blankets off and jumped out of bed.
Her door was still barricaded by the old train trunk she
usually kept loaded with shoes in her closet. She hadn't felt
comfortable sleeping with just the door lock between her
and her uninvited house guest. Just like she hadn't been
able to sleep in less than her tank top and a pair of sweat
pants on the off chance Verrin did burst in.

She shoved the trunk aside, leaving it against the
wall, and tore open the door. Feet flying down the stairs,
she ran down the hall and skidded to a stop at the
threshold of her kitchen.

Savvy looked up from where she sat at the kitchen
island, a coffee mug in one hand and her other casually
flipping the pages of a fashion magazine. Across from her
Verrin looked up from where he stood in front of the
stove, spatula in one hand as he flipped scrambled eggs
onto a plate.

"Hey, Cass." Savvy lifted her cup in salute and smiled wickedly at her. "Sleep well?"

Cass blushed, realizing what Savvy must have assumed.

"Good morning, Cassidy. Would you like some breakfast?" Verrin asked, smiling as he slid a plate with bacon, scrambled eggs and toast on it in front of Savannah.

Cassidy nodded dumbly as she stumbled over and sunk onto a stool beside her friend, dropping the cell phone she still clutched on the counter. Savannah grinned at her and lifted her coffee mug to her lips. "Long night?" She asked softly before taking a sip. Her eyes glittered with mischief.

Cass was sure her ears were red with how flushed she felt. "Uh...yeah." She croaked out.

Savvy chuckled and winked at her. Her whisper was conspiratorial as she leaned close. "I doubt I could have slept at all with that man in my house. But then he wouldn't be sleeping either. I think my panties nearly fell off of their own accord when he opened the front door."

Cassidy looked over at the man in question and had to agree. Verrin had turned back to the stove, cracking eggs into a bowl. He still didn't have a shirt on and she couldn't help the little sigh that tried to escape. Muscles shifted in his strong back as he moved around her kitchen and his black jeans looked as if they had been painted on. His dark hair was disheveled as if someone had been running their fingers through it.

He bent over briefly to put the eggs away in the fridge and both women leaned forward casually, ogling his rear. They caught each other looking and burst into giggles, earning them a confused look from the object of their ardour.

With a shake of his head, Verrin dumped the scrambled eggs from the pan onto a plate, put a handful of bacon beside it and two slices of toast before setting it in front of Cass. "I wasn't sure how you liked your eggs. Hope scrambled is all right. What would you like to drink?"

Cass blinked and looked down at the meal. An Incubus had cooked her breakfast. This was way too weird. "Um, juice?"

"Coming right up." Verrin turned back to gather a glass and poured her some orange juice.

"So..." Savvy started, popping a piece of bacon in her mouth and chewing as she looked Cassidy over. "Verrin here was explaining to me that you were nice enough to let him stay the night after his car broke down last night. How very thoughtful of you." Her pitch told Cass she didn't buy any of that ridiculous story.

With Cass's luck, Savvy probably believed that she had called an escort or abducted the poor man. Men with Verrin's model-worthy looks didn't generally go for nerdy, chubby librarians. At least not in her experience.

The house phone rang and their awkward conversation was put on hold. Cassidy got up and went to the phone that sat in its charger on one of the living room end tables. She turned her back on her guests so she could concentrate on the phone and answered. "Hello?"

"Oh hey, it's the chick!" The man on the other end had a pleasantly deep tone and he seemed surprised she'd answered her own phone. "Do me a favour, will ya? Just bang -"

There was a crash and a scrabbling noise on the other end, followed by a string of rather creative curses that had her pulling away to look askance at the receiver.

"Hello? Miss?"

Cass put the cordless handset back to her ear and frowned. "Yes?"

"I apologize for my brother, he was dropped on his head as a child." The male voice that took over the call had a charming European accent that Cassidy immediately fell in love with. It was the cultured caress of words that made you want to hear him say your name.

"Oh, okay." Cass murmured, unsure how to respond. "Who is this?"

"My apologies. My name is Merihem, but please just call me Meri. I believe my brother, Verrin, is in your company. May I speak with him please?"

"Yeah. One second." Cassidy walked back into the kitchen and held the phone out to Verrin, who was leaning against the counter devouring his own plate of eggs. "It's for you."

CHAPTER 8

Verrin had the sense to appear sheepish as he reached for the phone. "Thanks. Do you mind if I take this in the other room?" He gestured to the French doors off the entryway that led to the home office in the former parlor.

Cassidy nodded at him in bewilderment and he opened the glass paned door, slipping through and closing it behind him before putting the phone to his ear. He glanced back into the dining room where the women were now huddled together at the kitchen island, talking rapidly, before he answered the phone. "Hello?"

"Hello brother, how are things faring with your Lady?" Merihem asked cheerfully.

"She's *not* my Lady." Verrin corrected, striding over to sit in the office chair in front of the dark computer. "She summoned me without knowing what it was she was doing and now I'm stuck here until I complete the spell."

"Ah, I see. Is she not being responsive to your usual charm?" Meri asked, a hint of laughter behind his smooth cultured accent.

"Maybe she just needs an Incubus with skill!" Thius yelled in the background.

"Shut him up, Meri." He growled into the receiver. "This has nothing to do with my skills."

On the other end, Merihem sighed. "I understand that but can you quicken your pace a little? A swift seduction would be favourable considering the circumstances."

"Dammit, I know! But I'm not going to lure her into anything she doesn't want." Verrin hissed, getting up to pace. He peeked out the french door on the way past to make sure the women weren't listening at the door. The last thing he needed was to have Cassidy overhear him discussing his efforts to seduce her with his brothers. That definitely wouldn't help the situation.

"Is she a maiden?" Meri inquired thoughtfully.

Verrin rolled his eyes. "Meri, no one says maiden anymore. And no, I really don't think so. Can't say for sure but she doesn't look at me as a virgin would. Why?"

"To complete the summoning you need only to give her an orgasm. Sex is not necessarily essential. You could bring her to peak in any other manner of ways." Meri offered thoughtfully.

"Yeah, thanks, I'll keep that in mind." Verrin closed his eyes, suddenly tired of this vein of conversation. "So I see that Thius found you. Any luck hunting down Dantalion or word on Seir?"

Merihem sighed, obviously noticing his brother's abrupt change of topic. "Not yet. We are on our way to Dan's cabin currently. Once we collect him we will focus on locating Seir."

"Tell him he's missing all the fun!" Pithius yelled in the background, followed by the sound of feminine giggles.

"Thius brought a few of his paramours with him," Meri informed him needlessly.

"Good, Seir's going to need them." Verrin sighed and ran a hand through his hair. "Look I have to get back to Cassidy. Let me know when you've got Dan and you're going after Seir. With any luck, I'll be done here by then."

"Very good. Farewell brother." Merihem said and hung up.

Verrin stared at the phone in his hand and growled in frustration. He really wanted to be with his brothers, hunting down Empusa and rescuing their brother. He didn't like being left out.

On the other hand, he hated the idea of rushing things with Cassidy. Meri was right, he could just get her off and get out, but that wasn't what he wanted to do. He wanted to take his time, seducing her and making this good for her. The idea of squandering a chance with her seemed a waste to him.

Turning back he saw the women were talking animatedly about something, paying him no mind. He pushed one of the French doors open slightly to eavesdrop on their conversation, a smile conquering his lips as he listened.

***

"Oh. My. God! I have no idea where you found him but you need to get me one. He can be my Christmas present." Savannah exclaimed the moment Verrin shut the sunroom door behind him. "For the record, I am not buying the his-car-broke-down-and-you-helped-the-hunky-damsel-in-distress story. No way. No how."

Cassidy couldn't help but laugh. Savvy had always had a good imagination and Cass wasn't sure she wanted to know what scenarios her friend's mind had come up with to explain Verrin's presence.

"So, please tell me that you were attacked by Mr. Studly in some sort of home invasion gone pornographic last night and you asked him to spend the night with you to make up for the money he'll miss out on by not robbing you blind." Savvy sipped at her coffee and glanced over her shoulder at the office doors. "I can't say I would blame you for not calling the cops."

"It's nothing like that. In fact, I'm not sure I even know how to explain it." Cassidy twisted her fingers in her lap, trying to think of a plausible scenario to give to her friend. If she told her the truth, Savvy might just have her committed.

"Look, as much as I want to pry and find out all the juicy details, I won't ask if you don't want me to. As long as you're safe and whatever is going on is consensual, I'm happy." Savvy reassured, putting a hand over Cass's fidgeting hands. The blonde winked as Cass met her eyes. "I will, however, create all sorts of scenarios in my head as to how you drugged or hypnotized a male underwear model into shacking up with you until you tell me exactly how it happened."

Cassidy chuckled, only Savannah would take this so well.

"Now, you are sure you're safe with him, right? You can tell me if not and I will have the twins and their cop buddies drag him away in cuffs, no problem at all." Savvy inquired in a serious whisper, darting another look at the French doors.

Cass took a deep breath and looked around for inspiration. She honestly wasn't sure why she didn't want to accept her friend's offer but Verrin didn't really scare her. Not the way someone who appeared randomly in your house certainly should anyway.

His presence made her stomach flutter as if she'd swallowed a bag of goldfish. He was undoubtedly gorgeous with his crazy height, solid muscles and golden skin and damn him for running around shirtless. Who the hell cooked bacon shirtless anyway? It was like a form of torture to watch him move around and not rub yourself against him like a cat in heat.

Deciding to go with honesty, she told Savvy some of the truth. "He showed up here last night. Caught me by surprise. I can't say more but I thought the worst at first too. He promised he wouldn't hurt me, swore to it in fact, and he didn't do anything last night. He asked to stay and I put him up in the spare room."

"Wait, you let him stay the night and you put him in the spare room?"

"Uh, yeah," Cass replied, not really getting where Savvy was coming from.

"I think I just lost a teensy bit of respect for you." Savannah sat back and sighed. "You had a golden opportunity to have that man in your huge four poster bed – which was totally created with BDSM in mind, by the way – and you didn't take it. I just don't know if I can be friends with you anymore."

Cassidy rolled her eyes and laughed. They had

discussed the benefits of the antique mahogany four poster plenty of times. Cassidy loved it because it was classic and the perfect thing for the bedroom in her old Victorian house but Savvy was sure she'd seen its like in a porno before. Cass had tried not think about her bed being used in such a manner. Not that a little bondage wouldn't be hot, it just didn't make getting to sleep easy when you were thinking of what would make good anchor points for wrists and ankles.

"Well, it wasn't like he was all excited to jump into bed with me either," Cassidy informed her archly.

"Why would he be? You made the poor man stay all by his lonesome in the spare room! And he even made you breakfast!" Savvy pointed out, gesturing at the plates in front of them.

"I'll be impressed if he actually washes all the dishes he dirtied," Cass grumbled contrarily, staring at the plate in front of her. She couldn't think of a time when a man not related to her had deigned to make breakfast for her. She really wasn't sure how she felt about that.

"Honey, you should be impressed that I didn't have him down on the kitchen floor licking chocolate sauce off those amazing abs." Savvy gave her an incredulous look as she fanned herself with a hand. "Did you see those things? You could wash laundry on his stomach he's so cut!"

Cassidy snorted out a laugh and nodded, giving in to her friend's enthusiasm. "Yeah, he is pretty amazing looking."

Savvy turned on her stool and grabbed Cassidy's shoulder to swivel her so that they were facing each other. "Look, I don't know what's going on here but I trust you will tell me when you're ready."

Cassidy nodded again.

"I have spent the last hour interrogating him. He doesn't give me any creepy vibes and, by the way he talks, he doesn't seem to have any bad intentions. What do you think?"

Cass paused for a second, gathering her thoughts. She wasn't sure what she felt about Verrin but she really didn't get the vibe he was out to do her harm. "I – He doesn't give me a bad vibe. He almost gave me a heart attack at first but he did seem to feel bad about that. I don't really know what to make of him though. It's weird."

Savvy grinned at her and leaned close, lowering her voice. "That's just because he's a gorgeous man who has yet to back down when you told him where to shove it. Did you seriously mace him with vanilla air freshener?"

Cassidy flushed in embarrassment. "Yeah, right in the eyes."

Savvy threw her head back and laughed. "Oh, that's classic! Guess he likes it rough."

When she finally got her giggles under control she patted Cass's arm. "I know you're not overly comfortable getting close to guys after the whole Tyler thing," Savvy put a hand up to ward off her friend's denial. "Your ex was an ass who didn't deserve for you to give him the time of day, but not every guy is a cheating jerk. Verrin is really interested in you. He asked a ton of questions about you this morning."

"Oh god, what did you tell him?" Cass groaned.

"Just that your ex was an asshole who demanded that you change yourself, that this house was all yours and would make a perfect love nest and that if he made you cry I would have the cops arrest and cavity search him until his colon was squeaky clean."

"Oh Lord..." Cass groaned.

"I have to say it's quite an effective threat."The masculine voice broke into their conversation and both women froze, caught in the middle of girl talk. They turned in unison to see Verrin leaning against the kitchen door jam, a smirk on his face.

Good god, how much had he heard?

"Well, if you two aren't hungry for seconds, I'll whip up the dishes." Verrin walked over to the stove and started gathering the pans together by the sink.

"Thanks for breakfast, Verrin. It was lovely! But I really should be going." Savvy chirped happily, hopping off her stool and gathering her purse and cell phone from the counter.

"What? Why?" Cass stared at her in horror, appalled that her friend would bail on her.

"You're welcome. I love to cook." Verrin said, turning to face them with a dishtowel in hand. He leaned back against the counter, posing with the ease of those born sexy.

Both women stared for a second.

"Wow, okay. I have errands to run." Savvy recovered first, giving him a stunning smile, and turned to hug Cassidy. "Take two of him and call me in the morning. You'll thank me. I promise!" Savvy whispered sneakily in her ear.

With that, Savannah turned tail and left, the sound of the big oak door slamming behind her.

Cassidy turned and stared at the Incubus who now occupied her home. *Well, this is going to be awkward.*

CHAPTER 9

Seir's body crashed to the dirt floor of his cell face first and the air rushed from his lungs, strangling the cry of pain that tried to emerge. His arms were cuffed behind his back so he had to struggle to roll onto his side and gasp for breath. He didn't even hear when the cell door slammed shut and locked behind him.

Once he was able to breathe, although even to his own ears it was more of a wheeze, he started to catalogue his injuries.

His back was a collage of slashes in varying degrees of healing, some cutting deep and oozing crimson. His face was bruised and beaten, one eye swelling shut and blood still slowly seeping from his nose. The fingers of his left hand had been bent until they snapped. His head spun from a dizzying combination of hunger, blood loss and lack of female energy.

The bruises and cuts would heal on their own but those fingers...

With a grim sigh, Seir wrapped the fingers of his

87

right hand around his left index finger and straightened it to the best of his ability. The pain made his head swim but he clenched his teeth and breathed raggedly through the process of straightening the other fingers out. He had no way to splint them but hopefully they would heal fast enough.

Not like he had any plans besides laying here and wheezing.

His body may have been in pain but it was still humming with arousal. Now that he was away from any source of feminine essence his mind came back to him a bit more. He wasn't sure how long he'd been in Empusa's hands but he was guessing it was nearing a week. He'd never let himself get this far gone before.

His body was in a permanent state of arousal. Even laying here he was at half mast. If he caught the scent of a female now, given half a heartbeat, he would be rock hard and buried inside her. No questions asked.

He'd never been so happy to be locked in a cell.

He had heard the horror stories from his brothers and the rare other Incubi. In the early days, they hadn't really understood the consequences of abstaining. They had discovered that to be at peak capacity they needed a partner each day. His brother, Thius, swore by the motto 'an orgasm a day keeps the crazy away'. Thanks to their parent's intervention in the form of a magical seal tattooed on each of their children, they had better control of the lust. But better control wasn't complete control. After a few days the lust would become increasingly distracting, but still manageable. More than that though and the desire would start to take over. Their body would kick into survival mode.

At the worst, an Incubus would hunt a woman down and force himself upon her until he could absorb the energy of her orgasm. Sometimes once was enough to bring the male back to rational thought, sometimes not.

The most tragic story he'd ever heard was an Incubi who had raped his own half sister multiple times until he had awakened to the realization of what he had done. The poor soul had killed himself from the shame and horror he had inflicted upon a loved one.

As much as Seir wished he wasn't here at all, he was glad he wasn't anywhere near his girls.

Empusa wanted his blood for some gods forsaken reason and she was willing to drive him mad to achieve it. He remembered demanding why the blood she'd had spilled with her whip wasn't sufficient but she had laughed it off, refusing to answer.

Obviously, she needed his blood freely given.

With a wave of determination, he swore he'd lose his mind before he gave that bitch what she wanted.

***

"So, yeah..." Cassidy mumbled, trying to come up with something intelligent to say. She hadn't really expected to be left alone with Verrin again. When she had seen Savvy sitting at the breakfast bar, Cass had thanked her lucky stars. Savvy was an expert at providing social lubrication and knowing she'd have Savvy at her side had made the prospect of talking to Verrin much more manageable. *And then the wench bailed on me.* Cass silently vowed revenge and spit out the first thing that came to mind. "Thank you for breakfast."

89

"You're quite welcome," Verrin replied politely, bare back still turned to her as he washed dishes.

Cassidy sat there, watching the fine play of muscles shifting as he scrubbed at a pan. His back was amazing, broad shoulders that tapered down into a trim waist followed by the most amazing butt. There were two little dimples in his back, just above the waistband of his black jeans. Her mouth watered to lick them.

Whoa, girl! Time for a distraction!

She snagged a dishtowel and went to help him dry dishes. Proximity might be dangerous but sitting there fantasizing about him wasn't much better. At least this way her hands would be occupied.

"If you're intending on hanging around here for a while, we're going to have to get you some clothes. It's too cold to go around without a shirt or shoes for long." She pondered out loud, figuring it would do her sanity wonders to cover all that golden skin up. Maybe a turtleneck and baggy khakis and ugly boxers. Definitely ugly boxers. *And there I go, picturing him in his underwear. Argh!*

Maybe she'd pick herself up a chastity belt while she was at it.

"If you wouldn't mind." Verrin smiled at her over his shoulder and her girly bits perked up. Certainly her body wouldn't mind anything he wanted to do. "Both my phone and wallet are missing but if you wouldn't mind getting me a shirt and some cheap shoes I can pay you back. I do have the funds just no way to access them at the moment. My brothers will stop at my apartment in New York and bring me some stuff as soon as they can. They're kind of tied up at the moment." He assured her.

"Oh. Okay." She nodded, staring down at her

fidgeting hands again. Good god, to think there was more of him. His parents would have had a run for their money keeping the girls away.

"I'm perfectly fine like this but I get the feeling you might be more comfortable if I'm properly clothed." He pulled the plug out of the sink and turned toward her, drying his hands on the blue dish towel she handed him. The smile he offered her made her breath stutter. "So, now that you're awake, fed and we got the awkward introductions with your friend out of the way, what did you want to do today?"

Cassidy bit the inside of her cheek, not wanting to admit he was right about his lack of clothes. She racked her mind for something to say but what popped out surprised her. "So you're really an Incubus, huh?"

Verrin smiled and leaned back, crossing his ankles as he braced his butt against the counter top. "Yes, I am. Are you all right with that?"

"I guess." Cassidy murmured, looking out the patio doors toward the back yard to distract herself from staring at him. "It's kind of hard to believe though."

He chuckled warmly. "Yeah, I suppose so. Imagine our parent's surprise when they realized their little angels had become teenage horndogs. Teaching abstinence in our household was a no go."

Cassidy felt her lips twitch in amusement. "I never thought of that."

"Incubi didn't exist until we popped up," Verrin told her, a faraway look coming over him. "I can still remember my dad sitting us all down for 'the talk' when he discovered my oldest brother sneaking out at night to hook up with girls. I think he realized they would have their hands full with us that day."

She chuckled at that. "So you guys are the only Incubi?"

Verrin shook his head. "Nah, we're just the first. There's a handful of others but we're pretty rare." Verrin pushed off the counter and circled the island to drop into the stool Savvy had vacated. He towered above her even sitting and it was kind of intimidating. "I spent some time looking through that book you bought. I wouldn't try reading it again until I've had time to go through it thoroughly. I found a few pages I would recommend you stay away from if you don't want any other supernatural creatures appearing in your home."

"Oh, thanks," Cassidy said, surprised. She hadn't expected him to do that when she'd shoved the blasted thing at him last night. She leaned her hip against the island, happy to have its solid length between them.

Verrin gave her a reassuring look. "While we're bound together, you're under my protection. Having you summoning other critters, even other Incubi, would make this situation rather uncomfortable."

"Other Incubi? Why would anyone want to summon more than one?" Cass asked, appalled at the idea of random guys popping up all over her house.

Verrin's smile spread wickedly across his lips and he leaned toward her, voice dropping to a sensual purr. "I believe that old adage 'the more the merrier' would apply to that particular circumstance."

Cass felt the blood rush to her cheeks and she ducked her head, dark hair forming a wavy curtain between herself and his sex appeal. "Oh."

"Don't worry, little one," Verrin assured, reaching

over the counter top to tuck her hair behind her ear and reveal her face. "I don't like to share."

Oh lord. Cass was pretty sure her panties had just caught fire. His voice was like a silky caress down her spine, making her shiver delightfully. Not to mention having those brilliant blue eyes focused solely on you made you feel like the center of his world. The man had serious presence. His every movement oozed sensuality. Fumbling for a topic change she blurted out the first available question. "You said you had brothers?"

Verrin gave her an indulgent smirk, obviously recognizing her diversionary tactics for what they were, but followed along. "Yes, two older and two younger."

"Wow. Five boys. Your parents must have been busy. Do they look like you?" Now that would make quite the Christmas card, she thought giddily.

"Are you trying to upgrade? Not satisfied with your current model?" Verrin laughed, that wicked gleam in his eyes again. "And here you haven't even tried out all my nifty features." He pointed out with a wink.

Cass pushed off the counter, needing the added inches between them, and tried determinedly to stand solidly. Damn her knees for being weak. "Well since you can't answer a question without -"

"Cassidy," Verrin smoothly interrupted her, getting to his feet and coming to stand in front of her. He tucked a finger beneath her stubbornly set chin and tilted her face up until their eyes met. "I can't help but want to tease you." His finger ran across the red flush on her cheek and his smile was sweet. "This blush is precious, it looks so good on you. You tempt me to make it happen just so I can see it grace your features."

Cass felt her mouth open but she couldn't seem to get enough air. He was too close, his hands too warm. His very presence overwhelmed her senses and sent skittering jolts of excitement through her.

Taking pity on her, Verrin stepped back, letting her go and resuming his seat. "My brothers do look a fair bit like me. Most of us have dark hair and our dad's height but when our parents died we were split up so our personalities aren't all that alike. Dan is the strong, silent type. Thius will hit on anything that moves. Meri is a science geek and Seir is pretty much the white knight, always looking for a damsel in distress."

"And you?" Cass asked, intrigued. "Where do you fit in?"

"I don't know." Verrin shrugged. "I guess I'm the chef. When we get together I'm the only one allowed in the kitchen. The others aren't bad, but I'm better. Except Pithius. He would probably poison us."

Cass stared at him in silence for a moment before bursting out in a very unladylike snort. *Seriously? A chef? Not likely. More like wet dream.* When she caught his narrow-eyed look at her she tried to hold it in but a burst of giggles broke free.

"All right you cheeky little brat," Verrin grinned, standing up with fake menace and coming around the counter after her. "What's that laugh for?"

Cass sidled away from his seeking hands, circling until the island was between them again. Her cheeks hurt with the smile that dominated her face. No way in hell was she letting him know what a charmer he was. She wasn't about to give him that much of an ego stroking. "Nope!" She pressed her lips together and gestured as if she was zipping them shut. "You're not getting it out of me!"

"Aw, come on. Tell me." Verrin coaxed, leaning his towering height over the island and bringing his face closer to hers. "I'm sure I can convince you to open that pretty little mouth of yours for me." He intoned with a naughty grin.

Heat flamed up her cheeks and she put a hand over his face to give him a playful shove back. "Stop that!"

He flicked his tongue out and gave the center of her palm a little lick which had her yanking her hand back. Giving her a salacious smile, he licked his lips. "Tasty."

"Oh God!" Cass groaned, cradling the hand that still tingled from the touch of his warm tongue on her chest. *Escape. Escape now before this gets serious!* She cast about for her saving grace, mind frantically spinning. "I'm going to go grab a shower." She squeaked, backing away slowly as one would from a dangerous animal.

Verrin's smile got impossibly hotter and he opened his mouth, no doubt about to offer his scrubbing services, so she whipped a halting hand up to stop him.

"Alone. I'm going to shower alone." She informed him curtly, ignoring his knowing smirk. "Make yourself at home."

With that she fled, walking stiffly out the archway into the hallway. It wasn't until she reached the foot of the stairs and she knew she was out of his line of sight that she bounded up them as if the hounds of hell were snapping at her heels.

What in the world was she supposed to do with him?

She ran into her room, shut the door and made a point of locking it behind her before turning to face her room. Cass needed to stay away from him for a while. If she didn't clear her head the mental image of her climbing his tall body like a tree and ravishing his luscious mouth with hers was going to become reality.

A shower would help. Probably a cold one.

She went to her chest of drawers and pulled a pair of jeans and a black T-shirt out, rummaging around in the drawers until she found a bra, panties and socks. No way was she giving Verrin the chance to catch her naked.

She unlocked the door and poked her head out, listening carefully. The sound of the television downstairs flipping between channels assured her he was occupied so she padded down the hall to the bathroom.

Slipping in and locking the bathroom door behind her, she breathed a sigh of relief. Yes. A shower was a very good idea. She needed the relaxation to help her figure out her next actions.

Cass dropped her clothes on the counter by the sink and pulled her white shower curtain covered in little rubber ducks aside to turn on the water, letting it run until the temperature was satisfactory. She stripped out of her pajamas, leaving them on the floor to toss in her bedroom hamper. Pulling her hair from its messy ponytail she climbed into the shower.

The minute the warm water hit her she breathed deep and slumped against the wall under the shower head. Water ran down her head and back, plastering her hair to her cheeks and shoulders. The warmth and solitude were a balm to her frazzled nerves.

Verrin was a puzzle she couldn't figure out. His cocky attitude irked her as much as his confidence and sheer sexiness turned her on. He was an Incubus, a supernatural creature, and nothing like the men she had dated up till now. He seemed to enjoy teasing her, using clever innuendo to taunt her as well as pique her interest.

She knew she had refused to sleep with him last night but she felt that might be a hard line to walk going forward. His mere presence made all her female hormones sit up and take notice. She wasn't sure she bought this whole 'bound to her' thing, but she couldn't really complain about the results. Verrin would be staying with her until such time as the summoning wore off.

Yet he said he wasn't interested in her.

A nerdy girl with a fetish for books and a few extra pounds wasn't the kind of girl a guy with Verrin's looks usually went for. With his dark hair, Caribbean blue eyes and hard body he could pretty much have any woman he wanted. They only needed to glance at his towering gorgeousness and their clothes just miraculously fell off.

Savvy's words came back to haunt her then, reminding her that it wasn't often such a temptation was placed in front of her. Never in fact. She was a modern woman, she didn't have to be such a prude about sex. No one said love had to be involved for her to have a good time and she was pretty damn sure anything with Verrin would be a very good time.

The man could probably read her grocery list out loud and make her panties put out flood warnings.

She could do it. She could have sex with a man without getting her feelings involved. It wasn't a necessary element. All that was needed was her body and his. And perhaps a boat load of condoms.

Resolving to put on her big panties and take Verrin up on it if he offered again, she reached for the shampoo. She needed to get ready to go shopping with the most

97

handsome man she had ever seen.

CHAPTER 10

Verrin leaned back on his stool and chuckled as he heard her footsteps pound up the stairs. She had run from him like a frightened rabbit. It was a temptation for him to play the hungry wolf and chase her down.

Cassidy was a sweet little thing and his conversation with her best friend had been very informative. Savannah had sat down at the kitchen island and proceeded to threaten his family jewels with all sorts of nasty actions. She had sworn that if he messed with her friend or hurt her in any way the last mouth his dick would ever get the pleasure of would be his own when she choked him with it. Then she ordered him to make her coffee and waved him off to work with an imperial hand.

These women were highly unusual. Not only had he never had a summoner reject him flat out, he had never had a woman threaten to do anything to his manhood. Well, not that he wouldn't have enjoyed anyway.

Perhaps he had been talking to the wrong kind of women. If he had realized that bookish little geeks and their friends were this interesting, he would have spent a lot more time around them.

His instincts had long since kicked in, demanding he follow the trail of desire she had left behind her up the stairs and straight into her shower. The surprised look on her face when he threw open that ridiculous rubber duck shower curtain he'd noticed last night and took her hot, wet naked body into his arms would be priceless.

Gods, to feel her struggle against him even as her body succumbed so sweetly to his touch would be heaven. A groan rose in his chest, part rampant arousal, part torturous frustration. He really needed to get her under him. Maybe then he could get his head on straight. It wasn't like he didn't have other things to worry about. With Seir missing and Empusa involved he really didn't have time for a woman. Unfortunately Cassidy seemed to have this unusual ability to slink into the corners of his mind and stay there, taunting him with a delicacy he hadn't yet tasted.

Deciding this train of thought wasn't helping the hard-on he was sporting, Verrin adjusted his pants a little to give his zipper some relief from the pressure and went to watch TV. Snagging the remote off the coffee table, he sprawled on the sofa and started flicking through channels.

Commercial. Fishing. Paid programming. Televangelist. Dora. Paid programming. B movie. Christ, Sunday morning television sucked. He'd have to ask if she had Netflix.

Settling on good ole Scooby Doo, he grabbed the summoning book off the coffee table and kicked his feet up. He sat the book on his lap and flipped through the vellum pages carefully. Every one bore a different image, golems and kelpies and other such beasts filling the pages.

He might as well keep going on his earlier task. Last night he'd decided that going through the book to check for other summoning spells might be a good idea. The last thing he wanted was for Cassidy to summon – he flipped a page and frowned at the image of a lich – something malicious. He took another of the paper strips he'd created last night off the little pile on the coffee table and tucked it into the crease. Each one said simply 'Read this at your peril'. He was tempted to rip all the summoning pages out entirely but was pretty sure a woman who took her books so seriously would think such a thing was sacrilegious.

Passing over his own summons, he resisted the urge to remove it. The brothers had decided long ago to destroy the summoning spell any time they came across it in an effort to minimize the amount of summons they had to deal with. For some reason, Verrin wasn't bothered by the thought of leaving Cassidy in possession of his personal summons.

However his perusing did find two more incantations among the multitude of writings that he tagged with his handy notes. One was a chant begging Zemyna, a Lithuanian mother goddess, for assistance in the effort to get with child. The other was a spell to conjure a true demon which left out all reference to the circle you would need to contain said demon once it arrived. While he hated to imagine what would have happened had she summoned the demon instead of him, the image of Cassidy begging a fertility spirit to help her get pregnant was a potent one. He had always thought that pregnant women were gorgeous and the idea of Cass swelled with a child, namely his child, made him hard as a rock.

Damn, he needed to get his head checked. And not the one south of his belt either.

He closed the book and put it aside, realizing his focus was shot. He hit mute on the remote and listened instead to the faint sound of the shower running upstairs. His eyes drifted closed and he remembered how Cassidy had felt in his arms last night.

When he had scooped her up she had felt perfect, a viable weight in his arms. He believed women should be plump enough to handle a man affections. He wanted to feel her curves and her weight above him when she rode him. When he had sat her on the counter last night he'd had to stop himself from grinding his erection into her perfectly lined up feminine center. She was the perfect size for him, just small enough he could manhandle her a bit. The idea of tossing her over his shoulder, plump bottom high in the air, and carrying her off for some much needed pleasure was just what he wanted right now.

He listened carefully and heard the shower upstairs shut off. Gods she was naked above him, water trickling down soft skin that still bore the faintest hint of last summer's tan. He wondered if she would mind him licking those water droplets off her. Would she be wet from thinking about him in there or would he have to work for her sweet nectar? Perhaps he could convince her to let him make her dirty again so they would have a reason to get back into the shower – together this time.

Verrin moaned and flopped over on the couch to lie on his left side, head awkwardly mashed into one of the throw pillows. When had he become such a masochist?

"Verrin?"

His heart stopped at the sound of her voice beside him.

Apparently he had been lost in reverie far longer than he'd realized. So long that she'd had time to get dressed and come downstairs. Now Cass stood at the end of the couch, a slight frown on her face as she considered his sprawled form.

"Couldn't find anything to watch?" She asked, gesturing to the muted television.

Cass's chestnut eyes showed her amusement with him and her still damp dark hair was brushed back from her face even though it crept back over her shoulders in trailing tendrils. She was dressed in blue jeans and a black V-neck T-shirt with the words '3lau Me' scrolled across her breasts.

"Three Lau me?" He asked, looking for a distraction. He prayed to every deity he knew she didn't look down his body and catch sight of the massive erection trying to force its way out of his jeans. If the damned thing had a voice it would have already introduced itself to her and offer to shake her hand.

She glanced down at her shirt and a pained look flickered across her features as if his mangled pronunciation was hard for her to hear. "It's Blau. He's a DJ from Las Vegas. A pretty good one."

"Hmm, clever," Verrin grunted, sitting up and pulling the book into his lap as a shield. Stupid thing got him into this, he was damn well going to use it to cover his ass. "Haven't heard of him."

Cass seemed to take notice of the book and tilted her head, looking at him questioningly. "Find anything interesting in there?"

He glanced down, glad to get onto a different topic. "A couple more summoning spells to avoid. I've marked them." He flicked the top of one of the strips of paper he had used as a bookmark. "Don't read anything from these pages or you might end up with more unwelcome house guests."

"Thanks. One is more than enough!" She replied, coming around the sofa to sit beside him. "So what kind of creatures are we talking about?"

Verrin's brain stopped as she sat down, her body barely brushing against his left side. Damn, she smelled good, like strawberries and cream with the faintest hint of mango from her hair. He would kill to tunnel his fingers through that damp mass and drag her lips to his.

"Are you paying attention?"

He jerked, startled to realize he had been leaning toward her ever so slightly and now she was staring up at him, those milk chocolate eyes swimming with confusion. *She must think me mad.* And he couldn't even blame her.

He wanted her.

It had crept up on him so stealthily he wasn't sure what to do. It wasn't the pull on his sex drive that abstinence caused in Incubi. He'd had sex a mere two days ago and there was no way he'd be affected by its lack this strongly yet. It wasn't even that she was overtly sensual. It was just her. Her presence ramped his own desires up full force. He'd never felt anything like it.

He couldn't wait to get his hands on her.

***

Merihem slipped quietly through the woods,

dodging the branches his brother let fling back at him with abandon. Pithius stomped ahead through the woods, sounding more like a rampaging bear than his six foot two, 185-pound frame warranted.

Thius and Meri had decided to retrieve their eldest brother, Dantalion, to aid them in their hunt for Seir. They were almost to the cabin Dan used as his retreat, a perfect locale as it was buried in the dense Appalachian forest with no connection to the civilized world. No doubt their eldest sibling wasn't going to appreciate their interruption of his peace. Dan had once threatened them with bodily harm if they dared to bother him at his getaway.

Thankfully Merihem was certain Dan would redirect his ire from them to whoever had taken Seir when he heard the news they were bringing to his doorstep.

Dantalion had been raised as a warrior since he was an adolescent and, unlike Merihem, thought most situations could be solved at the end of a blade. No doubt that blade would get a workout soon. The brothers had all grown into very different people but loyalty to family was one thing they all stood by.

Ahead of him, Pithius started waving his hands about and cussing. "Goddamn mosquitoes! This is why I hate the outdoors! Leon's crazy if he willingly comes out here to get eaten alive." Pithius snarled, tearing a low hanging branch that dared to be in his path off and throwing it into the brush.

Merihem sighed deeply and slowed his pace, letting Thius storm off ahead of him. He really had no desire to drudge after his grouchy younger brother. The man was really only happy when he was buried in a woman or taunting his siblings. Anything he could do to get under someone's skin was exactly his goal. It had started many a fight among the brothers over the years and he wasn't about to goad Thius into another round.

Meri stepped over a fallen tree, making sure his black slacks didn't catch on any of the dead protrusions. This whole situation wasn't really his cup of tea either. He would much rather be tucked away in his study, pouring over books or staring through a microscope, but he would do anything in his power to help Seir.

Seir and Meri were alike in their less violent approach to most situations and that similarity brought them together even more than the fact that they were brothers. Seir was a kindhearted man who would do anything to help his brothers or adopted sisters. He hated to see someone upset and was a born defender of the weak. Meri was the mediator, constantly in the middle of arguments, trying to sort them out before the fists started flying.

His real expertise though lay with the art of bodily manipulation. With focus he could alter the way a body responded to different stimuli and also force its reactions to toxins and other outside forces. This gave him the ability to purge everything from bullets to cancer from another person, although it took its toll on him. This had been the motivation for his study to find cures for the sickness that plagued this world. The joy of being able to help the few people he had over the years made him determined to help those who needed it.

"Found it!" Pithius called from up ahead and Meri quickened his pace. He emerged into a large clearing with a small log cabin in the center, each of its tiny windows curtained from prying eyes. Thius was already striding across the well-trimmed grass toward the small porch. Meri hurried up behind him just as Thius banged on the door with the side of his fist, calling out.

The door wrenched open and their eldest brother, Dantalion, stood there in nothing but a pair of black boxers, a hunting knife in one hand and a half eaten apple in the other. "Why in the hell are you two here? I've heard you coming for miles."

Meri opened his mouth to break the news gently when Pithius blurted, "Seir has gone missing and some chick summoned V and is holding his balls hostage."

To his credit, Dan only blinked at them for a moment before gesturing them inside. "Get in here and give me the details."

They piled into the cabin, Merihem looking around in curiosity at the interior. Dan didn't let people in his haven often and Meri was surprised to see that the one room cabin was nicer than he'd expected. One wall had a kitchenette and a small wooden table with a single matching chair. The other wall had a bed large enough to comfortably fit Dantalion's great height that was covered in a handmade quilt. The center of the room held a well used maroon sofa and a coffee table littered with books. Five bookshelves stood around the room, bearing titles varying from the Art of War to a book on cognitive behavioural therapy.

Pithius threw himself onto the sofa so Meri decided to take the chair at the table. He couldn't help but smile sadly at the little wooden horse toy with its faded paint that sat beside a loaded Glock and the hunting knife's leather sheath on the table top. Dantalion may have seemed like the untouchable one but he carried his sentimental memories around with him.

"Tell me," Dan demanded, turning to lean against the counter with his arms crossed. Pithius sat forward, the look of an eager puppy on his face, and opened his mouth to talk before Dan shut him down. "Not you." Dantalion snapped before turning to Merihem. "I need details."

Meri nodded. "Verrin went to check on Seir when none of us had heard from him in days. The harem was missing when he arrived and he found a group of nymphs in the villa instead."

"Mmm, nymphs..." Pithius interrupted with a dreamy murmur.

Meri rolled his eyes and continued. "Verrin was drugged and taken to where Seir is being held. Empusa is apparently holding him although she would not tell Verrin exactly why. Before he could get them out, Verrin was summoned. He called us from an island in Canada. He said Seir was not doing well, that he had obviously been there a while and Empusa had refrained from letting him have a woman."

Dantalion's frown had deepened. "Did he have any idea where Seir was being held?"

Pithius shook his head. "Nope, but he mentioned it looked like a dungeon. I looked into it," His grin was devilish and Meri knew that research was the questioning of ladies in the throes of passion. "It sounds like Empusa has been causing quite a stir, fighting with Gorgons and other nasties. Even going so far as to claim some of their hideouts. Any one of them could have a dungeon. There's a pretty good chance that's where she's holding Seir."

"All right," Dantalion stood tall, his face settled into determination. "Let's go get Seir. When will Verrin be joining us?"

Merihem's "Soon." was run over by Pithius's "When he can convince the chick he's with to let him into her pants."

Dan raised an eyebrow but refused to ask. Instead, he went about gathering weapons and getting dressed. Their eldest brother didn't believe in useless conversation and now that they had a pretty good idea what was going on it was time to follow Dan into whatever was to come.

CHAPTER 11

Cassidy looked up from the book Verrin held open on his lap to see his gaze fixated on her. His beautiful features were drawn, blue eyes dark with roiling emotion. "Verrin?" She asked carefully, studying him in return.

His eyes closed and he took a deep breath, turning to face forward again. When he exhaled he let his head fall back to rest against the sofa. When he spoke his voice was so low she had to strain to hear him properly. "Cassidy, could I kiss you?"

Cass's heart stopped for a second before kicking up to double time. Had she heard him right? Last night he seemed not to care if they ever had sex and now he was asking her in an almost shy manner if he could kiss her. "I-I thought you weren't-" She stumbled, unsure how to handle this.

"Interested?" Verrin's eyes opened but he stared at the ceiling instead of meeting her eyes. His lips twitched with a self-deprecating smile. "I lied. I didn't want you to worry about being alone with me. I may be an Incubus but

I'm not a beast. The lust is something I have control over, not the other way around. I choose who I want to be with."

Cass just stared at his regal profile, outlined by the golden sunlight from the living room windows. She really wasn't sure what to say. She had just finished promising herself upstairs that she would go for it if the opportunity arose and now that it was here, she was unsure how to follow through. She wasn't even sure she truly believed he was an Incubus, just that he seemed to believe it. She never got the chance to voice any of that because Verrin plowed on ahead.

"It's okay if you say no." Verrin rambled, "I would never pressure you into anything. I just, well I was actually happy to see who had summoned me last night. I thought I'd lucked in to get a curvy little thing like you."

"Yes." She said softly, forcing it out past her nervousness.

"It's not like we get summoned that often anymore. We destroy the incantation any time we come across it and – wait, what did you say?" Verrin turned now, facing her. Those sea deep eyes were wide with pleasant surprise.

"Yes," Cass repeated, the word sounding a bit like a question even to her own ears.

A devastating grin spread across his lips and his eyes took on a boyish glint. "I'd ask if you're serious, but I don't want to give you the chance to back out." His hand reached out, catching her chin and drawing her mouth up to his as he bent forward. Firm, full lips brushed hers softly in the barest of touches and Verrin groaned, sounding pained. Their lips met again, his kiss firmer this time, melding their mouths together.

Cass's breath stuttered as he turned toward her on the couch, the summoning book dropping to the floor absently. The fingers of one hand buried in her long hair and held her as he plundered her mouth. He ravished her, slipping his tongue in on a gasp and exploring with skill. When he nipped her bottom lip she couldn't help but moan his name.

"By all the gods, your mouth is sweet." Verrin crooned against her lips. He kissed the corner of her mouth before licking across her bottom lip and then sealing his lips to hers again.

Cass's mind was blank. His kiss had stolen all the air she needed to think. Her hands came up to push him away and instead got distracted stroking the smooth skin that covered his hard muscled chest.

His lips trailed off her mouth, following the line of her jaw to her ear. Breath, warm and sensual, ghosted over her skin causing a wave of shivers. "Cassidy. Dear, sweet, devastating Cassidy. I've been dying to touch you since I first saw you." His words were a dark timbre murmured against her throat.

"I – I don't..." Cassidy stuttered, mind clouded with passion. Her body was begging her to let him do anything he wanted, but she couldn't do it. Even after her earlier inner pep talk, she just couldn't do it. She'd barely known him 24 hours, but the way he made her feel was extraordinary. No matter how much her libido was on board, her heart just wasn't sure this was a good idea.

"Please, Cass." Verrin pleaded, slipping his hands deep into her hair to massage her scalp gently, the promise of absolute pleasure lurking in his every touch. "Just a little. You can tell me to stop any time. I just – I need you. In any way I can have you." He stared into her eyes, those gorgeous blue eyes glowing and serious.

She waited a heartbeat, trying to think of a good reason why she should listen to reason and ignore the lust racing through her body. He was an Incubus for God's sake. He was built for sex.

That should turn her off and yet somehow it worked in his favour.

She nodded shyly and his big body surged fully into her personal space, conquering it. His firm hands gripped her hips, turning and lifting her enough so he could drag her towards him. He pulled her across his lap until they were face to face, her knees fitting beside his hips perfectly and her core hovering over his own. His lips caught hers and then his hands were in her hair, sifting through it as he devoured her mouth.

The man was an expert. No kiss she'd ever had could compare with his. He possessed her fully, her body begging to become his. When his hands began to roam, slipping down her back and sides, massaging her neck and scalp, she moaned into his mouth. "Verrin..." She breathed against his cheek as he kissed his way across her shoulder.

"Yes, little one?" He murmured, kissing up the column of her throat to her ear. "Tell me what you want..."

His arms were wrapped tight around her, holding her to the solidity of his chest, and she shuddered against him when he bit her neck gently. "Oh God, Verrin..."

His chest vibrated and it took her a startled moment to realized he'd growled at her. The sound was deep and unearthly, but also sexy as hell. One of his hands slipped up her side and gathered her hair, twisting it around his hand to anchor his hold. He pulled gently, tugging her head back, then leaned forward to kiss across her collarbones and the scant amount of cleavage revealed by her shirt.

She moaned, gripping his shoulders, needing more. Her core was snug against the hardness in his jeans and she rocked her hips against him, giving them both pleasure. His hands trailed across her body, tempting her through her clothes. He groaned and dragged her in for another deep kiss before cupping her butt and grinding her against his jeans covered erection. The whimper that escaped her was pure frustration.

"Dammit woman, you could tempt a saint to sin." Verrin breathed harshly against the skin of her throat. His arms tightened around her, pinning her to his broad chest and halting the rhythm of her body against his. "I could do this with you for hours." He growled as he seemed to try to calm his raging body.

Cass's head cleared slowly from the daze his kisses had plunged her mind into. When she spoke her voice was still breathless and sounded disappointed to her own ears. "You mean we won't?"

Verrin laughed, his body shaking with the harsh sound beneath hers. "Sadly no. As much as I would like to I don't want to rush this. This is something that needs to be savoured." He pulled back a bit to smile at her, blue eyes twinkling with mischief. "Don't think I wouldn't have you under me in seconds if my libido had its way, but if I did that you wouldn't be leaving this house for a few days and I know you had things you wanted to get done. I saw the list tacked to the fridge."

The pathetic chuckle that left Cass echoed the

frustration she felt in that moment as well as the amazement at his virility. She dropped her head forward until it was buried in his shoulder. He smelled amazing, warm male and dark coffee with the slightest hint of vanilla in his dark hair. Her lips quirked. Apparently, it was going to take a while for the air freshener to wear off.

"I suppose I should find you some clothes." She murmured grudgingly. It really seemed a shame to cover up any part of him but the winter weather outside wouldn't be forgiving to all that bare skin.

Verrin chuckled. "I would appreciate that."

Cass climbed off his lap awkwardly, appreciating his big hands on her hips as she tried to stand steadily. Her knees were still a little weak from their kisses and she wasn't altogether certain how she'd think straight for the rest of the day. With a tug of fabric, she righted her shirt and turned to head for the hallway. "I – uh - I should have something upstairs that might work for you."

Verrin stood, adjusted his jeans, and followed as she padded down the hall and up the staircase. "Um, no offense, but I don't think any of your clothes are going to fit me."

Cass grinned and shot him a naughty smile over her shoulder as she reached the top of the stairs. "While I'm pretty sure I do have a large periwinkle t-shirt with kitties all over it if you really want, I actually have another idea."

"One that doesn't include periwinkle kitties?" Verrin asked, smirking.

"Uh-huh." She stopped in the middle of the hallway and jumped up, trying to catch the pull string that dangled from the trap door in the center of the ceiling. Verrin casually reached over her head and snagged the cord, pulling it down until she could reach it. With a smile of thanks, she tugged hard and moved to let the foldaway stairs to the attic come down.

"My grandma could never bear to part with granddad's things so instead of sending them all to goodwill she packed it up bit by bit," She climbed the little stairs with Verrin following until she stood in the attic surrounded by train trunks, boxes and sheet-covered furniture. "And stored it all up here."

Verrin crested the steps and looked around the dusty room in awe. "Wow."

"Yeah, grandma was kind of a hoarder. On the upside, that might work in your favour." Cass headed over to a pile of steamer trunks tucked beneath the roof pitch and flipped the closures on one, opening the lid. With a quick peek she saw her grandfather's military uniform and its accoutrements. Moving on to the next, she flipped the lid and started to rifle through the clothing that filled its cedar lined belly.

"I take it your grandfather was in the military? This looks like a world war two uniform." Verrin noted as he eyed the contents of the first trunk.

"Yep," Cass confirmed, moving piles of pants and slacks to the side as she tried to find a suitable shirt. "He joined toward the end, was only seventeen when he went over. Grandma was his sweetheart back then and swears she worried every minute of every day until he made it home safe." She held up a large blue button down shirt and turned to eye the breadth of Verrin's shoulders before pulling out a polo shirt and a turtleneck as well.

Verrin was hunched over, head brushing the ceiling beams. His eyes were locked on the contents of the trunk in front of him and he moved things around within it with a careful hand. She watched him lift the lid on an old shoe box and stare at the photos and news clippings within. Removing one, he held up the black and white photo of a young couple dressed in their modest wedding finery. "Your grandparents?"

Cass nodded and pulled a rubber maid bin toward her. She popped the top and saw the multitude of shoes that she herself had dumped in here when she'd claimed the house. Digging in she hunted for the pair of penny loafers Grandma had gotten her husband just before he'd gone into the hospital. Never worn, they still had the tags on them when she uncovered them at the bottom of the bin. "When he came back he was different. The war had changed him. Grandma Lillian tried but she had to move on. A few years later, he must have come to his senses and he hunted her down and begged her to marry him." Cass left the shirts onto the top of the trunk with the shoes and went over, taking the picture from his hand. With a soft smile, she eyed the happy faces of her grandparents, forever frozen in time. "Grandma Lil said he chased her around for a week before she'd even give him the time of day. He'd broken her heart and she wasn't fond of letting him do so again."

Verrin chuckled, grinning at her. "I'm assuming by that photo the wily man managed to talk her into it."

"Yep. Apparently, he could charm the pants off a horse."

Verrin quirked an eyebrow at her. "Not sure if you've noticed, but horses don't wear pants."

Cass laughed. "Exactly. They don't anymore. Grandpa's doing so I've been told."

117

Verrin smiled and shook his head. "So did you find something or am I going to have to start a new periwinkle kitty fashion trend?"

Cass tucked the photo safely away again and closed the trunk. Turning, she tossed the shirts at Verrin and closed the other trunk. "While I do think periwinkle is your colour these might be a better choice. We'll wash them up and they should fit all right. Might be a bit tight, but I think they'll do the trick."

"As much as I think it's a travesty for me to wear clothes, I appreciate the fact that my nipples won't get frostbite if I step outside. How do you people survive here?"

Cass laughed as she led the way down the attic steps again. "It's not so bad. When we're not shoveling, we're cuddled up watching TV." She had almost made it to the bottom of the stairs when she caught his murmured retort.

"I'm surprised Canadian birth rates aren't higher." He mumbled as he followed her down the stairs.

118

CHAPTER 12

Seir startled from sleep, coming awake to the sound of his cell being opened. He wanted to jump to his feet, but his head throbbed and his body refused to listen to his demands. Instead, he listened to the footsteps get closer as he watched a rather large ant lead a few of its fellows along the edge of the wall inches from his face.

Strong hands caught him under the arms and hauled him up, dragging his body over to the bars that made up the front of his cell. Two of the blank-eyed guards held him up against the barred wall as a third threaded the chain of his cuffs through the bars, making it so his hands were chained behind him.

A cool golden chain looped around his neck from behind, pulling his head back until he couldn't pull forward from the bars without choking himself. They did the same to his ankles next, keeping his legs spread shoulder width apart. The guards released him once he was bound and defenseless.

Seir growled hoarsely as one of the men withdrew a

knife and used it to cut through the fabric of his dirty blue jeans, starting at the ankles and working his way up. His body froze as he felt that blade moving between his legs and hissed as the edge slice across his inner thigh, far too close for comfort.

The guard caught Seir's flesh again while trying to saw through his leather belt and he felt the trickle of blood running down his hip. With a few rough tugs that strained the healing flesh of his back, the guard tore his pants from him, ridding him of the last of his clothing.

For the first time, Seir cursed his habit of going commando. Perhaps if he'd had boxers on it would have delayed what happened next just a little longer.

The guards stood aside, not leaving but obviously staying out the way. The creak of the dungeon door opening let the sound of female voices filter in and the soft tap of shoes across the rough stone came to him.

As the scent of feminine musk rushed into his nose Seir jerked as if electrified, cock rising hard and fast at the slightest hint of female presence. He pulled hard against the chains that held him until his breath came in pants and his skin chafed against his bindings.

Gentle fingers stroked across his bunched shoulders, moving around the bars to offer smooth passes. Empusa came around the cell wall through the open door and stood in front of him, a deceivingly sweet smile on her face. "Hello, little demon." She said it conversationally, as if this was the most normal thing in the world. She ran her dark nailed fingers over the taut muscles of his abs in admiration. "Mmm... Aren't you a fine specimen."

Seir growled, the sound animalistic and the only noise he could grind out in his haze of lust. His body was ready to fuck her even as his mind fought so hard focus on the situation.

"Are you ready to give me what I want, Seir?" Empusa asked, brushing a strand of her fiery red hair behind her ear. Her dark amber eyes held a fiendish fire that didn't bode well for him.

Seir bared his teeth, a rumble of snarl rising in his chest. His mind didn't get much of a say anymore. Thankfully even his body wouldn't agree with anything that didn't involve her beneath him, taking his every thrust.

"I'm going to assume that's a no." She sneered and nodded at someone over his shoulder. Stepping into him, she reached forward and caught the erection that strained in her direction in her palm. It's hard length throbbed urgently in her warm palm. "Well, not that it matters to me either way, but you're probably going to wish you hadn't gone with that option."

Seir groaned as he watched her head sink down as she slipped to her knees before him. Her position and the warm caress of her breath across his head made his balls ache in frustration. Her hands reached around his hips, grabbing his ass and drawing him forward, cock almost breaching her lips. She smiled just before she would have made contact and looked up at him with a nasty smirk on those ruby red lips.

"I know how much you need a woman's pleasure so I hope it gives you some relief to know that I will get a great deal of pleasure from watching what's about to happen." Empusa gave a nod to someone behind him before swiping her tongue out, licking up the precum that had beaded at his tip. She purred like a kitten before slowly rising to her feet, letting his erection drag along the curves of her breasts and abdomen as she went. With another longing stroke to his hardness, she stepped back, gesturing for her place to be taken.

A pixie-like woman with a cap of dark, silky hair came to stand before him. Her eyes were the colour of swirling mist and when she smiled it showed a mouth filled with sharply pointed teeth. She reached out and rubbed her small, pale hands up his abs and over his chest, testing his flesh gently with the long pointed nails on her fingers.

"Go ahead, Mara." Empusa encouraged with a grin. "Show our guest what Nightmares are really like."

The hands on his chest started to push against him harder and he glanced down to see her hands sinking slowly into his skin. There was no blood or pain, just the unsettling image of her fingers delving into his body. Seir bared his teeth as the oily feel of her touch filled him, penetrating him in the most disturbing violation.

Suddenly there were voices whispering at the edges of his mind, talking so low he couldn't quite hear what they were saying. The shadows that inhabited the cells dark corners grew, stretching out gnarled talons, wanting a piece of his flesh. His skin crawled as if something stirred beneath it and he shuddered all over, his stomach roiling with nausea. His heart thudded wildly, its rhythm stuttered by the feeling of her hands compressing his chest, crushing it from the inside.

His eyes met Mara's, caught by their swirling gray depths and he couldn't look away. His vision narrowed until it was nothing but her horrifying smile and eerie gaze.

Empusa's voice seemed to come from a distance, even so, it chilled his bones to hear. "Mara here is a rare breed. Her people feed on the terror they cause in their victims. That pressure you're feeling, it's the press of the Mare. Mara is one of the original Nightmares and that gives her some very unique talents."

A cool, slithery tongue pressed into his ear, licking the length of the whorl before withdrawing. Cold lips brushed his cheek. The voice that followed was soft and eerily deep, completely wrong for the small woman it issued from. "There is nothing you can hide from me, Incubus, blessed son of Sariel." She breathed. "I can find all the hidden corners of your mind. Nothing will be left unseen when I let you go."

His vision darkened as the shadows in the room shot forward to devour him. The image of his mother's brutalized body appeared in front of him, her dark hair pooled in the blood that covered the ground beneath her. Her gray-green eyes were blank, still fixed on the spot where she'd hidden her youngest son. Her eyes had been the one thing that held the sobs that racked his small body at bay, frozen in his chest as he watched her always smiling face display shock, pain and despair. They had toyed with her before finishing their task, a far cry from the merciful death that had been ordered. He'd been too young and frightened to stop them when they dragged her battered body away.

The picture changed and he was looking at the bruised face of a young woman with bedraggled blonde curls. Her split lip and the lid that was swelling shut over her tear stained blue eyes were testament to the brutality of her ward. Seir had urged her to come away with him, had fought with her all night.

Nothing he said mattered. The next time he'd laid eyes on Victoria, they were fishing her body out of the canals in Venice.

Before his eyes her face mottled and rotted, eyes paling until her gaze was a vacant milky stare. Her half eaten, waterlogged hand rose up, reaching for him, and her voice called his name as if her lungs were still filled with water.

Image after image, memory after memory, flashed through his mind in high definition. His oldest brother, Dantalion's, tortured screams after discovering the death of his family. Pithius, ever the playboy, reduced to a slave in the hands of the Sirens. Being surrounded by vicious Wendigos and feeling his own flesh bitten from the bone. Finding Verrin's trembling body bound to a table as he was vivisected in a crazed series of sick experiments. Farhina's rape and attempted suicide before Seir had convinced her to join his household. The smell of Merihem's scorched flesh as they kicked the burning wood away from the stake the villagers had attempted to burn him upon for witchcraft.

Each horrible recognition was dramatized, brought to life in ways that made his heart stop and his mind scream in horror. They replayed, again and again, interspersed by terrors that didn't come from his memory.

True nightmares.

He finally understood what Empusa was going on about. His worst fears, his biggest shames, his hidden secrets were trotted out on display in front of his terrified eyes.

He needed it to stop but he knew there was no chance in hell Empusa was going let him off that easy.

***

"How did I let you talk me into this?" Cassidy grumbled at the tall hunk strolling down the frozen food aisle beside her. The cheerful grin he cast upon her just made her frown.

"I'm pretty sure you decided leaving the house was the safest bet when I found the chocolate sauce in your fridge and offered to lick it off you." He replied smartly, casting her a lascivious smile. "Then you said you were done clothes shopping when I asked you to come into the changing room and help me out of my pants."

Cass growled softly and hunched over the push bar of the cart, trying to hide her flushed cheeks. "Could you possibly announce that any louder? I don't think the people in the bakery department heard you."

Verrin opened his mouth to say something and was suddenly striding away to dig through one of the freezer cases. When he turned back around he was grinning madly. "Look what I found!" He singsonged like an excited child, waving a tub of Tiger Tail ice cream at her.

Cass sighed and dropped her head forward to rest on her crossed arms. This may have been a very bad idea. He'd been rather tame clothes shopping, just getting a few essentials, but once they got to the grocery store Verrin had let loose. He was going to town, gathering snacks and foods he swore you couldn't get anywhere else in the world. The cart she was currently pushing was filled with ketchup chips, Nanaimo bars, butter tarts, hickory sticks and a smattering of coffee crisp and crispy crunch bars along with her regular groceries. The devilish rogue had even convinced her to get the makings for poutine, touting that he needed to try a Canadian staple. If he kept up this way, she'd be broke by the time this stupid bond with Verrin was through.

She bypassed him where he stood eyeing the frozen pizzas and turned into the next aisle. Gathering cheese curds and a dish of margarine, she tossed them in the cart.

A crashing sound drew her attention and she looked up to see Verrin striding down the aisle toward her. Behind him, a woman was looking embarrassed as she drew her cart away from the display of canned food she had knocked over in her preoccupation with Verrin's backside. The woman's longing glances followed Verrin as he walked up to Cass.

"Couldn't find anything else you wanted?" She grumbled, finding herself irritated by the other woman's desirous looks.

"I know exactly what I want," Verrin smirked and leaned down until his lips were close to her cheek, speaking only for her ears. "I'm just waiting for you to let me have it."

Cass could feel the colour flaring in her cheeks as Verrin gave her forehead a chaste peck and turned to examine the contents of the cart. "There seems to be a serious lack of maple cookies in here. Can we remedy that?"

Cass nodded, turning the cart to follow him down the aisle obligingly and grabbing a bag of French fries on the way. She had to admit she understood why Verrin had caught the eye of every female and even a few males they had walked past. His dark jeans moulded to strong thighs and a butt that belonged on a calendar model. The midnight blue turtleneck she'd dug up was a little too small but that only succeeded in contouring the fabric to his hard frame.

The image of him in that tiny changing room, begging for her assistance with the massive bulge in his jeans while wearing his customary naughty smirk rose in her mind and she forced it back down. The hour they had spent clothes shopping had been one of the longest of her life. With Verrin offering up suggestions on how each article of clothing could be removed by her, she had been wet and needy before they'd even reached the dressing room. His request for help, delivered bare-chested and with his fly invitingly unzipped, had been one straw too many. She had turned away, ignoring his laughter and the attendant's swoon, and told him she'd be by the registers when he was done.

Essentials in hand, she'd told him they were going grocery shopping, mainly so she didn't have to be alone with him while the image of his incredible erection pressing against his jeans still haunted her.

As she came up beside him, he put two bags of maple leaf cookies in the cart with a bright smile that forced her own lips to curve up. He looked supremely pleased with their haul. "Thanks for doing this. It's been a while since I've enjoyed Canadian food. I promise to pay you back when my brothers get a chance to bring me my things."

Cass nodded. She wouldn't have normally spent this much on groceries but she'd discovered it was too hard to say no to this man.

"Have I mentioned how awesome you are?" Verrin asked, grin shining. "Because you are."

She smirked, giving his arm a swat. "Stop sucking up. Let me finish shopping and you can eat your cookies in the car."

He leaned down, dropping his mouth to her ear. "Can I eat something else in the car?"

Her heartbeat picked up as she tried to keep the bolt of heat his words sent through her from showing on her face. With careful nonchalance she reached into the cart and snagged a coffee crisp, smacking it to his chest. His hand came up to catch it, grazing her fingers as she withdrew. She gave him a sweet smile and turned her cart toward the toilet paper aisle. "Enjoy!"

His amused chuckle followed her, warming her insides.

Which is the exact reason she didn't notice the bane of her high school years turning into the same aisle. Felicia Murphy sashayed into the aisle in her kitten heels, black dress pants and a bright blue winter dress coat. With her short blonde hair perfectly smoothed into one of the newest trendy cuts and her makeup expertly applied, she looked like a fashion model on the lam. The black grocery basket dangling from her elbow was the perfect prop.

Those baby blues blinked at her before narrowing slightly. "Cassidy." The word wasn't a greeting, merely an acknowledgement of her existence.

Cassidy stopped a few feet away, wanting to keep enough room between her and the other woman that she could get a good running start if she needed to mow the snooty wench over with her grocery cart. "Felicia."

Felicia's eyes traveled the length of her and Cassidy suddenly wished she'd done more than throw on her old black parka and winter boots before they left. A little makeup certainly wouldn't have hurt. Perhaps an evening gown. And diamond earrings.

"You must still be working at that little library."
Felicia guessed, switching her basket to her other arm.

Cassidy nodded, trying not to give away how
inadequate Felicia always made her feel. It may have been
years but she still thoroughly remembered all the nasty
remarks Felicia had tossed her way going through school.
Her weight, mousy brown hair, plain features, shyness and
general geek-ness had all been blazing targets for the
teenage harpy.

"You really should expand your horizons. You'll
never meet someone buried in a dusty library all day."
Felicia sighed as if the troubles of commoners were so easy
to spot from her high horse. "But then, you always were
better with books than people."

Cass wanted to tell her to kiss off, that she was the
reason Cass had spent every high school lunch hour in the
library but didn't get the chance. Felicia's haughty gaze
shifted to something over her shoulder and Cass nearly
jumped out of her skin when a strong arm wrapped
around her shoulders.

"There you are, gorgeous," Verrin said casually,
pulling her into his side and tossing a box of instant
popcorn in the cart. "I almost forgot the popcorn. Movies
just aren't the same without it." His smile flashed up and
he caught sight of Felicia. "Who's this?"

Cass opened her mouth to talk, but Felicia stepped
forward, giving him a winning smile. "Hello! I'm Felicia. I
know Cassidy from school." She gave him an appraising
look, like a rancher checking out a new stud horse and
beamed. "You can't be from around here. I'm sure I would
have recognized you."

Cassidy wanted to gag. She had seen this exact act

played out a hundred times on the unsuspecting boys in school. Felicia would act all sweet and lure them to her like flies to honey. Only some of them figured out it was a farce and escaped her conniving clutches.

Verrin gifted the nasty woman with one of his stunning smiles. "No, I'm visiting with Cassidy for a while. This is my first time here."

"Oh, well then," Felicia batted her eyelashes at him – batted her freaking eyelashes! - and tried to look demure. "I'd love to take you out and show you around. Perhaps this evening? There are some amazing restaurants in our little town I'm sure you'd enjoy."

Cass's stomach hollowed out.

Felicia, the perfect plastic Barbie doll, had just hit on Verrin right in front of her. As if she wasn't even here. Verrin had his arm around Cass and yet Felicia went for it as if Cass was a non-entity.

Nothing more than a minor inconvenience.

Cass bristled, her ire rising. *What the hell? Did the evil wench think she could get away with pretending she wasn't even here? Like hell!* Cass opened her mouth, ready to set the pretty blonde and her stupid ideas straight.

CHAPTER 13

Merihem pulled out a chair and released the two buttons holding his suit jacket closed before sitting. The wood of the seat to his left creaked when it accepted Dantalion's muscled bulk and the two of them sat there quietly, Meri checking his Rolex and Dan examining every corner of the quiet pub with an experienced and watchful eye.

The little pub was quiet this early in the afternoon, just a few old men in a corner trading stories and Pithius at the bar, hitting on the bartender as she made their drinks. Pithius had talked them into making the trip to Inverness, Scotland, assuring them that one of his contacts had some information they could use to locate Seir.

Dantalion leaned back in his chair, stretching his legs out as he drummed his fingers on the scarred wooden table top. "When did Thius say these contacts of his were coming?" He grumbled low enough only Merihem would hear. "I'm getting sick of waiting."

Meri smiled at Dan's impatience. "We arrived

twenty minutes early so it will be a little while yet."

Pithius sauntered over, three glasses of dark ale pinned between his hands and a little piece of paper sticking out from between his grinning lips. He set the glasses on the table between them and pulled the section of torn off receipt paper with a phone number scrolled across it from his mouth, stuffing it in his pocket. "I like this place." He announced, sending a brilliant smile to the redheaded woman manning the bar.

Dantalion snorted and snagged a glass, taking a long pull of the brew.

"Are your contacts local?" Meri inquired, wondering how long Dantalion's patience would stretch if they were late arriving.

"Yeah, they are." Pithius nodded absently, still eyeing the bartender. "Got a castle and everything."

"The Sinclairs, correct? Are you sure they are men for hire?" Meri murmured over a drink of the dark beer. "I am surprised such a long-standing house would stoop to such tasks."

"Jesus, Meri!" Pithius groaned, turning his attention fully back to their table and leaning forward on his elbows so his brothers could clearly hear his quietly spoken words. "They're bounty hunters, not rent boys! You make it sound like they're doing something dirty. Look, Iain is the heir to the Sinclair clan, but as long as his grandfather is well enough to run things Iain's duties are pretty light. He and his brother use their skills to hunt down rogue supernaturals and pad the coffers." Pithius sat back again, finger tapping the rim of his glass lazily as he finished. "It's not a bad gig really."

"That brother of his is a vampire, right?" Dantalion

asked, slowly tracing the wet ring his glass had left on the table.

"Half," Pithius confirmed. "Solain is also half human."

Meri made a considering noise as he thought that through. "I am surprised he still breathes. The Vampire council does not look highly upon hybrids, and with a name like Solain, it is obvious they found him lacking."

Pithius nodded, confirming his brother's thoughts. It was common knowledge that Vampires gave their society's pariahs sun based names in the hope that the sun would cleanse their dark culture of the taint by burning the offending creature to ash. The practice was frowned upon by most other races and it was just one more reason the Vampire race was so insular. "Iain's grandfather found Solain staked out in a field one day. Guess the poor kid had enough of his human daddy in him to withstand the sun. Grandpa Sinclair took the kid home, making him an official Sinclair and Iain's brother."

Meri had just opened his mouth to comment when Dantalion grumbled crankily beside him. "Are these contacts of yours ever coming? It's ten after three already and I'm growing impatient. We have spent all day chasing your contacts and their dubious leads all over the world while Seir languishes in a dungeon somewhere!"

"You're just pissed because you missed out on all the frequent flyer miles." Pithius shot back snidely.

Meri watched as his eldest brother's expression darkened as his hand curled into a fist on the tabletop. No one could push people's buttons like Pithius and it looked like today wasn't about to be any different. Before the siblings broke into their very own bar room brawl Meri waved a hand between the two and cut off their stare down. "Gentlemen, please. We do not have time for this nonsense. Seir is missing, but we will not locate him by beating each other blind here." He looked pointedly at Pithius. "Do not needle him. He spent the whole day teleporting the three of us all over the globe to look into your leads. He is exhausted and frustrated and your teasing is not lightening the mood."

Merihem turned on Dantalion next, putting a hand on the man's thick shoulder. He delved in with his powers, trying to diminish Dan's cortisol levels even as he spoke calmly to him. "I know you are worried about Seir. We all are. We will find him, but there is nothing you can do at this very moment. Relax, eat something and regain your strength. When we have a location we will need you to get us there and you need to be up to the task."

With his stress under Merihem's regulation, Dantalion took a deep breath and seemed to relax. "You're right. I just..." Dan trailed off, running a hand through his dark hair in frustration.

"I know." Merihem acknowledged, giving his wide shoulder a squeeze before releasing him.

"Look, they have great fish and chips here. Hand cut fries and everything." Pithius offered, obviously trying to make up for being an ass. "How about I grab you some?"

Dantalion nodded, apology accepted with his acquiescence. "Thanks."

"No prob." Pithius got to his feet before looking askance at his other sibling. "Meri?"

"No thank you, I am well." Merihem waved him off. Teleporting never did sit well with him and he'd long ago found that doing it on an empty stomach was the only way to retain his dignity.

Pithius nodded and headed for the bar, the woman behind it smiling widely at his approach.

"Do you think we'll find him in time?" Dantalion asked once Pithius was out of earshot.

"Yes," Merihem assured, completely confident in their success. "We will get him back and he will be fine. Empusa is not stupid. She knows that an Incubus lost to lust is a dangerous creature. No doubt she has our brother well secured. Verrin said he was in a dungeon and Empusa would not be dumb enough to let him loose." Meri smiled as the door to the pub swung open and the light was blocked out by a massive figure. "Looks like the bounty hunters have arrived. Perhaps with their help, we will have Seir back home by tomorrow."

Across the bar Pithius shook hands with the new arrivals and ordered them drinks before gesturing them over to the table Dantalion and Merihem occupied. The men came over, each carrying a drink, followed by Pithius who placed a large platter of beer battered haddock and fries covered in rich gravy in front of his eldest brother before regaining his seat.

"All right, time for introductions." Pithius gestured at the dark-haired man seated to Merihem's right first. "This is Laird Iain Sinclair, next in line as leader of the Clan Sinclair wolves."

A broad smile curved Iain's lips and his brogue came out strong as he brushed off the title. "Just call me Iain. I'm no' Laird yet so doona bother with the title. I leave that honour to my grandsire. He takes care of the running of the clan." He took a swig of his ale and grinned.

"Canna say I'm all that eager for the headache being Laird to a bunch of wolves brings about anyway."

Pithius smirked and nodded toward the lithe blond man who occupied the seat to Iain's right. "And this bloodsucker here is Solain, the bane of necks all over Scotland."

Solain gave him a wicked grin that showcased two rather sharply pointed canine teeth. "I prefer Sanguinarian, thank you."

"More like human-itarian." Iain snorted, setting his glass down as he teased his brother. "Bitey little bastard has a peculiar diet. Doesna like drinking from wolves."

"You try picking dog fur from your teeth and tell me how well your dinner sits with you after," Solain grumbled wryly.

Merihem couldn't help but chuckle at that. It was probably good none of the Incubus brother's had a vampiric lover. The jests about sucking would be endless.

"Now, let's take care of business. We have a flight to catch this evening and need to pack." Iain said, redirecting the conversation to the task at hand.

Dantalion, who had been quietly devouring his meal with proficient ease, set his fork and knife aside and took a small drink to clear his palate before he started. "Our brother Seir has been taken by Empusa. She needs his blood for some reason and evidently, he doesn't wish to give it up. From the information we've gathered she was hired by someone else although who is still unknown. We've checked with -"

ACDC's Back in Black trilled out in the quiet bar and Pithius frowned, digging his cell phone out as he apologized to the table. "Sorry, gotta get that. Go ahead and continue. I'll be right back." He got up and wandered away to answer his call.

"We checked with a few of Thius's other contacts, but haven't had much luck."

"Who'd ye talk to?" Iain questioned, sipping his ale.

"We spoke with the Oracle in London this morning," Dantalion informed them.

"I love Dolores." Solain murmured, a wistful little smile on his face. "Her cookies are to die for."

Dantalion nodded, having already been treated to the grandmotherly ways of Dolores Burgess, descendant of the Oracle of Delphi. Tea prepared to exactly to your preference and perfectly cooked chocolate chip cookies could endear that sweet woman to even the most stalwart of warriors. "She didn't have much for us, just some prophecy that 'those bound within the earth would walk again' that doesn't really seem to apply to our current situation."

"Hmm... How odd." Iain mused.

"The proprietress of the voodoo shop Spectre in New Orleans didn't have any useful leads for us either." Merihem put in, remembering the sensual Cajun woman who had directed them to a room in the back of the shop that wasn't for the tourists and sold the true magic supplies. Abella hadn't had much to give them, just rumors she'd heard in passing.

"She's a handsy one," Solain added with a grin before taking a swig of his ale.

"Yes, so I discovered." Merihem grudgingly admitted. The spirited woman had grabbed his rear before he left and told him she needed some essence of Incubi for a love spell, offering her body to help acquire it.

"If Empusa is under orders from a client, I doubt she'd leave behind her two mercenary pals." Iain wondered aloud, putting pieces together. "Lamia and Mormo are rarely far from her side and if they have a paying client there's a good chance they're all involved."

"I was thinking the same thing, but no one has seen hide nor hair of Mormo and Lamia," Dantalion confirmed.

A wicked smile spread across Iain's face and he glanced at his adopted brother, finding the same shit eating grin on his face. "Lads, I think we've got ye covered," Iain announced triumphantly.

Meri cocked an eyebrow and Dantalion just sat there, waiting for them to have out with it.

Iain leaned in, his voice falling to a conspiratorial whisper. "We've been on the hunt for a little nightmare demon. Seems she got into someone's dreams she shouldn't have and now daddy wants a little payback. We almost had her two days ago while she was waiting to meet a contact at a coffee shop in Edinburgh. Turns out that contact was Mormo and before we knew what was going on, the two of them had stolen into the bathroom and teleported away."

"Do you know where they were going?" Dantalion demanded, obviously thrilled with this news.

"Got something even better!" Solain announced, pulling out his phone and tapping away at the screen. When he turned the device to them a map of the world showed with a little blinking light over South America. "We bugged her."

"Ye take us with ye to South America and we'll go in together," Iain suggested easily, amber eyes alight. "We get our mark and ye get yer brother. Everyone wins."

Merihem glanced at Dantalion to see his older brother now grinning wolfishly. "You've got a deal!" Dan agreed, more than ready for the hunt to begin.

Pithius strode over, stuffing his phone in his pocket as he sat. "That was Amelia. She called to let me know that Seir's girls are all accounted for. They've split up into groups and are hiding out at a few of Seir's safe houses. Apparently, Seir told them to run for it when they got home to a bunch of the staff walking around aimlessly and sporting bite marks. I told them they can head to my place if they want to regroup and we'll bring Seir to them when we have him." Pithius looked around the table at all the pleased expressions. "What did I miss?"

CHAPTER 14

Verrin was sure if he looked to the side he would see the sparks of outrage coming off Cass's compact body. She nearly vibrated with fury at the blonde's undisguised offer. He was sorely tempted to revel in her jealousy a little longer but didn't want her to think he might actually accept this painted up harlot over her.

He tightened his arm around Cass, both to show his affection and to keep her off the blonde, and smiled broadly. "Thank you for the offer but I'd rather spend the night with my girlfriend. We have quite the evening planned."

Felicia's welcoming features stiffened. "Your girlfriend?" She asked slowly. She said girlfriend with the same inflection one would say road kill.

Verrin nodded, tugging Cass's smaller form in front of himself and wrapping his arms around her. He rested his head on top of hers and grinned at Felicia. "Yep. It took me a while to get her to say yes, but she eventually gave in and I'm so glad she did."

"I see." Felicia grated out.

"So thank you for the offer but Cassidy is far more delectable than anything I could get from a restaurant." He turned Cass toward the cart and gave her bottom a little pat to get her going in the right direction. "It was so nice to meet one of Cass's teachers from school! Have a good evening, ma'am!" Flashing a stunning grin at Felicia, he gave her a little wave before he turned his back to the woman who was now spluttering at his sly insult. Sauntering off after Cass, he tried to hold back the chuckle that wanted to escape.

He found Cassidy stopped two aisles over, peering around the corner past a display of lip glosses. He shot her a wink, loving the look of surprised delight on her face.

"I can't believe you just did that!" She hissed quietly, glancing around to make sure no one was watching them.

Verrin grinned and swept around her, nabbing the cart and turning it toward the cashes. "I just did what needed to be done. She was a snooty bitch to you and needed to have her nose rubbed in it. So I did."

The peal of laughter that broke from Cass was joyous. She lunged into his side, wrapping her arms awkwardly around his larger frame and squeezed tight. Her spontaneous hug lightened his heart and he wrestled his arm free of her hold so he could wrap it around her and pull her fully into his side, draping it across her small shoulders. Her puffy winter coat made him feel like he was snuggling a mini marshmallow man.

"I did good?" Verrin asked teasingly as they got in the line for the self-checkouts.

The smile she turned up to him was 100 watt and her beautiful chocolate eyes glittered with mirth. "You did so good! Did you see her face? Priceless!"

Verrin chuckled and leaned down, lowering his voice to an intimate whisper. "What's the good of having a demon lover if you can't use him to get back at evil bitches?"

She giggled, ducking her head to hide her flushed cheeks.

They checked out without too much fuss, although Cass kept looking around seemingly checking that Felicia wasn't on her way back for more, and headed to the car. The tiny red compact had made him wince when he first saw it in her driveway and he certainly wasn't looking forward to cramming himself back in the little sardine can she called a car.

Snagging the bag she'd just lifted from the cart, he waved her off. "It's freezing out here. You get the car warmed up. I got these."

She gave him a sweet, surprised smile and went around to climb in front, starting the engine. He opened the hatchback and tried to remember not to clock himself off it as he put their grocery bags inside with his clothing bags. With everything stowed, and his head safely out of the way, he shut it and returned the cart to the corral.

He grimaced as he climbed in the passenger side, folding his more than six-foot frame in as well as he could. He really would have preferred to drive but one glance at her car and he knew there was no way he could have crammed his legs up under that steering wheel. Well, not without it becoming some new form of torture anyway.

Cass was flipping through radio stations, spending mere seconds on one before moving to the next. Finally she decided on a tune he recognized from the 80's and smiled at him. "Ready to head home?"

"And have you all to myself?" Verrin teased.
"Definitely!"

Her blush was the most tempting reward he'd ever
gotten.

***

"Have you informed the client of our success yet?"

Empusa looked up from the enchanted scroll she
had uncurled in her lap and grinned at her accomplice's
entrance. "Yes, just finished sending the message." She
rolled up the scroll and waved it at the other two women.
"I wish we'd get a client that used modern means of
communication. I'm getting sick of having to figure out all
this magical crap."

Mormo snickered darkly, her voice a chilling
intonation. "But the old ones pay the best to get the job
done." The tall woman in her fashionably distressed black
clothes and goth makeup straddled a long wooden bench,
fingers tapping her knees as her booted feet thumped out a
steady rhythm on the stone floor.

"So true!" Empusa grinned before turning her gaze
to Lamia. "Our bounty is secured?"

Lamia nodded her elegant head, her plaited golden
hair falling over her shoulder. "It's all secure." She said
softly, her deceivingly demure voice dragging out the S in
each word ever so slightly. "The key and the blade are
locked away."

"Well, ladies, it took us a while but we finally got
the job done! I think we should have us a little
celebration!" Empusa announced, setting the

communication scroll on the side table and unfolding herself from her chair.

Mormo stopped her drumming, looking excited. "With the Incubus?" She asked, dark eyes flaring red with hope and a lewd grin crossing her face. "I haven't had an Incubus yet. I'd love to sink my fangs into him."

Lamia adjusted her rimless glasses, a pinched look on her face. "They taste off. I think it's the angel in them. Their blood is too..." She waved a hand in the air as she searched for the best descriptor. "Good." The word was said with serious distaste.

Empusa held back a snicker at her friend's expense. The two vampiric demigoddesses were always trying to one-up each other by sinking their fangs into stranger and stranger creatures. It seemed that this time the prim and proper Lamia had beaten Mormo to yet another delicacy.

Mormo glared at Lamia before pinning Empusa with her dark-eyed stared. "So? Can we nibble on the Incubi?"

Empusa shook her head. "Not yet, I want to make sure the client doesn't need more blood. They never gave us a quantity. I'm hoping the vial will do the trick, but if not I need him whole and cooperative to provide more."

"Aw, come on Emmy! Just a little bite?" Mormo whined, trying to give her the puppy dog looked. With her black lipstick and mass of eyeliner, she looked more like a dead dog than a needy one.

"Not yet. Just leave him alone for a while. As soon as the client is satisfied you can do what you want with him." Empusa assured her.

"Fine." Mormo huffed, flopping back onto the bench and kicking her knee high combat boots up to rest on the end. "Spoil sport." She murmured under her breath.

"When will the client be picking up the items?" Lamia asked, pulling a tablet and stylus from the stylish leather messenger bag slung across her body. In her knee length black skirt, thigh high stockings and white blouse she looked more like someone's fantasy secretary than the famed queen turned monster she was. Her only tell today was the black snakeskin stiletto heels she wore.

"Soon hopefully. I haven't gotten a response back from the scroll yet, but seeing as the client was in such a rush to get this done, I can't imagine it will be long." Empusa sighed. She thought carefully for a moment before broaching her plan. "I'd like both of you there for the exchange."

Lamia looked up from the screen, the light catching the rough lines of the scars that crisscrossed her eyes, and arched a regal brow. Mormo stopped throwing the apple she'd somehow acquired up in the air, catching it with a soft *thuk*. She voiced the question they were both wondering. "Why?"

"I just get a bad feeling about this. The client has been working through a third party, obviously wanting to keep their identity hush-hush, but the components we gathered were all angelic based. If our client wants to fuck with the angels that's a mess I want nothing to do with."

Lamia tucked her tablet back into her bag and focused on the others. "I noticed the same connection. They obviously need those items for something pertaining to the angelic host, but I can find no reference to any enchantment that would require those ingredients."

"Okay, so we all show for the exchange, get our just

desserts and then we can come back here to get a taste of Incu-boy while the dumb ass who paid us gets smoted by the winged wonders!" Mormo grinned at the other two. "I love it when a plan comes together!"

Lamia glanced back at Empusa and they shared a look. Neither thought it was going to go quite so easily. There was a good chance that whoever was hunting for the items they currently possessed wanted to keep their acquirement of them a secret. That would make the people who went through all the trouble of getting those items loose ends.

Empusa was highly uncomfortable being one of those loose ends.

***

Merihem crept through the undergrowth carefully, trying his hardest not to disturb anything with his passage. The last thing he wanted was to alert any of the guards surrounding the temple that they were being spied on.

After their rather productive meeting with the Sinclairs, the brothers had wanted to get going as soon as possible. Iain had sent word to his grandfather that they were leaving and met the brothers in the alley behind the pub. The look on the Sinclairs faces when they weren't met with a vehicle of some sort was comical and only got better as Dantalion put his flattened palm out in front of himself and opened the portal. With a flowing ripple, the air distorted, looking like heat rising from hot pavement as it spread into a wide circle.

It took a bit of cajoling, but everyone finally went through, Dantalion following to close it behind them.

On the other side, they walked out into dense jungle and moist warm air.

They had taken the rest of the day to established a camp of sorts a few miles from the location of Iain's GPS locator. Now, with Dantalion teleporting Pithius to collect a few women for Seir and Iain watching the camp, Merihem had volunteered to scout out Empusa's base of operations. With darkness swiftly falling, Iain had sent his brother to accompany him.

Which was how Merihem ended up fighting his way through the darkness with a half vampire.

"Hell, demon, could you make any more noise?"

Merihem started as the smooth amused voice curled out of the darkness and with a rustle of leaves, Solain jumped down from his perch among the branches. The half vampire settled his long, lean form against a tree trunk and ran a hand through his spiky blond hair, appearing for all the world as if he was a bored to death GQ model on a jungle photo shoot.

Meri took a deep breath to try and keep his irritation buried before inquiring, "Have you found anything?"

Solain shrugged and gestured flippantly to a crumpled body near the base of a nearby tree. "I found a snack."

Merihem couldn't keep the grimace from his face.

"Oh, don't give me that look." Solain sighed, disgruntled. "I needed a bite and you're not my type. Plus, he's one of Empusa's sentries."

Merihem forgot all about his disgust with the vampire's eating habits and whipped his head around, looking at the ancient vine-covered stone walls with new

147

appreciation. "She's here?"

"Judging by the things Snack-n-Go over there was thinking, Empusa and her cronies have made themselves a little bunny ranch out here with your brother as the star attraction," Solain informed him, sounding vaguely amused.

Ignoring the bunny ranch comment for a moment, Merihem studied Solain. "You can see the thoughts of those you drink from?"

"Most have the ability to erase the memory of their bite, but some vamps have the skill to do more." Solain shrugged as if it was nothing. "Guess I'm one of the lucky ones."

Meri narrowed his eyes at that but didn't comment, instead deciding to research the phenomenon when he had time. "Can you tell me anything else about where Empusa is hiding Seir?"

"Well, this place isn't hers for starters. It belonged to a local group of snake shifters, but it seems like Empusa took control of it and allowed her vampire buddies to bite the shifters. They're all in thrall."

"Thrall?"

"Good lord, have you ever met a vamp before?" Solain griped.

"In battle, yes." Meri pointed out. "I have never sat down for tea with one. Your race is rather antisocial if you haven't noticed."

Solain gave a derisive snort as if that image amused him. "Fair enough. All right, vampire crash course time. One. Vamps with enough power can overtake the minds of their prey and make them compliant to their every whim. Thus, a thrall. Two. Old vampires or halfborns like myself can usually stand some degree of sunlight without issue so don't expect a UV bulb to be of any help. Three. Your enemy, Empusa, has two seriously ancient vamps on her payroll. Mormo is a demigoddess and Greek boogieman with her very own cult, and Lamia is a god-cursed former queen with a penchant for blood and terrifying little children."

Merihem just blinked, absorbing all this information. "How in the world did those three get together?" He murmured thoughtfully.

"Apparently they all got shafted by the gods. Guess they weren't allowed to take their place on Olympus when the gods receded and were forced to stay here with the rest of us. Guess they met up at demi-whiners anonymous." Solain admitted while carefully examining the nails of his left hand. "Gotta say, when your brother finds the crazy bitches, he goes for the craziest of the bunch. It wouldn't surprise me if they've drained him dry by the time we find him."

Merihem's head jerked toward the fortress as the faint trill of female laughter filled the night air. Images of Seir struggling as the vampire women sunk their teeth into him clouded his mind and darkened his thoughts. With a determined step, Meri began toward the fortress, adamant on getting his younger brother out of their clutches.

"Whoa, hold on there! I didn't mean it like that!" Solain soothed, getting in front of him and holding his hands up in a placating gesture. "They aren't going to kill Seir. They need him for something. Not to mention, that castle has almost a hundred bespelled guards, three crazy demigods and a nightmare demon. We need a little bit more of a plan before we bust down the door if you want to pull your brother out in any recognizable form. We have the time to get it right."

Merihem heard the logic in Solain's words, but it beat against the desire to retrieve his youngest sibling with reckless abandon. Frustration boiled up and Meri whirled, slamming his fist into the nearest tree trunk.

Solain blinked. "Oh-kay. So now that we have shown the trees who's boss, why don't we gather up the others and take care of business."

Merihem nodded slowly, the pain in his hand barely a distraction as he turned and stalked off into the darkness toward their meeting point. Once Dantalion picked them up they'd need to regroup and plan out their next move at the Florida penthouse Pithius had appropriated.

"So..." Solain started awkwardly, following him and trying to find a topic to distract the touchy demon. "Tell me, what's it like to have a dick that's catnip to women?"

CHAPTER 15

The alarm went off for the third time at quarter after seven and Cass finally had to give up the idea of sleeping in. No matter how many times she hit the snooze button she still had to work at nine and her boss was the nicest woman in the world until you didn't show up to open her beloved library on time. Cassidy flopped over and tried to work up enough motivation to get her butt in the shower.

Instead, she remembered exactly why she was exhausted and couldn't help but smile.

They had come home from shopping yesterday and settled into making the largest batch of poutine Cass had ever created. She had never cooked with a man before but found bumping around in her kitchen while they shredded cheese and retrieved dishes was actually rather enjoyable. It didn't hurt that Verrin kept stealing sweet little kisses every time he came up with a reason to reach past her. When it was done, she spooned up heaping bowls of fries smothered in cheese and gravy and settled in to watch funny videos online on the living room TV. They had laughed, winced and giggled over the horrible crashes, hilarious trips and silly pets until the sky had darkened to night.

Around eleven they had finally gathered up their dishes and filled the dishwasher, wiping down the counters and putting the leftovers away. Verrin had decided to clean up the recyclables so Cass popped herself up on the counter to talk to him as he worked.

"So you're welcome to hang out here tomorrow while I'm at work." She told him as she picked at the frayed edge of a dishtowel in her lap. "I'll try to be quiet in the morning so I don't wake you up."

Verrin turned off the tap and set the last of the pop cans aside to looked straight at her. "That won't be a problem. I'll be coming with you."

"What?" Cassidy stared at him in surprise. "You realize I work in a library right? You'll be bored out of your mind having to spend the entire day there. Why not just relax here?"

Verrin's gorgeous lips tipped up at the corners and he tugged the dry dishcloth from her lax fingers to dry his wet hands. "Cass, I could never be bored around you, but more than that, I can't be parted from you. You're kind of stuck with me."

"I don't understand."

Verrin stepped in close, putting his hands on the counter on either side of her, effectively boxing her in. It was a move he seemed to enjoy. "I can't leave your side until I've done what I was called here to do." His smile turned wicked and he leaned in close, putting his perfect lips by her ear. "So, unless you're willing to let me have my way with you tonight, I'm coming with you to work in the morning."

At that memory, she shot up in bed. Oh god, Verrin was coming to work with her! Cass scrambled to the edge of the bed and climbed out, not worried about making her rumpled bed. She went to the door and poked her head out. Not hearing anything, she raced down the hall to the bathroom and threw open the door.

Her breath caught as she revealed a very muscular, very wet, very nude Verrin who was just lowering a towel from his wet hair, leaving its short length sticking up in all directions. His eyes widened slightly when they met hers, brightening with the intense light she associated with his rising lust, before that wicked grin was graced his lips. "Good morning, Cass. Did you need in the bathroom?"

Because of Verrin's tendency to discard his shirt she had thought she'd be better prepared when and if she saw the whole package. Now she knew she had been brutally wrong. His thickly muscled thighs were amazingly contoured and the left one bore a strange dark circular tattoo that wrapped around to the back of his leg. She wanted to focus more on it, but her attention was drawn instead to a much more prominent facet of his male physique.

Cass had never seen a more beautiful cock.

It was large, thick and cut, and even as she watched it began to harden. Her hands twitched and her mouth watered as she stared, fixated, on it.

Oh lord, that's one way to spice up a Monday morning.

"Would you like to lend me a hand?" Verrin asked, the tone in his voice alluring. He held his damp towel at his side, not embarrassed at all to be completely naked in front of her.

"Uh, nope." She squeaked, backing up slowly, hands raising as if to ward him and that amazing erection off. "I'll, uh, just wait till you're done." Her cheeks heated as she recognized the double meaning of her own words and she rushed to corrected her phrasing. "With your shower, I mean. Oh god." She shut the door gently and bolted for her room, the sound of his low masculine laughter echoing after her.

"Dammit all to hell!" She cursed quietly once she was safely locked inside her empty bedroom. The image of Verrin, every solid inch of him, dripping wet and aroused in her bathroom was going to haunt her erotic daydreams for the rest of her life.

Daydreams she'd rarely had until his unexpected arrival in her life three days ago.

She hung her head. This couldn't be happening. She'd never fallen for a guy this fast. She'd never fallen for a guy period! Cass was no untried virgin, but most of her dalliances into the matters of the heart had been nothing more than... nice. Nice men, nice dates, nice sex, nice breakup. Nothing messy. No heartbroken tears over chocolate ice cream. No man trying to convince her he was in love with her. Just two people amicably parting ways. Hell she was still casual friends with most of her exes.

Tyler, her most recent ex, was the only one who stood out in the mire of niceness and that was only because he'd turned into such a jerk at the end.

And yet, here she was. Her heart pounding in her chest at the mere idea of going back into that bathroom and plastering herself to Verrin. She wanted to offer herself up as a demonic sacrifice. She'd even volunteer to lick every rivulet of water from his deliciously golden skin.

Cass groaned at that carnal mental image and threw herself face down across her bed.

Where was the unruffled Cass she'd always been? She had calmly gone to a community drawing class with Savvy just so her friend could ogle the nude male model and felt nothing more than artistic appreciation. Men, even beautiful men, didn't do this to her! They never made chills race down her spine at a mere glance. Her insides had never fluttered at a single hot touch.

Her heart had never ached just seeing a man smile.

This was dangerous uncharted territory.

She had to remember that Verrin was an Incubus, it was in his very DNA to be able to turn a woman inside out. She was just one in a long line of women. On top of that, Verrin was in a situation. He could wait for this stupid bond to wear off or he could sleep with her and go back to his regular life. She might be highly attracted to him, but Cass had no desire to be a means to an end.

It was time she got her act together.

Forcing herself to take a deep cleansing breath, Cass rubbed at her eyes, trying futilely to rid the image of Verrin from her memory and exhaled. She had to steel herself. All she had to do was wait out this bond and he'd walk out of her life, never to come back.

She certainly wouldn't let him walk out with her heart in tow.

She got to her feet and went to her closet, determined to focus on something else. Cass gathered a fuzzy black sweater with a cowl neck and a pair of classic black jeans from the closet. A sensible bra, boy short panties and a pair of knee-high rainbow socks from her dresser completed the outfit. She listened with bated breath at the door for a moment before opening it. The clink of dishes and sound of running water came from downstairs and she stealthily opened her door and hauled her armful across the hallway to the now unoccupied bathroom.

She dumped her burden on the counter that was surprisingly clean considering her last boyfriend had a habit of leaving water, towels and remnants from shaving everywhere. Verrin was a rather awesome house guest. The view he provided was in his favour too.

Shaking her head, Cass stripped off her pajamas and threw them in the laundry hamper before turning on the shower. Once it was warm enough she got in and quickly washed her hair and body, trying not to linger as her mind tended to drift under the showers warm influence.

Within twenty minutes she was out and drying off, dragging a comb through her long chestnut hair and getting dressed in the confines of the steamy bathroom. It wasn't her first choice, but the way her luck had been holding out on her she wasn't willing to risk Verrin catching her in the almost buff on her way to her room. Socks in hand, she hung her towel on the hook on the back of the door and headed downstairs. At the top of the stairs she steeled herself to face Verrin again before jogging down and into the kitchen.

Verrin was standing in front of the stove, flipping french toast in a frying pan. Plates were laid out on the counter beside him just waiting to receive their bounty. He seemed so at ease in her kitchen it was almost as if he'd always been there.

Cass slipped onto one of the stools at the island and watched his muscled body move as he flicked two golden brown slices onto a plate and turned to set it in front of her. This was starting to become a rather enjoyable part of her morning routine.

"I figured you could use a good breakfast before we head off for the day." Verrin smiled and tilted his head toward the fridge. "Grab a drink. I'll get the syrup."

Cass just stared at him, taking him in for a moment. He turned back to her, syrup collected from the cupboard, and she couldn't resist voicing what was on her mind any longer. "You're an unusually willing cook."

Verrin chuckled. "Isn't that a good thing?"

Cass nodded. "I'm just surprised. A lot of men aren't into cooking and yet you just go ahead and do it. Not only do you make good food, but you actually clean up afterward too!"

"Well, I am an immortal bachelor. At some point you realize that paying for meals gets old quick. It's easier to learn to make food for yourself." Verrin shrugged. "Having four hungry brothers who will eat almost anything means that very little goes to waste, even if you screw it up during practice."

Cass grinned. "I guess that would help." She poured syrup on her french toast and took a bite. Cinnamon and maple blended on her tongue. "Mmm...you really are too good at this."

Verrin, who had turned to watch her eat, smiled wickedly and winked at her. "Wait till you see what else I'm good at."

Cass ducked her head, hoping he wouldn't catch the

blush on her cheeks, and tucked into her breakfast. A few silent minutes later Verrin set his plate beside hers and sat down to eat.

"So I'm curious..." Cass started hesitantly, needing to get her mind off the daydream of licking maple syrup from Verrin's golden skin. "You said you're immortal so exactly how old does that make you?"

Verrin glanced over at her quizzically and shrugged. "Good question. You got a calculator? I hate numbers."

Cass brought the calculator app up on her smartphone and turned it towards him, waiting to see what he came up with. "Go for it."

He poked at the buttons for a moment before turning it back to her so she could read the screen.

2376.

"That's an approximation. Calendars tend to vary so I might be a year or so off give or take." Verrin stated blandly, popping a piece of syrup covered french toast in his mouth.

Cass's eyes widen and her head jerked up to stare at him. "Y-you're ancient!" She squeaked, stunned.

Verrin snorted indelicately and put a finger out to push her gaping mouth closed. "I told you I was immortal."

"Yes, but I didn't realize you were so old!" Cass shot back.

He laughed and put a hand to his heart as if hurt. "You wound me, lovely lady. I don't look a day over a thousand."

Cass gave him a flat look and smacked him in the arm lightly. "You know what I mean!" She leaned toward him, excitement flowing as she really started to think of the things he must have seen. "You were around at the same time as Alexander the Great! Did you see the building of the Colosseum? Oh, did you get to explore the new world? See the Mayans and Aztecs when their cities were still populated?" She leaned forward in her excitement, voice lowering to a confidential whisper. "Did Atlantis really exist?"

Verrin seemed surprised by her enthusiasm and chuckled, "Calm down, little one! One question at a time." He popped the last bite of french toast into his mouth and chased it with a swallow of coffee before continuing. "Now, yes I grew up under the rule of Alexander. In fact, my eldest brother was in his army. I was there with Seir and Thius when they held the opening ceremonies for the Colosseum. That place was not for the faint of heart." He informed her with a grimace. "I did get to the new world but I waited until the travel arrangements were a bit more common. As for Atlantis, I have no idea."

"Oh," Cassidy said, only slightly dejected.

Verrin leaned close and grinned at her. "Although I have heard tell that it was real."

Her eyes widened. "Really?"

Verrin nodded, "One of my uncles once mentioned it. He said that Atlantis had been drawn into a conflict. When they knew all was lost they did something and withdrew from the world."

"Withdrew from the world?"

He shrugged. "That was all Penemue told me."

Cass quirked an eyebrow at him. "Penemue?"

Verrin sat back and grinned. "One of my uncles. Angels don't have the same family ties humans do. My uncles and aunts are every angel to ever grace the heavens, although most of them won't talk to me now because of my father's decision to come to earth."

Cass made a little thinking hum as she contemplated this and went back to her food, eating without tasting as her mind raced. The things he'd seen, the changes the world had gone through, the rise and fall of civilizations. It was just too much to imagine.

She quietly finished her breakfast and gathered her lunch, her mind still buzzing. Verrin helped her into her winter coat at the door and they left for work.

CHAPTER 16

Verrin had carefully watched her on their drive along the snow covered streets to the library. Cassidy hadn't said a word to him the entire way, but her lovely lips were pursed flat and her forehead crinkled slightly in consternation. Obviously, their little conversation about his extensive past had gotten her thinking and he could only guess where that mind of hers would go to.

She pulled into a parkade and drove up a couple of levels until she found an empty spot. She parked, grabbed her purse and the tote she'd sat in his lap and got out. He pried himself out and she locked the car doors, already turning toward the stairway that would take her back to street level.

He sighed and jogged up beside her. He may have been around women for the last two thousand and some years but he still couldn't figure out the way their minds worked. The only thing he did know was that silence was bad. Very, very bad. Taking a deep breath, he braced himself and went for it. "Did I do something wrong?"

Cass stopped as she reached the bottom of the stairs and just blinked at him. "I don't know. Did you?"

Verrin rubbed the back of his neck and stared down at their shoes. Gods, he hated situations like this. Women were so complex he was pretty sure he'd never figure them out. "Well, I – ah, hell! You're being really quiet and I'm worried I said something that made you that way."

The corner of her lovely lips tipped up and she graced him with a small chuckle. "No, that's not it. I just – I guess I'm a little stunned by what you told me." She glanced around to make sure they were alone in the stairwell and lowered her voice. "I know you told me the first night what you were, but I guess it didn't really kick in."

Verrin frowned. "Does my being different bother you?" He asked carefully, following her lead while trying to not announce his supernatural status in public.

"Not really." Cass shrugged. "I mean it makes sense, sort of. There's all those stories and myths of other beings in the world. Some of it had to be the truth. What gets me is that you've seen so much of the world. You've been there to see things I can only read about in books." She shook her head in amazement.

"So it's my age that gets you." Verrin assumed, arching an eyebrow at her. "I can assure you, you're not the first younger woman I've been with." He stated blandly.

Cassidy flushed red but she held up one finger. "First off, you have not *been with* me yet." She held up a second finger. "Secondly, isn't sleeping with someone my age a form of cradle robbing?"

Verrin threw his head back and laughed. Damn this woman, she had the strangest way of looking at things.

When his laughter had faded to a chuckle he leaned forward into her space and grinned. "I'm a firm believer in the age of majority. And if you think about it, in my day, you'd have been married off years ago and have a herd of kids following you around by now."

She narrowed her eyes at him and he just grinned back at her. He swept up her hand and tucked it in the crook of his arm. "Come now, my Lady. Let a gentleman escort you to work."

Cass rolled her eyes and leaned into his arm. "You are such a pain in the ass."

"And yet you say that with affection." Verrin grinned and opened the door onto the street for them. "Now, where are we headed?"

Cass gestured with a black gloved hand to the left. "The library is just down a couple of blocks."

They started off and Verrin got his first real look at the town Cassidy lived in. The buildings were all turn of the century brick monsters with windows accented in lighter stone. None of them were over five stories high as if they had been built low to endure the strong island winds. Streetlights in an old fashioned style lined the streets and every corner had a brightly lit Christmas tree on it. They walked the two blocks, past decorated shop windows and early morning shoppers, until they reached a large set of stone steps that led up to the largest brick building yet.

The library must have taken up an entire block, it's bulk sprawling and intimidating. He followed Cass up the steps and paused while she unlocked the double doors to let them into the grand entrance. Cassidy veered left, past a circle of comfortable looking chairs, toward a long counter.

She opened a waist high door at the end of it and stepped through, leaving Verrin on the other side.

An elderly woman looked up from a computer behind the counter and smiled, "Good morning, Cassidy." Her eyes narrowed at Verrin where he leaned against the counter behind Cass and her lips thinned. "We're not open yet, young man."

"Oh, sorry Mrs. Miriam, he came in with me," Cassidy said, trying to come up with an excuse as she looked between the old lady and her new demon companion. "He... uh... He's here to..."

"Good morning, Madam." Verrin smiled smoothly, walking down the other side of the counter until he was even with the elder librarian. He met her powder blue eyes and turned on the charm. "I apologize for coming so early. Cassidy and I got into quite the debate over dinner last night and seeing as we're planning on doing dinner again tonight I need to study up." He leaned onto the counter and gave the old woman a wink. "I'm afraid she had an unarmed opponent yesterday and I'd rather not hand her a second victory quite so easily. If it wouldn't be a problem, I was hoping to get started early."

"Oh." Mrs. Miriam sat up straighter and smiled back at Verrin. One wiry hand came up to plump her short silvery curls. "Well, there's nothing wrong with a little dedicated study. There are closed study rooms on the second floor if you like."

Verrin gave her a bow of his head and another smile that radiated his charm. "Thank you so much, Madam." He met Cass's eyes and gave her a grin. "I'll be upstairs if you need me."

With that, he turned and headed for the stairs. Time

to find something to keep himself busy. Maybe he could track down the sexuality section. He'd been meaning to figure out that whole Tantra thing anyway.

***

Cass scanned the last of the returned library books from the drop box back into the availability system and then dumped the lot of them on a cart to be shelved. Verrin had given her a lot to think about that morning, not the least of which was the fact that her house guest was an immortal supernatural creature with supposedly unbelievable sexual skills.

It hadn't really hit her until this morning that he was truly different. Sure, he was unlike any man she'd ever met but the idea that he was truly an Incubus just seemed like a formless idea before. Now her brain was kicking over his words repetitively, obsessed with the idea that he might very well be what he said he was. Ancient. Immortal. A creature of human myth.

Cass shook her head to try and clear her thoughts. She needed a little bit of normal before she was overwhelmed and there was no better place then work to get that.

She pushed the loaded cart out from behind the counter and headed into the stacks, shelving books along the way. When she finished all the fiction books she headed for the elevator and pushed her cart inside, hitting the button for the basement level where they kept all the reference books.

As the elevator descended a low hum of arousal ran through her and she shifted slightly where she stood. The elevator dinged and the doors slid open so she brushed it off as she pushed her cart out and continued to shelve books. A few books later and she was positive something must be wrong with her. What had started as just a slight hint of arousal was now a curling ache of desire that spread through her and made her stomach flutter.

Needing a minute, Cass pushed her cart into a rarely visited encyclopedia section and leaned against the shelving. Her body was almost shaking with the arousal coursing through her veins and, for the life of her, there was no viable reason why.

Could she really be that hard up for sex? Or was there a perfectly good reason for this? Was this some sort of side effect caused by being around Incubi?

Wait, hadn't Verrin said they were bound together? That implied that they could only go so far apart. Was this some type of sexual calling card telling her not to leave Verrin's vicinity?

Cass eyed the end of the long aisle and made her decision. Taking one hesitant step after another she approached the end of the aisle. Every step was a jarring strum against sensitive nerves, but she continued until an ache so sharp it made her double over, her steps faltering.

Holy hell, her sex clenched with every heartbeat, making her core feel disturbingly vacant. The sensation was so consuming that she had to hold back a needful moan.

Cassidy leaned her weight heavily on the bookshelf to her left and tried to breathe evenly. Each rise of her chest dragged her nipples the scantest bit against the soft inner cups of her bra and nearly undid her. She needed to move back, get within range of Verrin so this horrible needy ache could ease.

If only she could make her legs work.

Her knees shook so bad she was seriously afraid her legs would give out beneath her. She looked longingly over her shoulder at the book cart at the other end of the aisle and the distance felt like miles instead of feet.

Cass couldn't help it, her eyes welled. It was inexplicable and she hated it, but all of a sudden she wanted to rail at Verrin for not telling her about this. For not warning her that their so-called bond would turn her into this needy, quivering mass of sensations and desires. Damn him! He was probably sitting upstairs, cool as you please, while she suffered down here alone.

It was then she heard the rhythmic thudding on the tiled floor. Cass glanced up, lashes spiked in tears, just as Verrin skidded to a stop at the end of the aisle. She hated to admit it, but with his tousled dark hair and flushed features, he was the most welcome sight she'd ever seen. Like a hunting predator, he strode toward her. Those gorgeous blue eyes started to glow with a cool blue light and his full lips were thinned into a pensive line.

With each of his steps her breath came easier, but the wanton heat in her body didn't abate. Cassidy slowly eased up to stand on her own, letting go of the bookshelf. "Verrin - " She started, worried he was mad at her.

He reached out, hard hands catching her arms, and dragged her into his chest. One hand caught her chin, tilting her head up so his lips could take possession of hers. The kiss was desperate, fevered with a passion that nearly burned her up. His lips both tamed her mouth and made her body go wild. She writhed against him until he dug one hand into her hair and ran the other down her back to grip her bottom. With a tug at her hair, he pulled her hungry mouth away just far enough that he could speak.

"Jump." The order was growled out and without hesitation, she did just that.

The firm hand on her rear caught her at the top of the jump and pulled her tight against his body. The hand in her hair loosened to drag her hand from where it caressed his male nipple through his shirt and brought it behind his head. "Hold."

Again her body was his to command and she clasped her arms behind his neck as he caught her legs and wrapped them around his hips, taking her weight easily into his arms. She moaned as his hardness came up tight against her center and rubbed deliciously at her through their clothes.

"Oh, Cass..." Verrin purred against her lips, his hands holding her backside tight so he could rock into her, rubbing her into a frenzy. "Fuck, Cass, what you do to me."

"I - " She started again, not even sure what to say as his lips trailed nipping kisses down her throat.

"Hush. I won't take you here, little one, even if kills me not to. I just need you in my arms for a few minutes. I need your heat against me." He nipped the spot where her shoulder met her neck and then sucked the small hurt away until she shuddered in his arms. Her hips bucked against his and he groaned into her hair. "Sweet Hades woman, I could feel you moving away from me and it almost drove me mad."

"I'm sorry." She breathed, the words a groan of appreciation.

"Don't apologize. Just don't do it again." One of his

hands trailed up her body and grasped her breast, circling the nipple. "I doubt I'd be able to control myself a second time. Your colleagues are lucky there was an elevator in my way."

Cass couldn't help it. She giggled. "Couldn't find the stairs?" Her merriment turned into a surprised squeak when his big hand came down on her butt in a swat. Her eyes got big and she stared at him in shock. "Did you just spank me?"

Verrin's predatory look faded in the wake of a smug smile and arched brow. "I did indeed. In fact, I would go so far as to say you liked it."

Her cheeks heated and she buried her face in his neck, shielding herself from his amusement. How could this incorrigible man know her so well after so little time?

After a moment of quiet calm, Verrin touched a kiss to her now disheveled hair. "I suppose I should let you get back to work." He sounded put out as if the idea of letting her out of his arms was a trial.

"Probably." She murmured, in no hurry.

Verrin buried his head in her shoulder and inhaled deeply, his arms tightening around her in a big hug, before lowering her enough to set her on her feet. Even so, he didn't seem to want to let her go completely, finding a reason to touch her as he ran his fingers through her hair and settled her clothing back into some semblance of acceptable. "There, beautiful as always."

Cassidy flustered and needing to clear her thoughts, she stared at the cart of books yet to be shelved. "I really should get those finished." Anything to distract her from the fireworks in her blood.

Verrin nodded. "I'll stay down here until you're

finished. I don't think we need a repeat just yet."

Cass nodded, heading back to her cart. She was having enough trouble getting the first time out of her head, a second might just fry her circuits permanently. She was pretty sure she would never look at encyclopedias the same again.

CHAPTER 17

Verrin managed to let Cassidy shelve the rest of her cart. It wasn't an easy task by any means. Every time she bent down those black jeans of hers moulded to her perfect heart shaped rear and he had to hold himself back from crawling over and begging at her feet for a taste of her feminine core.

He glanced around and seeing no one casually adjusted himself. He was starting to worry that his erection would develop a mind of its own and best the fly of his jeans for freedom. The last thing he needed was for his cock to go into Godzilla mode and storm the city until it found happiness inside his little librarian.

And on that note, he started to fantasize about taking her against the stacks. She looked so innocent and comfortable in her jeans and soft sweater, but she had turned into a firebrand in his arms. Writhing and grinding her hips against him until he wanted nothing more than to take her where they stood, Gods damn whoever saw.

It was only the fact that this was her job that held

him back. As sure as he was that he could make her forget that fact in the whirl of pleasure, she would be pretty pissed at him afterward. And he found himself highly interested in the afterward with Cass.

So he held back.

"I'm all done down here," Cassidy said, pushing the empty cart toward the elevator where he'd waited for her.

"Great." Freed from visual torture, he turned and hit the button to call the elevator back to their floor. They waited silently side by side. Afraid he would do something unforgivable at her workplace, Verrin jammed his hands deep in his pockets and tried to keep his mind on anything but the lovely woman beside him.

The ding of the elevator was both a good thing and a bad.

When the door slid open, he held it so Cass could get her cart through and then stepped in, hitting the button for the main level and the second as well. He leaned against the back wall, hands in pockets and eyes ahead as he waited for the door to slide closed.

"Did I do something wrong?"

His own question from earlier parroted back at him made him start. He turned to look down at the woman at his side and saw the apprehension in her chocolate eyes.

"What? No! Absolutely not! You did nothing wrong. Why would you think that?" He was appalled that she might have even got that idea.

"Well, you haven't said a word to me since..." She made a hand gesture to indicate their little meeting in the encyclopedia aisle.

Verrin shook his head wryly and turned, boxing his little librarian into the corner of the elevator. Leaning down, he touched her forehead with his and gave her a wolfish smile. "I spent the time since our little tryst imagining myself stripping your clothes off and taking you right there, bent over your cart. It's taking all of my restraint not to do just that right here."

Her voice was breathless when she uttered a shocked little, "Oh!"

The elevator dinged that they had reached the main level and Verrin stepped back, giving her space. "I suggest you get going before I decide to take you up to the study room with me."

Her cheeks flushed and she scooted past him, pushing her cart rapidly. He still managed to give her butt a swat as she went and Cass shot him a surprised look over her shoulder.

Verrin grinned and gave her a little wave as the elevator doors slid closed, blocking her from view.

Once out of sight, he dropped his head back until it thudded against the elevator wall. Gods above, how in the world was he going to make it through the rest of the day.

***

Merihem stared at Pithius' master plan and felt his stomach drop. This was never going to work.

"What? Don't give me that look, Meri! I didn't see you coming up with anything better!" Pithius grouched from where he stood behind the sofa. In front of him, squished together on the brocade couch, sat three absolutely stunning women, two brunettes and a golden blonde. The women, all of them nymphs, were volunteers for the position of Seir-bait as Pithius had so eloquently put it.

When Dantalion had reappeared in their makeshift camp an hour ago it had been to inform them that Pithius had secured willing females. Figuring the poor women wouldn't enjoy the jungle accommodations they currently had to offer, Pithius suggested getting them a hotel room in a nearby city and letting them stay there until it was time. Now they sat in a palatial suite in the grandest hotel Buenos Aires could provide, gathered together in the sitting room. Iain and Solain had left soon after they'd been teleported in, claiming to be on a foraging mission.

"I truly doubt this is a good idea," Merihem stated, staring at the women. "Seir will be lust crazed and dangerous."

"Exactly!" Pithius cheered, coming around the sofa. "You think that Seir is going to be pleased as punch to see us? We're dudes! Without a vagina, he has no use for us. He'll toss us aside and hunt down the nearest available female." He gave a displaying gesture toward the women that would have made Vanna White proud. "I give you the nearest available females!"

"Hi." One of the brunettes said with a dazzling smile and an awkward little wave.

Merihem dropped his head into his hands. "What do you think Dan?" He murmured.

Dantalion straightened from where he leaned against the wall and came to stand by Merihem's chair. Arms crossed, he considered the three nymphs. "This is something you truly wish to do?" He asked, eyeing the women carefully.

A chorus of yeses and nods.

Dantalion narrowed his eyes at them. "Why?"

The blonde haired nymph was the one to answer, scooting forward in her seat until she was perched on the edge of the sofa. "Your brother, Seir, is an Incubus too, right? You guys are the stuff of legends! You were built for pleasure! Compared to a human male, being with a regular Incubus is the difference between driving a Hyundai and a Benz. An Incubus lost to lust is even better! Like a custom made Ferrari! Who wouldn't want to ride that?"

"Damn..." Pithius muttered, looking lustily at the blonde. "I love it when beautiful girls talk cars."

Dantalion sighed and glanced at the other women. "You feel the same way?"

The other two nymphs nodded vehemently.

"Come on, Leon!" Pithius pressed. "If the ladies want to ride a Ferrari, who are we to deny them?"

"Only you can make such a lewd comment sound reasonable." Merihem murmured, rubbing at the bridge of his nose.

Pithius ignored him, opting instead to push his advantage with Dantalion. "Look, I didn't see either of you coming up with anything better!"

Meri held up a finger. "I suggested we sedate him."

"Pfft!" Pithius scoffed, brushing the suggestion off. "Just what we need, an unconscious Incubus with a raging hard on. I don't know about you, Meri, but I'm not going to be the one who carries his horny ass home!"

"So you are suggesting we let him rut on these poor women?" Meri growled, starting to get pissed off.

"Uh, we are volunteering..." One of the brunettes spoke up hesitantly, earning herself a beaming smile from Pithius and sharp look from Merihem.

"See that?" Pithius gestured at the women wildly.

"They are volunteering, Meri! Vol-Un-Teering! I explained the whole thing to them and they want to do this! We could dope the living hell out of Seir and it won't do a damn thing to help him until he fucks someone!"

Merihem took a deep breath, rubbing his temple with one hand. "Must you be so crass?"

"Oh, I'm sorry Mr. Polite!" Pithius hissed at him, his hazel eyes taking on an amber glow. "When you said you wanted to rescue Seir I didn't realize our plans had to pass our propriety tests! I just figured that getting him out in one piece was the goal!"

"This is not about propriety!" Merihem shouted, coming to his feet. "This is about putting our brother, who is already mentally compromised, in a situation he would not choose for himself!"

"Come off your high horse, Meri!" Pithius growled back. "Don't drag your own sad history into this! We're not using him! We're letting him use them!" He shouted, pointing at the women who sat on the sofa, looking uncomfortable between the feuding brothers.

"Do not bring my past into this, Pithius!" Merihem, green eyes shone laser bright in rage.

"Why? Because you're a pus -"

Dantalion stepped forward, getting directly between the two younger men. Putting a hand to each of their chests, he gave them a little shove backward. "Stop it, both of you. Neither I nor Seir has time for your childish bickering. Get your shit together."

Pithius and Merihem glared at each other around their brother's large body but backed off. Merihem sat down again, crossing his legs at the knee and Pithius sat on the arm of the sofa, gathering a section of the blonde's

176

long curling hair as a fidget toy, curling it around his fingers again and again.

"We'll use the women," Dantalion said, laying down the decision in the same tone he'd sent legions into battle with. "Meri, keep a portion of the tranquilizer drug with you in case he doesn't respond accordingly or he wears out the women before he's sane."

Merihem nodded, accepting this idea.

"Pithius, since they were your idea, you're in charge of the women," Dantalion ordered, turning on the blond man. "We're bringing them into a dangerous situation. Guard them with your life and prepare them for Seir."

Pithius cocked an eyebrow at his big brother. "By prepare do you mean...?"

"Mentally and physically. They need to be a hundred percent sure this is what they want to get into and when they are, prepare their bodies. Seir will not be in his right mind and will waste no time sating himself on their flesh whether their bodies are ready to take him or not. You'll make sure they are prepared."

As Dantalion turned away from Pithius, the blond brother fist pumped and childishly stuck his tongue out at Merihem, his smile gigantic.

Merihem ignored him. "What about Verrin?"

"We're going to need to collect Verrin. I don't think going in there with anything less then full force is a good idea." Dantalion admitted. Always the military man, he knew there was strength in numbers.

"What if he hasn't banged the summoner yet?" Pithius inquired, rubbing a section of the blonde's smooth tresses back and forth against his bottom lip in an unconscious action.

"Dear lord..." Merihem muttered, disgusted at Pithius's vocabulary.

"Then we inform her of what's going on and give them half an hour to end the summons. Time is of the essence. If Verrin wishes to tarry with his lady after we've retrieved Seir, I'll return him."

"Sounds like ye lads have this all planned out." Iain Sinclair drawled, stepping into the room, a stack of pizza boxes in his hands.

Pithius stared at the pizza boxes with the same lust that the nymphs focused on Iain as they ogled his broad body. "What you got there, wolf?" Pithius asked, coming around the sofa as if he were going to offer Iain a hand.

"Meat pizza," Solain called, kicking the door shut and sauntering in to dump a large paper bag and a couple plastic ones on the far table. "Also got beer, soda and enough wings to make our own chicken graveyard."

"Awesome! Come here you beautiful thing!" Pithius crooned, stealing the top box off the stack and dropping down into an armchair. He flipped it open, inhaled deeply and grab a slice. Looking around, he caught the surprised looks from the nymphs and the disgusted looks from the others as he stuffed half a steaming slice into his mouth. "What?" He asked around his mouthful, completely oblivious.

"I thought you guys were supposed to be completely irresistible to women," Solain said sarcastically, eyeing Pithius.

"That particular charm is lacking in a select few," Merihem stated blandly as he got to his feet and went into the kitchen to retrieve plates.

"Are you making fun of me?" Pithius asked, staring

at the vampire and his brother questioningly, a second piece of pizza halfway to his mouth.

"No, of course not. We're just trying to determine what makes you so stunningly charming." Merihem commented, snagging a box of pizza and putting it, a stack of plates and napkins as well as a varying smattering of drinks on the coffee table in front of the nymphs. "Here you are, ladies. If you need anything more, please don't hesitate to ask."

Pithius smirked. "It's just in my blood!"

"Oh?" Solain perked, turning to take Pithius's measure. "Is that so? I could always use a bit more charm." He stepped toward the rambunctious Incubus and bared his lengthened fangs. "Mind if I have a bite?"

"Sweet baby Jesus!" Pithius scooted back in his chair so fast he almost tipped it over. "Stay the hell away from me you fang banger!"

Iain snorted. "Fang bangers are the lassies who consort with vampires, no' the vampires themselves. Get it right Incubus."

Solain snickered, fangs fading to their normal, slightly pronounced length. "Not that I don't love to bang myself."

"Now, ye could call him a leech, bloodsucker, sun sadist, humanitarian and my personal favourite," Iain suggested, grinning impishly. "Sparkles."

CHAPTER 18

When five o'clock finally arrived Cass had to resist cheering in glee. She packed up her things, grabbed her coat and threw a parting wave at Miriam on her way to the elevator. She pushed the up button and waited impatiently, mind churning.

After their interlude among the stacks, she hadn't been able to get Verrin out of her mind. The feel of his hands on her body and his mouth claiming hers had haunted her all afternoon. She was still worked up hours later and couldn't wait to get home with the gorgeously seductive Incubus.

She had spent the afternoon daydreaming about continuing their little tryst. Part of her was still hesitant to get involved with him, the risk of getting hurt was serious, but her inner-Savvy demanded she let go and take a chance. With her courage and libido equally worked up, she was determined to see where this was going to go.

An abrupt shiver rode down her spine and she glanced over her shoulder, startled to see Verrin's darkly handsome countenance looming behind her. A hand rising unconsciously to her chest as if to keep the suddenly pounding organ suitably housed, she breathed out in relief. "You scared me." Flashing him a beatific smile she teased. "I guess you found the stairs."

Verrin gave a slight nod and gestured to the front door a couple of paces away. "Let's go home."

Abandoning the elevator, they exited the building into the cold evening air and walked the Christmas-lit streets to the parkade in silence. At first, Cass thought it was companionable silence, figuring Verrin may just be lost in thought, but as he held doors for her and got her safely into her car it stretched into awkwardness.

The drive home was nothing but silently stewing tension. She wanted to ask him what was wrong, if maybe he was mad at her for testing the bond earlier, but every time she glanced at his stark features her nerve died on her tongue. As they pulled into the driveway she grabbed her purse and popped out before Verrin had a chance to make it around the car to open her door. Unsure what to do about her plans and frustrated with his prickly silence, she stormed to the front door, jammed the key in the lock and blew into the house.

At least if she was going to be a disgruntled mess she was doing it at home.

Dropping her purse on the little hall table, she pulled her phone from it and laid it on the tabletop, quickly checking for missed messages. Nothing important. Cass shrugged her coat off intending to hang it up when Verrin caught her eye.

Her Incubus house guest had his back pressed against the large oak door, head down so his eyes were shadowed and body was almost vibrating with leashed tension. As she watched, one of his strong hands rose and flicked the deadbolt into place.

The snap of that little metal latch sliding into place made her pulse spike uncomfortably.

"V-Verrin?" Cass asked hesitantly, cringing inwardly as her voice came out shaky and unsure.

Verrin's dark head slowly rose, his blue eyes luminous and bright enough to cast shadows in the darkened entryway. That glow was something she had come to associate with him being seriously turned on and the sight of it made her stomach clench in an irrational surge of lust. Taking a step toward him, she reached out hoping to easy him. "Verr-"

"Run."

Cass froze, startled by the rough timbre of his voice. "What?"

"Run, Cassidy." Verrin's blazing blue eyes flicked over her body from head to toe before returning to meet hers. "Run now."

Confused, she stepped forward and gasped when he growled at her.

"I promised myself I would treat you right, take you in a bed like a proper gentleman, but if you don't get to your room right now, I'm going to fuck you right here on the floor."

Cass's mouth fell open in shock. His voice, although warning, hit her like a physical jolt, kick-starting every female hormone in her body. She was torn, wanting to feel his hands on her and yet wanting to follow his wishes. She took a step back, toward the foot of the stairs and his demonic eyes watched her as if she were prey.

My god, she was done for.

She made it up three steps when she glanced over her shoulder. As she watched, Verrin let go of the door frame he'd clenched in a death grip and took one determined step forward.

"I'm coming, Cass." He warned her darkly, eyes locked on her retreating form.

She ran.

Cass tore headlong up the stairs, feet flying and hands gripping the banister to propel her flight faster. She was just swinging around the railing to lunge for her open bedroom door when the raucous thud of Verrin's footsteps pounded up the stairs.

Her heart raced, reminded of the last time they had done this. How fitting was it that instead of running from her bedroom, this time she was running toward it with her gorgeous demon lover at her heels.

Cass tore into her room, slapping the light switch out of habit, just as his thundering tread reached the landing. In the next heartbeat, she could feel his heat behind her, his big body looming over hers.

She froze. It was ludicrous, but to be within the sights of such a predator made every thought flee her mind. Cass now knew what a rabbit caught in the headlights felt like. Her heart pounded a staccato rhythm as it tried to escape her chest and her breaths were ragged pants for oxygen that seemed in rather short supply. The skin at her back tingled in hyper-awareness of him and her core ached in need.

"Verrin..." Her words were a mere breath, small and quiet in the stillness of the moment.

His arms snaked around her from behind, one

183

curving over her shoulder and between her breasts while the other curled around her midsection. His big body engulfed hers, drawing it in until everything was warm and smelled of sensual male spice. "You're mine now Cass." He informed her harshly from where he nuzzled his nose into her hair. A fine tremor ran through his body at the announcement. "I let you get away earlier because it was your workplace, but I'm not letting you go here. There's no escape tonight."

Cass couldn't help it. A whimper escaped her. It was full of need and desire and begged wordlessly for more of him, all of him.

His fingers caught her chin, turning her face up and to the side so he could kiss her without turning her around. His lips tempted and tamed hers, kissing her until she swayed in his arms. With a purring growl, he hefted her up, turning her in his arms until her length was pressed flushed to his from chest to thigh. Those glowing azure eyes gleaming in triumph as he looked down at her in his arms. "It's time I get to enjoy my prize."

With three long strides, they were at the side of the bed and he dropped her with a bounce that broke a giggle from her. Cass tried to sit up, but the infuriating man pushed her back with a gentle shove to the breastbone. "Verrin, let me up." She demanded, smiling up at him from her sprawl on the comforter.

"No." Verrin grinned as he reached down and pulled his T-shirt over his head. His jacket was already gone, lost somewhere in his headlong race after her no doubt, and as she watched he started working on the fly of his jeans. "You're going to stay right where I've put you until I've had my fill. There are only eight words I want to hear from you."

"Eight words?" She breathed, confused.

He shoved his jeans down his thighs, revealing that intriguing tattoo and the straining erection he was sporting as he shucked them off. "God. Yes. Please. Verrin. More. Harder. Faster. Coming."

Cass tried to pay attention. Really she did. But the minute those tight jeans of his had dropped to his knees and his cock had sprung out to point directly at her like she was its next target, her mind had gone blank. Thankfully her libido took over the free airtime with relish.

Fingers twitching to get her hands on him, she jerked to a sitting position and reached out, just needing to feel his hard steely length for herself.

"Tsk, tsk, little one. That's not where I put you." Verrin chided, catching her wrist with a wicked smile. "Do you know what happens to bad girls who don't listen?"

She slammed her thighs together and wiggled her hips as an incessant ache took root inside her. She wanted to know. God almighty, Cass would kill to know! Whatever this big man with his hard body and wicked mind had planned, she certainly wouldn't have any objections.

Verrin bent and hooked an arm behind her knees, knocking her back and dragging her closer until her hips were at the edge of the bed. With one hand he started to undo the button fly on her work jeans and tugging them down.

Cass pushed at his hands with her free one, getting a sinking feeling what he wanted to do. "Verrin, wait. I can't _"

Verrin looked up at her and his face was serious. "Is

185

there a reason you're using more than the eight words I gave you?"

Heat flooding her cheeks, Cass ended up in a small tug of war with Verrin's unmovable hold on her jeans. "I – I'm not comfortable...with that."

Verrin cocked one dark brow at her and smirked. "With what, little one?"

Giving up on her jeans, she fluttered her hand between them to encompass their position. "You know. This."

He leaned in until she was forced back on her elbows, his smile broad. "Are you embarrassed?" At her nod, his smile took on an indulgent look. "Okay, I understand." He leaned down and kissed her belly, giving it a nuzzle with his nose.

Cass was so sure she had deterred him when all of a sudden her vision was blinded by fuzzy wool. The sneaky bastard had flipped her shirt over her head! She pulled it back down only to have one of her pillows plopped onto her face. "What are you doing?"

Her free hand came up to pull it away but Verrin tipped the pillow back so he could meet her eyes and grinned. "I get it. You're shy. So use the pillow."

"That's ridiculous. We just won't - " She hated to admit it, but she'd had a stab of anxious terror that he might see her naked in all her less than perfect glory and decide he could do better. She wasn't fooling herself, she knew she had some extra weight on her petite frame, added to the fact that her few lovers had never been eager participants in the oral Olympics, and she was fraught with worry that he'd find her lacking.

Obviously, Verrin intended to lick that fear for her.

"Oh yes, we will!" He flipped pillow back down and positioned it so it didn't cover more than her eyes. When her hands fought to move it he encircled her wrists in one of his big hands and pressed them into her stomach slightly to keep her still. He fidgeted until she realized he was finishing tugging off her jeans and panties and she squeaked when she felt him press a kiss to her now bare mound.

"Verrin! What the hell!" She squealed as she felt him wedge his big body between her thighs.

"I understand you being shy, Cass, and I'm okay with that. Think of it like a blindfold. This way you can be as shy as you want hiding under there, while I devour this perfectly delectable little pussy over here. Everyone wins!" With that logic, the wicked man licked directly up the center of her slit and her hips jerked off the bed in surprised delight.

"Oh god!" Cass moaned as he settled in to lap and suckle at her tender flesh. Thought blanked from her mind. She groaned and wished he'd free her hands so she could sink them into his hair. His amazing tongue darted into her entrance before rising to circle her clit. When his lips circled the bud and sucked, she writhed against his face and moaned. The intrusion of a thick finger made her keen as he worked her well, finding a spot inside her that made her hips buck.

"More! Please!" She pleaded breathlessly, body shaking as she endured his oral assault. Her whimpering pants heated the air and she tossed her head. Suddenly her hands were free as his own circled her thighs and hiked her up until her legs rested over his shoulders, pussy sealed to his face.

The pleasure that had been building skyrocketed as he thrust a second finger into her tight core and rubbed that magical spot that made her see stars. Stomach clenching and body strung tight, she tunneled her fingers through his hair, terrified he'd pull away from her when she was so damn close to coming.

He groaned into her wet flesh and she could hear the slick slide of his fingers. With a final deep thrust of his fingers and a brutal suckling of her overly sensitized clit, she cried out, shuddering as she came. The wicked beast at her core devoured her just as he had threatened, ringing every keening cry and shaking breath from her body until she lay limp and exhausted, legs splayed wantonly in front of him.

The pillow moved and she blinked open bleary eyes, trying to focus through the waning haze of pleasure. Verrin leaned over her, his smile huge, lips swollen red and gleaming with her wetness. "You okay?"

Cass groaned and nodded. Her body felt like it was both electrified and floating. Everything seemed more intense and at the same point she couldn't muster up the energy to care. Somewhere deep in her chest a tightness she hadn't realized she was carrying loosened like a knot being untied.

Verrin grinned, blue eyes twinkling in mirth instead of glowing, and bent to kiss her. His taste combined with the flavour of her orgasm on his lips made her moan and kiss him harder, arms circling his neck.

Breath returned, she broke from the kiss. "That was..."

"Tasty?" Verrin supplied with a wink.

Cass gave him a mock stern look and a swat to his

big buff shoulder that turned into a giggle and her feeling up his broad pecs. "I was thinking more along the lines of amazing."

Verrin shrugged nonchalantly. "I'll take what I can get, I guess." He patted her thigh as he sat back on his heels. "Sit up, little one. I want you naked for this next part."

Cass's eyes widened as she struggled to sit, her muscles lazy after their orgasmic workout. Catching the hand Verrin provided, she managed to sit straight and lift her arms so he could tug her sweater off. Her head dropped forward onto his shoulder limply, making him chuckle, as he took care of the back clasp on her bra and eased it down her arms.

"I'm not sure I'm up to a next part. That last part was pretty intense." She murmured, only half joking. Her inner muscles were still twitching.

"Oh, you'll be okay for it. Really all I need you to do is lay there and moan." Verrin told her with a saucy wink.

She laughed and wrapped her arms around him, drawing him into a nude hug. "What about those eight little words?" she whispered against his ear.

He chuckled. "Those wouldn't hurt either."

CHAPTER 19

Empusa straightened the golden bracer on her forearm as she examined herself in the full-length cheval mirror she'd found in the former chief's rooms. The Amazonian fortress had once been an ancient temple by Lamia's best guess but had been inhabited by a tribe of snake shifters when they'd come across it. It hadn't taken much work to overpower the slithery miscreants and take it for themselves. She had to admit it was a vast improvement over their previous domicile.

And lucky them, the former tenants had brought some improvements to the ancient building.

She turned to the side to make sure the tight black leather pants she wore perfectly accented her amazing backside and then strapped a holster to her right thigh before sliding a knife in. With a black tank under a battle hardened leather corset and golden breastplate and combat boots that tied just below her knee, she looked like a LARPer's wet dream. The outfit was affectionately termed 'Emmy's Xena cosplay' by her friends, but she knew she looked good. With her red hair pulled into a thick braid and bristling with weapons, Empusa felt every inch the mercenary demigoddess she was.

With a last approving smile at her reflection, she turned and left the room she'd appropriated, heading for the central hall of the fortress. Her client would be arriving shortly and she wanted to make sure she made a good impression. There weren't many immortal mercenaries in their world and once you were on top of that small brutal pile you needed to stay there. Sometimes good looks and a hefty dose of professionalism were the only things standing between you and a bad customer review.

She was a few turns away from the main chamber they were planning to entertain their client in when the satellite phone clipped to her belt chirped out a tinny version of Nicki Minaj's Anaconda. She silenced it before it could get stuck in her head and didn't bother with a greeting. "Remind me to kill Mormo. She changed my ringtones around again. That girl as a twisted sense of humor."

Lamia ignored her entirely, instead trampling her words with an almost excited tone. "The client is here!"

"Already?" She panicked, starting down the corridor again at a faster pace. Her black boots thumped with every hurried step.

Lamia's normally clear tone seemed almost conspiratorial when it came across the line. Emmy could just picture the normally businesslike former queen hunched over her phone in a corner somewhere. "Yes, and you are not going to believe who it is. Are you almost here?"

"Yeah, I'm just about there."

"Good. I need you here before Mormo does something stupid. The little leech is literally quaking with the desire to offer herself to him." Lamia warned softly.

"Okay. Give me a sec." Hanging up, Empusa clipped the phone back on her belt and broke into a run. She skidded to a stop at the side door to the main room that led directly onto the dais and took a deep breath to gather herself. Whatever awaited her inside had her girls all up in a frenzy. Knowing those two it could be anything from a really hot guy to a phlebotomist with a martini bar full of blood samples.

They had spent yesterday having the thralls clear out this main room, moving the St. Andrews cross she'd had Seir on and the workstation Lamia had set up elsewhere. They had needed an audience chamber and with the benches and tables cleared out, this hall was perfect. They had sat three ornately carved chairs on the dais, one for each of them and directed the thralls to have the room cleaned thoroughly by morning.

Thankfully it looked like their word had been followed to the letter when Empusa strode in. Gray stone floors were swept free of debris and the only places to sit were the three chairs on the dais. The room was open to a bright sunset, beams cutting through the jungle's green to fill the room with light.

Lamia and Mormo stood beside a towering blond man, chatting amicably. With his back to the dais, all Emmy could see was his finely tailored black suit stretched over a broad shouldered, lean hipped body. He chuckled at something Mormo said and a shiver clenched Emmy's insides. Good lord, the male was crack to female hormones. Maybe she should sit down for this meeting.

Sauntering over to the middle seat, she crossed her legs at the knee, took an appraising glance at herself and then gave a delicate cough to garner their guest's attention.

Amethyst. Bright amethyst eyes cut to her and she was very glad she was sitting all of a sudden. Emmy wasn't sure how the other women had managed to talk to such an enchanting male specimen without aid. A glance over revealed Lamia had leaned against a stone pillar carved with some ancient fanged beastie and Mormo had braced her feet apart, her hands on her hips fisted with white knuckled appreciation. No doubt she was trying to keep herself from grabbing at the man.

"Hello, Empusa. Nice little operation you have going here." The client said, his voice a curl of smooth chocolate over her senses as he gestured around the audience room. "You three are doing quite well for yourselves."

Gathering her wits, Empusa pasted on a pleased smile. "Why thank you, Murmur, how nice of you to notice. It's been quite some time since we've made acquaintance with an angel of your status."

"Not much of an angel anymore I'm afraid." The blond man smiled wryly and gave her a wink that nearly set her panties ablaze. "It turns out I've gone to the dark side."

Behind him a scuffle broke out as Mormo opened her mouth to no doubt say something lewd and inviting and Lamia tried to slap a hand over her companion's big mouth. It quickly devolved into hissing and the snapping of fanged teeth at one another.

Murmur paid them no mind, his focus now solely on Empusa. "I was informed by my client that you had the three items that were requested ready for pick up. May I see them?"

"Your client?" Empusa's brows drew down as she sat forward, pinning the beautiful man with a hard stare. "I was led to believe the client would be picking them up herself."

Murmur chuckled, his tone turning patronizing. "No, my client prefers to have no dealings with the lower forms of immortals. She sent me out to collect the items she requires and deal with the - and I quote - 'riff raff'."

Emmy ground her molars at the insult. Behind him, both Lamia and Mormo looked like they wanted to hand Murmur his angel ass on a silver platter. And not in a sexy way.

Murmur sighed dramatically and checked the gold watch on his left wrist. "Look, ladies, I hate to rush things along, but my client is a nasty cow who dislikes when I delay getting her what she wants. If it wouldn't be too much trouble, could I have the items you've been contracted to obtain? Then I can transfer the funds and we can all get the heifer off our backs."

Somewhat mollified at Murmur's mutual dislike of their client she gestured at Lamia. "Show him the goods."

Mormo snickered, her sick mind turning that into an innuendo no doubt, as Lamia stepped aside to roll a draped silver cart that would usually hold a tea service closer. When it was between Emmy and Murmur she withdrew the black cloth covering it and revealed the items beneath.

An ancient looking golden skeleton key carved with symbols, a black-bladed, jewel encrusted dagger with a crimson handle and a vial of red Incubus blood.

Murmur raised a golden brow. "Is that all the blood you have?" His voice was chilly, a clear sign that the former angel was not impressed.

Empusa bristled, but Lamia spoke up first. "We were not given a quantifier. However, we did keep the being who gave us that sample. We can always obtain more."

Murmur's model worthy features returned to their normal state of cool detachment. "You have an angel's child here? Is it full grown? Most of its blood will be required for the ritual."

"You intend to kill him?" Mormo asked, coming to stand beside Lamia.

Murmur gave a careless shrug. "Not I. That will be left to the client. I prefer to keep my hands unsullied."

Lamia let out a barely covered scoff that sounded a lot like 'angels' and Mormo shot a glare over her shoulder at Emmy, mouthing words that looked suspiciously like 'Should've fucked him when we had the chance'.

"I'd like to see the angel child. Without proof that you have a viable source for the blood, the deal is incomplete." Murmur declared, checking his watch again.

Empusa sat forward in her chair, eyes darkened with malice. "You know, I've decided I don't like your attitude. You can see the Incubus when we get what we're owed. Not a second before."

Murmur's amethyst eyes flashed dangerously and a pair of huge silver wings flared into existence behind him. The lustrous platinum feathers shimmered in the light, darkening until the very tips of his wings looked like they'd been dipped in black ink. "You will show me to him now or I shall find him myself!" He commanded, voice booming in the large room.

The three women, powerful beings in their own rights, cringed at the power inherent in the male. Former angel or not, he didn't appear to have maintained their good demeanor or godly patience.

"Very well." Lamia piped up, recovering first. "This way." She gestured to an archway that led into another hallway and Murmur gave the others a curt nod before following her out.

The troupe of them stalked down the hallways until the air cooled and the stone walls barred the last vestiges of sunlight from getting in. Flickering torches set in brackets along the walls lit their way as they took another passage, going deeper into the structure. When a large wooden door appeared along the wall, Lamia produced a key and let them in. A set of stairs descended into the dungeons and a small hall led them to the line of barred cells. There in the very first cell, unconscious with large manacles clamped around his wrists and ankles, lay Seir, the fifth son of the angelic Watcher Sariel.

"You've damaged him." Murmur pointed out, eyeing the mass of deep gashes, dark bruises and bloody rivulets making up the Incubus's skin. "The blood needed to be freely given, not beaten out of him."

Mormo growled at him as Empusa stepped forward, taking control. "It was freely given. He just took a while to break."

"I can see that." Murmur sighed with distaste. Turning his back on the cage, he pinned Empusa with a determined stare. "It matters not. He will not last long. I'll need another."

"Another?" Emmy gawked, horrified. "Do you

realize what a pain in the ass it is to find one of these guys? The whole species is rare because the angelic host tried to wipe them out and now you want me to hunt down another one and break him to give you more blood? You're nuts!"

Murmur looked bored, giving her a flippant hand gesture as if brushing off her worries. "Believe me, I know full well how rare they are. I'm an Angel, remember?" His amethyst eyes went hard as he continued. "Regardless, this one won't last long enough. I'll need another to make my client happy. You get me that and you get your payment."

"And how are we supposed to find another one?" Mormo bit out, fangs bared as she spoke.

"It just so happens I've heard one of this one's brothers is shacking up with a human woman. Get her and he'll come to you." Murmur pulled a smartphone from the inside pocket of his suit and tapped away at it for a moment before putting it away. "There, I sent you the information. Good luck with the retrieval. I'll stay here until the job is completed successfully."

With that Murmur turned on his heel and headed back up the stairs, leaving Mormo and Lamia cursing behind him as Empusa looked at her phone and glared at the picture of the human female that had popped up on her phone screen.

Cassidy O'Neill, age 27, was the latest play toy of Verrin, third son of Sariel, and the newest pawn in her game.

***

Cassidy sighed as she watched Verrin walk across

197

her room to the light switch. He had lifted her up the bed once she'd calmed slightly and placed her so she could lounge against the pillows. The position gave her the perfect view of his smooth gait and the slide of firm muscles under bronzed skin as he flicked off the overhead light, leaving the bedside lamp to cast a golden glow over the bedroom.

The return trip was just as sweet.

His long legs stretched to thick thighs, the left one bearing that intriguing black and red circular tattoo. She really had to ask him about that sometime. Any current questions she may have had faded before the sight of his impressive cock. It strained toward her as he came closer, the head reddened in its eagerness. Cass licked her lips as her mouth watered to taste him. It was difficult but she managed to drag her eyes up to his ridged abs and the solid slabs of his pectorals. Broad shoulders and muscled arms topped off the man's prime physique.

"Like what you see?" Verrin asked, stopping in front of her and gesturing at his body. His smile was radiant as he looked down at her from his nearly seven-foot height.

"Uh-huh." She nodded, sure a silly little grin was spreading across her lips

Laughing, Verrin gave her a slow spin before facing her again and striking an Adonis pose, flexing those awesome muscles of his.

"You know, if you ever get tired of being an immortal Incubus, you could make a killing as a stripper." With a grin, she opened her arms to welcome him to her.

"Sadly I have no real desire to fish twenties out of my underwear." He laughed, putting a knee on the foot of the bed and slowly, predatorily, crawling up the length of the bed to hover over her. He leaned down and dragged his lightly stubbled cheek against hers like a cat marking their scent. "Currently the only thing I want to do is you."

"Well then," Cass laughed, throwing her arms wide to make a proper sacrifice of herself. "Do with me as you will, foul demon beast!"

Verrin snorted out a laugh and dropped his head between her breasts, shaking it between them until she giggled. Catching one of her nipples between his teeth, he gave it a little nip in punishment. The moan this elicited was the sound of their love play switching from carefree and humorous to passionate and hungry.

"Mmm... Do that again." Cass moaned, tunneling her hands through his thick dark hair and pulling him in tighter.

Rising up on his elbows, Verrin used one hand to toy with the nipple he'd just nipped, rolling and pinching it gently between his finger and thumb, while laving the other with his tongue. Another quick nip broke a moan from her and her hips rubbed temptingly against his.

"Gods, Cass, you almost killed me this afternoon." Warm lips trailed up her chest to her neck, leaving a path of kisses and nips. His hand stroked her trembling belly, slipping down to cup her mound and slide a finger slowly through her wet slit. "I spent every moment in that little cubicle imagining taking you in every possible way. In my mind I had you bent over that desk, taking me deep inside you. Straddling my lap while you bounced and I stroked this little gem." He circled her clit with a fingertip before rubbing over it. His lips curled up into a smile against her own as she moaned into their kiss.

"Oh! Verrin..." His name came out as a breathy plea.

His wicked chuckle tantalized her nerves and he kissed down her jaw to her ear, whispering hotly against it. "Can I have you, Cassidy?"

She shivered and nodded, mind going back to the translation of his summons he'd told her days ago. She rubbed her cheek against his lightly roughened one. "Verrin, I seek the pleasure of your touch."

He pulled back, blue eyes catching hers, and she got to watch as those amazing irises lit from within and a broad smile broke across his face. Verrin's words were a sensual purr as he responded with the ritual words. "I offer my body for the use of your pleasure, my Lady."

One of his hands grasped her thigh and pulled it up, hooking it over his forearm as he leaned in, dragging the head of his shaft through her wetness. Verrin gave a few short thrusts, rubbing himself tantalizingly along her slit.

Cass bit her bottom lip and rocked her hips, trying to catch his shaft. "Stop teasing." She complained only to gasp as he slipped the crown inside her. "Oh, yes..."

"Fuck, you're tight." Verrin let go of her thigh, letting her wrap her legs around his hips and caught her wrists, pulling them above her head and holding them with one hand as he plunged deeper inside inch by inch. He glanced down and groaned, obviously loving the sight of his length sinking into her.

Cass whimpered and squirmed on his impaling shaft. He was thick and hot inside her, a branding she wasn't sure another man could ever surpass, and she wanted more of him desperately. Thankful she was so very wet, she bit her lip again and moaned as he bottomed out inside her, his pelvis grinding into her clit. She trembled with anticipation beneath him as he looked her over.

"You okay?" His words were a growl, giving away the strength he used to hold back this moment to check on her.

She nodded frantically, not trusting her voice, even as she met the eyes of the Incubus hovering over her.

His fingers moved up, lacing with hers to hold her hands, as he withdrew until he was almost entirely out before plunging back in.

Oh god. Somehow she'd found heaven in the arms of a demon.

He pumped into her and she writhed beneath him, crying out. His hands held her even though she was sure she had dug her nails into his skin and his lips found hers, twining their tongues until their movements became too frantic to keep up.

Cass could feel her muscles tightening, straining for the release that was just out of reach. Verrin freed her hands and she immediately dragged them across his back, kneading the shifting muscle beneath. He braced one arm above her head and the other pressed a large palm against her lower belly, pushing slightly as his fingers played her clit with experience.

All of a sudden his cock seemed to grow inside her as if his hardened rod touched every possible millimetre of flesh within. The pressure and fullness were a delicious sort of strain. His fingers plucked and twisted her slick little bud, sending zings of sensation racing through her.

It was all too much.

With a cry, Cass's body clenched around him, hands gripping his back as she came. Her mind flew, all thoughts zeroing in on the pleasure, as she felt Verrin hunker down over her body, his hips bucking wildly as he groaned into her hair. His body tightened with impending release and he growled, his seed spilling like warm honey inside her.

Her shaking limbs held on, almost afraid this amazingly sweet, lust inducing, gorgeous man would disappear from her life if she dared let him go.

CHAPTER 20

Verrin roused slowly to wakefulness, not wishing to move from his warm position in Cass's bed. He glanced down and saw Cass's chestnut hair spilled across his chest, her head pillowed on his pec and his arm around her shoulders. He wasn't usually one to sleep through the night with a woman, preferring not to confuse his summoners that their connection might be lasting, but Cass felt right snuggled into his side. She just fit.

Last night, after they had made love for the third time, Verrin had reigned in his lust and dragged his petite bed partner down to rest. For her part, Cass had collapsed into him, letting him sort out the blankets and draw them up to cover their bodies.

When she slowly started tracing the lines of the seal on his left thigh he twitched. Her small fingers were torturous as they followed the inner and outer circles as far as she could reach.

When she spoke it was in a voice tinged with sleepy curiosity. "What does your tattoo mean?"

Verrin smiled into the dimly lit room and stroked a hand down her tousled hair, petting her. "It's a seal my parents gave me. Each of my brothers has one too. They created it to try to help us deal with the conditions our birthright created in us."

"What kind of conditions?" Cass asked, not moving her head away from his attentive hand even though her voice came across more interested than before.

"Well, you see the text between the two rings?" Verrin asked, twitching the sheet that covered him out of the way of her view.

"Um, yeah. The ones with the words between them. What language is that? I can't read it." She murmured, stroking her fingers along the outer ring.

"It's an Angelic script. Those words are my summoning spell and the ritual answer to it. You've actually already read half of it." He chuckled warmly, remembering her earlier repetition of them. "My parents gave me the summoning spell and the seal so no one else could try to bind my soul."

"Bind your soul?" Cass repeated, tilting her head up to meet his eyes.

Verrin nodded. "Djinn can be forced to follow the will of another if their true name is bound using a spell. My parents never considered that their children could be bound so they never worried about hiding our true names." He gave a slight shrug. "When they realized it was possible, they sealed us themselves, binding our names so no one else could."

"So your name is in here somewhere?" Cass inquired, gesturing at the tattoo.

"Yeah, you see the big black line symbol in the

middle?" He told her, staring at the strands of her hair as he sifted it through his fingers.

"The one that looks like a double-crossed T in a V?" She mumbled, shifting her fingers to trace it.

Verrin made a little noise of affirmation as he twirled a lock of her hair around his index finger and let it spring off only to begin coiling it again.

"What about the two little symbols on either side of your name?" She poked her finger at the one she could reach, two interlocking figure eights crossed at the center to form a flower-like shape. "Like this one."

Verrin chuckled. His girl was an inquisitive little thing. Indulging her, he explained. "The other one is actually magical birth control, so I won't leave a string of halfing children through the ages, and that one is my out clause."

"Out clause?" She repeated in query.

"Apparently, our parents put a sort of release into our seal. If one of us meets our perfect mate, we can activate it and stop ourselves from being summoned in the future."

She lifted her head, finally inspired to move it seemed, and rested her chin on the back of her hand on his chest. "So essentially you can stay with one woman? No more appearing in the beds of different women."

"Yep." He confirmed, tracing her jawline with a fingertip.

"Why not trigger your out clause now? Then you wouldn't have to be summoned anymore." She inquired, brown eyes intent.

His mouth thinned to a sad line. "I can't yet. I need to meet certain... criteria first."

"Oh. That sucks." She looked suddenly downcast, burying her head back into his chest until he couldn't see her face. With a yawn that had seemed forced, she asked. "Will you turn out the light?"

He did as she'd asked and they'd curled together in the darkness, sleeping away the rest of the night.

Glancing over at the clock Cass had on her bedside table, he realized he'd woken up before her alarm. He had about an hour before she'd need to be up for work. Detaching himself carefully, he made sure Cass was settled and covered to her ears with the thick comforter before grabbing his clothes and heading out the door.

Quietly letting himself out into the hallway, he slipped his jeans on before padding barefoot down the stairs. He went into the living room where he'd left the bag of clothes they'd bought and switched yesterday's shirt for a clean one.

Wandering into the kitchen, he poked through the fridge and tried to figure out what to make Cass for breakfast. If he played his cards right, he could feed her and have a quickie before she had to get ready for her day.

Verrin had his nose buried in the pantry when the doorbell rang. Frowning, he strode toward the front door, hoping to catch it before the noise woke Cass. Flipping the dead bolt and turning the knob, he got ready to enjoy the company of Cass's best friend Savannah once again.

Hopefully this time with a few less threats to his manhood.

"Hey Savvy, I was just about to make - " Verrin's voice died as he saw the men darkening Cassidy's doorstep.

His brothers, with the exception of his youngest

sibling, stood with varying degrees of pained looks on their faces.

"Come on, man! Let us in! It's freezing out here!" Pithius whined, rubbing the bare skin the arms of his blue T-shirt didn't cover. "You should have told us this chick lived in the freaking arctic! I would have dressed warmer!"

Ever polite, Merihem elbowed Pithius aside so he could step forward. "Might we come in, brother. We have much to tell you and little time to do it in."

Verrin nodded, stepping aside and opening the door wide so they could file in.

Deep inside a little part of him growled at letting not just other males, but other Incubi, close to his woman. That little territorial beast was torn between parading his beautiful Cass out for every male to see the wonderful woman that he'd claimed or hiding her away as if she was the most prized possession in a dragon's hoard.

It was a startling dichotomy to have and one he'd never fathomed before. He found he kind of liked it.

Well, so long as Cass didn't come down those stairs behind him looking adorably rumpled in her pajamas and his brothers didn't eye fuck her when they saw her. Then he might be tempted to toy with his homicidal tendencies.

***

Cass rolled over in bed and reached out, stroking a hand across the indent Verrin had left in her bed. His side still had the faintest traces of warmth and she snagged the pillow he'd used last night, bringing it to her chest to hug. Mmm... it smelled of spice and man, Verrin to a tee.

Nuzzling her nose into the purple pillow case, she

marveled at how easy it was to be with him. The simple act of sleeping with him, for actual sleeping purposes, had been a snap. Like two people who'd been doing it for years, she'd snuggled into his chest and he'd wrapped her in his arms and they'd cuddled. There had been no sorting out who got what side or arguments over snuggling.

Then again, the sleeping with him for non-sleeping purposes had been pretty easy too once she'd let him past her barriers.

Verrin had been an intense lover. He'd overwhelmed her senses and just when she thought it would be too much he pushed her over the edge and she loved it. He could be sweet or rough depending on his mood at the time and his kisses had a sneaky way of derailing her thoughts.

She supposed their bond was over now with him having completed what he'd been summoned for, but he hadn't said anything about it. It certainly hadn't stopped him from going for another two rounds. She absolutely wasn't done with him.

Flipping to her back, Cass stared at the ceiling and listened for Verrin downstairs. He was probably down there making breakfast as he usually did. The man might be an immortal sex god, but he loved to slave away in the kitchen. She hated to admit it, but she rather liked catching him in the kitchen, cartoons on the TV in the background while he cooked.

The rumble of Verrin's voice and the shutting of the front door caught her attention and Cass froze in bed, breath halting while her ears strained to listen.

Other male voices replied to Verrin's, one cajoling and the other seemingly more serious. They volleyed back and forth with a fourth, deeper voice breaking in a few times to give short answers. Unfortunately, no matter how hard she listened she could make out what they said.

Curious, Cass got up and threw on a loose black T-shirt and her purple flannel pajama bottoms before easing over to the door and opening it a crack, listening intently to Verrin and their unexpected guests.

"Have you had any luck finding Seir?" She recognized Verrin's voice as he asked the others.

"Thankfully, yes. They have him locked away in a fortress in South America." This male voice was cultured and smooth, a slight European accent tingeing his words.

"When are you getting him back?" Verrin inquired.

"We're going to get him back tonight. That's why we're here." This one's voice was brisk and commanding.

"Have you banged the chick already? Cause we'd like to get this show on the road." This one ended in a crass chuckle.

Cassidy's blood chilled, her heart seemingly stilling in her chest. She waited, opening the door wide as she stood there, straining to hear what Verrin would say next.

"Shut up, Thius," Verrin growled.

"So you haven't broken the bond yet?" Thius bit back. "What's taking you so long? You've been here almost a week! It's never taken you that long to get your dick wet before."

"Gods, Thius! Be quiet!" The cultured one hissed, sounding frustrated.

"Well, if Verrin doesn't want her, can I have her for a round? I haven't had my fill yet today. I'll be quick about it." Thius asked in a playful tone.

"Leave her out of this," Verrin demanded. "The

209

bond is broken. That's all you need to know."

Cass brought a hand to her mouth, covering it so she didn't make a sound. Verrin's brisk reply cut through her and she sank down onto the top step as her knees went weak. Was that what last night had been about? Him needing to break their bond so he could leave? The idea he might have used her made her chest ache.

"Oh, come on, V. Tell us! All you had to do was make her cum. Did she scream like a good girl when you put it in? Or did she cream on your fingers before you even got that far?" Thius inquired in lascivious delight.

"Fuck off." Verrin bit out harshly causing the rude one to burst into laughter. "I'm free to leave whenever. Let's just go and get Seir. I want this whole thing over with."

"Do you want to speak to your Lady before we go?" The cultured one asked.

Thius barked out a derisive laugh, "Seriously? I thought the terms of the summons were completed. Oh wait, did you have to love talk your way into her bed? Is that what took you so long? Did you have to convince her you were head over heels before she'd let you get some?"

"I swear to God, Pithius. Shut the fuck up!" Verrin hissed. "It's over. The summons is complete and I'm free. That's all you need to know."

"Ooh touchy, touchy." Thius taunted and the sound was followed by that of scuffling and flesh hitting flesh.

"Stop it you two!" The commanding one ordered, voice booming. "Pithius, shut up and step outside. Stop instigating trouble. Verrin, go thank your hostess and we'll leave."

Cass jolted when she realized Verrin would be

coming up to find her. She dashed a hand across her suddenly damp cheeks, refusing to acknowledge why they were wet in the first place. She shot to her feet and took a deep breath before starting down the stairs. *Okay. I can do this.* She had made it three-quarters of the way down when Verrin and the other men came into view.

The four men all turned to stare up at her and her breath caught. They were the most beautiful men she had ever seen in real life. They were all tall and muscular, perfect specimens of masculinity, but they were all unique.

The one who was being pushed out the open door had dark blond hair, standing up in spikes in all directions, a sardonic smirk on his face and a wicked glint in his green eyes. The one pushing him had longer straight mahogany hair, pulled back in a cue. His black slacks, white button down and long black peacoat gave him an air of sophistication the others lacked.

She paled in comparison.

Verrin stood beside a man even taller than he was, whose hair and eyes could give the darkest night sky a colour match. His face was stoic and his manner that of someone used to being obeyed.

Verrin stepped toward her, mouth opening to say something, when she held up a hand for his silence. "It's fine. Don't worry about it. Just go."

Verrin's brows drew down in a frown and he stepped closer, coming to the base of the stairs. "Cass, please, can we talk for a minute? I just - "

"No." She shook her head, knowing the other men were watching their exchange. "I think I've heard enough. Just go."

"Cass..." Verrin's voice took on a pleading tone as

he reached toward her.

"I don't want to hear it right now, Verrin." She went up another step, putting herself farther out of his reach, and raising her hands as if to ward him off. "Just go. I- I just need some time to myself and I think it's best you go."

Verrin's azure eyes darkened to the deepest midnight and his normally smiling features hardened. "I'm not letting this go. I'll give you some time, but I am not letting this go." He gave her an assessing once over and turned away, gesturing to the other men out before he walked toward the door himself "Let's go."

Cass breathed deep, waiting for him and the others to get out of here before the dam holding her tears back gave way once more.

The other men filed out her front door to congregate in the driveway and Verrin followed them to the door. He didn't look back, just kept his head high as he paused on the threshold. "This isn't over, Cass. When we're done retrieving Seir, I'm coming back and you're going to talk to me."

"Sure, whatever." She'd agree to anything as long as he'd leave.

"See you soon, Cassidy." He stated flatly and walked out, shutting the door behind him.

Cass's eyes stayed dry just long enough for her to get one last look at him through the window beside the door, stepping out into the predawn darkness. His back was strong and she fleetingly noticed he wasn't wearing a coat. His dark hair was still mussed from her fingers.

Sinking down onto the stairs she put her face in her hands, letting the tears fall. *How had this all gone so wrong?*

CHAPTER 21

Cass grabbed her cell phone off the hallway table and stared at it, unsure who to call. She wanted to call her mom, seeking the comfort only a mother can give, but dreaded trying to explain her relationship with Verrin. She doubted her mother would approve of her sleeping with a man she hardly knew. Instead, she hit the contact for Savannah. Her friend was relatively informed about the situation and would be able to commiserate. She waited, wiping at the betraying tears that streaked her cheeks as her friend's phone rang.

On the fifth ring Savvy's sleep roughened voice came over the line. "Cass? What's wrong? It's like 6:30 in the morning."

Cassidy winced, feeling bad for waking her friend but needing someone to talk to. "Verrin just left." She stated simply.

"What? Oh, Cassie." Savvy's voice became clearer and a rustling came over the line as if the blonde was sitting up in bed and getting comfortable. "Tell me everything, honey."

Fresh tears welled and slid down her cheeks as she went to sit on the bottom step again. "I just - I thought that maybe we were more, you know. We made love last night and I thought -" A sob hiccoughed out of her and she pressed her lips together to hold the next in, angry at herself for being this affected by him. "God! I'm acting like such a girl!"

"Oh, honey..." Savvy soothed through their connection, a tinge of laughter colouring her voice. "You are a girl so it's okay if you act like one. Verrin's a jackass if he didn't realize what he had in you."

"He just – he says he's coming back. That he wants to talk."

Savvy gave a hum of consideration. "Maybe he's not such a jackass after all."

Cass sniffled, heart in her throat as she tried to explain to her friend what had happened. "I – I just don't get it. His brothers made it sound like being with me was some sort of trial, a task to check off the list before he could do other things."

"Did Verrin say anything like that?" Savvy inquired.

"Well... no. Not really. It was mostly his brother. It seemed like that anyway."

"And Verrin didn't stand up for you?" Savvy asked, a dangerous edge to her voice. Cass was sure there was a good chance her friend was contemplating gelding Verrin with a rusty spoon the next time she got near him.

"I guess he did, sort of," Cass admitted, remembering the f-bombs he had dropped in the process of telling his brother off. "He told him to shut up."

"Okay. Did he say anything else?" Savvy queried,

her voice radiating calm through the phone. "Just that he was coming back and he wanted to talk." Cass rubbed the bridge of her nose, her head now aching. "Oh god, did I just blow this whole thing out of proportion?"

"Maybe, maybe not. I wasn't there. But you know I have your back either way." Savvy stated. "I will call in sick this instant and come over if you want. We can spend the day alternating between picking out lingerie for makeup sex and plotting where to bury the body if it would make you feel better."

"Savvy..." Cass almost choked on a watery giggle. "I don't know. Give me a little time to think. I -" She stopped as an odd sound filled her home.

The thump of boots on hardwood. Boots with a heel. Too light to be a man's tread. It was a rhythmic sound any woman who'd ever worn them would recognize. And it was coming closer.

Cass leaned her head around the banister to look toward the kitchen. Eyes still bleary with tears she saw a stunning red head round the doorway from the kitchen and smile charmingly back at her.

"Hello, little mouse."

Standing up, Cass blinked at the strange woman in her house. "Who are you? How did you get in?" From her hand, Savvy's voice could be heard from her cell, asking what was happening.

"My friends call me Emmy and I just let myself in to pick up my bargaining chip." She smiled, examining her neatly polished crimson nails.

"Bargaining chip?" Cass was getting a very bad feeling in her stomach. "What bargaining chip? What are you talking about?"

215

Ignoring her, Emmy continued talking as she came closer. "You, foolish human, are my bargaining chip. I get you and Verrin comes to me willingly. Poor soft soul."

"Verrin? But he's gone." Cass told her, taking a step back toward the front door as Emmy got a little too close for comfort. "He just left. He's not coming back." She blurted, hoping this woman would buy her worst fear as the truth.

Emmy blinked before breaking out into a tinkling laugh. "Silly mortal, even if he is through with you, he wouldn't allow you to be hurt at my hands." Her smile turned into a sadistic grin. "And, believe me, you will be hurt at my hands."

Cass whirled, lunging for the front door. Dammit, she was getting tired of being chased through her own house! If she could just make it out...

Cass had her hand on the doorknob when she was slammed bodily into the solid oak panel. The breath whooshed from her lungs and she gasped as pain exploded in her chest. Her phone fell from nerveless fingers, bouncing until it settled on the hardwood floor.

"So predictable. Prey always runs." Emmy purred, tangling her fingers into Cass's hair and yanked her head back until Cass feared the crazy woman would snap her neck. "Why are humans so painfully stupid?"

"Screw. You." Cass ground out as she caught her breath.

The redhead laughed, a lyrical sound that verged on maniacal. "Just remember when you wake up, we could have done this the easy way." With that, Emmy drove her hand forward, plowing Cass's face into the oak door. Pain exploded across her cheek and forehead as she turned at the last moment, taking the brunt of it on her left side. Dark sparkles flickered before her eyes and widened until her vision was just a hazy blur.

She felt her limp body being hefted up and slung over a delicate shoulder. Everything was indistinct, sensation fading as the sound of high heels walked away from the front door. Cass fought to stay conscious, but her head had taken on a drum beat to match those heels and every note dragged her farther into oblivion.

In their absence, the foyer echoed the tinny sound of Savannah's voice as she screamed for Cass through the abandoned phone.

***

Murmur sighed as he looked out the window of the room he'd appropriated in the mercenaries fortress. Below him the jungle spread out in lush greens and browns, butting up against the sturdy walls that made up the building. While the structure itself was nice the location left a lot to be desired. The air was far too hot and muggy, leaving one's clothes sticking to the skin, and the bugs were not only plentiful and voracious but varied too. Almost made him miss the days of being a true angel when lowly mortal beings wouldn't dare touch him.

Having shucked his suit coat and his fine Italian loafers, he pushed the sleeve up on his white dress shirt and glanced at the gold Patek Phillipe watch that graced his left arm.

Everything was going according to plan.

He felt mildly bad about setting Empusa and her buddies on Verrin's little human, but he'd known it would come to this. The minute he had opened the door to that used bookstore and the diminutive brunette almost ran into him he'd realized which path they were on and knew what he had to do. Getting in good with his new client, annoying the mercenaries and avoiding Sariel's sons at all cost until the time was right had become his plan of action. Throwing the little human under the bus might make his stomach turn, but it was fated to happen.

Better that he do it then let destiny take the reins. At least when it was him there was some control over the outcome.

Destiny was always so messy.

Shaking off the guilty feeling, he turned and surveyed his space for the night. The room was relatively large considering most of the rooms he'd come across reminded him of closets. At least this one had a real bed, complete with mosquito netting and a low wooden stool. Lamia had informed him there was a washroom down the hall, but thankfully he didn't need it as long as he avoided mortal food.

With a sigh, he unbuttoned the soft dress shirt and pulled it off, hanging it on a hook by the door so as not to wrinkle the fabric. In the two millennia since he'd descended to earth he'd enjoyed shedding his plain white angelic uniform and wearing all the different styles the human's had available. Unfortunately, human apparel didn't leave much room for his wings and he quickly got tired of putting slices in perfectly good shirts just to let the feathered buggers out.

Enter the best deal he'd made to date.

About a hundred years ago he'd met a rather prestigious sorceress with a penchant for glamour spells.

218

Two months of vigorous bedding and a few hundred gold pieces later he had an amulet that would make his wings appear whenever he wanted. The glamour wasn't functional for flight, but it mirrored his real wings and made quite an appearance when necessary. Not to mention, saved him from constantly wandering around without a shirt.

After all, he wasn't some romance cover hero and, in his opinion, perky nipples were only sexy on women.

Bare-chested, he shrugged under the mosquito netting that covered the bed and tossed himself belly down on the not so soft mattress. Scooting up until he lay diagonally so his feet were the only thing dangling off, he clutched a pillow and dragged it under his head. Not the most comfortable he'd ever been, but it would do in a pinch.

His shoulders twitched and with a soft sound that reminded him of fluffing a down pillow, his wings unfurled, their great expanse arching slightly over his head and falling to his stretched out toes. With a few settling flutters, the giant silver wings gently blanketed his body from head to toe.

Forcing his eyes closed, he readied himself for what experience had told him was coming. His breathing evened out, taking on the steady rhythm of sleep. He slowed his heart until the cadence was a relaxed thump and his muscles succumbed to their frozen sleeping position.

It took a while as he drifted, letting his mind slowly sift clear of the day's stimulus until it was able to open to the much more important information available to him from the ether. Scenes played past him, ones he'd been witnessing for years as he waited for their time to come upon him. A sable haired man reaching out a beseeching hand. Blood being dripped from a red and silver goblet into a gaping mouth. An emerald-eyed woman with terror etched upon her features, cringing from a blow. A dark cavern filled with soft, mournful sobs. A small boy with open arms and disheveled brown hair, a streak of purple on his cheek, racing forward in joy.

There, amongst all the older visions, was a new one. It was hazy, its picture dim and distorted in a way that told Murmur this one wasn't certain yet.

Murmur turned his back on it and examined the other visions. As he ignored the new one, older ones started to fog over, the little boy, the green-eyed woman, the brown haired man all became hazy and uncertain. So the new one was a catalyst, somehow affecting the probability of the others.

Whirling, he lunged into the new dream and felt it solidify around his consciousness.

A room of stone walls and metal bars. A beaten and broken man curled into the fetal position on the dirt floor, blood making tiny pools around him as his wounds cracked open with the tight posture. A shadow in the darkness, observing. The sounds of a battle in full swing not far away. A hand, hazy and indistinct, reaching out to open a latch. Blue-violet eyes, glowing with an unnatural light, raising to stare out of the darkness of an opened cage.

Murmur's body jerked all over, hands propping his big body up so he could glance around the room. His wings had ensconced him in silvery feathers, moulding themselves to him like a blanket, and he had to push one aside so he could make sure the door was still closed.

Assured he was alone he dropped onto his pillow,

mind reeling. His wings rubbed against his skin softly as if trying to reassure him with the soothing gesture.

He had seen it. The vision had been clear. Someone was going to let Seir, maddened as he was with lust, free within the fortress. He had no doubt in the world the shadowy figure had been himself, watching to make sure the future played out as it should.

Dear God in Heaven, he didn't envy the soul that released that man. There were women in this place that would be in immediate danger. Perhaps if he was there watching he could guide Seir into something less harmful.

Then again, perhaps it was one of the women who released him.

Regardless he would wait for this person to show at Seir's cell so he could do as much damage control as possible. After all, he wouldn't stop this from happening, Seir's release affected too many futures to not let it run its course.

Murmur climbed to his feet and tucked his wings away, getting dressed once more.

***

Verrin stepped through Dantalion's portal and stopped dead, staring at his brothers. Dantalion came through after him, sealing the portal back to Cass and leaving him trapped in a hotel room hundreds of miles away from where he truly wanted to be.

He could feel their eyes on him, but he had no desire to talk to them. If they hadn't appeared he would still be with Cass, would even now be telling her how much he loved her as he sunk himself into her body.

He wasn't even sure how he could explain his feelings. No one but Cass had ever inspired them in him. Then to have her demand he leave, Gods, it made his heart ache.

Dantalion, his eldest brother, stepped over to where Pithius and Merihem stood watching him and swung out a hand, smacking Thius in the back of the head hard enough to make him stumble forward. "Idiot. You just had to mouth off and act like an asshole."

"What the hell?" Pithius growled, regaining his balance and rubbing the back of his head. He spun on his older brother and held his ground. "How was I supposed to know the chick was more than a bag and tag? V doesn't do relationships. None of us do!"

"Evidently, he does now," Merihem stated, rubbing the bridge of his nose as if the whole scene was too much drama.

Thius rounded on Meri, about to start fighting with his younger brother, when Dantalion bellowed. "Quit it! You're all idiots! You," He pointed to Pithius. "For opening your big mouth when it was not called for. You," He pointed at Merihem. "For not getting his dumb ass out of there sooner. And you," He turned on Verrin with dark fury. "For not taking better care of your woman and telling her how you felt from the get-go."

Verrin gaped at Dan. "My woman?"

Dantalion crossed his thick arms over his chest and glared at him. "Deny it all you want, but you wouldn't look so shaken up if that woman didn't mean something to you. Unfortunately, we don't have time for you to figure this all out right now. The others are waiting for us. Let's go get Seir and you can come back to make it right when we're done."

Dantalion turned his back to them and put a hand up, palm out. The air in front of it wavered as if from a heat wave and spread until it was large enough to accommodate someone walking through. Dan stepped to the side and gestured his brothers to go through the portal he'd created before leaning down to grab a black duffel bag off one of the room's little chairs.

Merihem went through, giving Verrin a sad half smile before he disappeared, followed by Pithius who offered him a disgruntled, "Sorry man."

Dantalion stood there waiting for him, but Verrin couldn't move. He had no desire to put any more distance between himself and the feisty woman who had stolen his heart. When his voice came out it was nothing but a harsh murmur. "I don't like leaving her behind."

Dan took his measure for a moment before stepping forward and putting a big hand on his shoulder, giving him a slight shake. "Let her calm down. Get your head together. Approach her once you know what it is you want with her and tell her exactly what that is. She may shoot you down at first, but if she means something to you, she's worth fighting for."

Verrin let that percolate a moment, knowing that out of all his brothers Dantalion had the most experience with relationships. The breath he let out was both an exhale and an acknowledgement that there was nothing he could do at the moment to make things right with Cass. "Okay, let's go get Seir."

Dantalion gave him a grim smile and gestured him forward through the portal.

CHAPTER 22

Empusa hefted the unconscious human higher on her shoulder as she stormed down the fortress's hallway. She wasn't pleased she had to stoop to human retrieval, but with Murmur watching her every move it wasn't worth letting someone else bungle it up.

Better she do it right the first time.

With a wave of her hand, two glassy-eyed thralls scrambled to open the door and let her into the room she'd picked to house her little human captive. There wasn't much inside, but the room itself was strategically placed. Far away from any entrance, one tiny window, a single door and close enough to the audience room that the thralls could drag the human in swiftly when required.

Hopefully, the human would be needed shortly.

Empusa had left her calling card right beside the girl's phone, a simple marble sized crystal sphere with a soul bound minor demon inside. When the Incubus returned for his woman, the demon shade would give him her message. With any luck, Verrin would be trading himself for the girl in just a few hours.

Then she could hand the whole affair over to Murmur and rid herself of the winged wonder.

Empusa knew that she really shouldn't be so leery of Murmur. He was just an angel after all and she dealt with much bigger and badder deities on a regular basis in her line of work, but he still gave her the creeps.

Maybe it was the fact that no one in all the realms knew what he was plotting. He was always doing things that apparently benefited his game plan but made no sense to anyone else. Add to that the fact that he was precognitive and probably knew what you were going to do before you did it, and that shit was freaky as all hell.

Emmy shrugged the unconscious girl off her shoulder and let her body fall across the bed limply. She shoved the girl's head back onto the mattress when it threatened to fall off the edge and turned to go.

Lord, she couldn't wait to wipe her hands of this entire mess.

Without a backward glance at her unconscious captive, Empusa walked out and let the guards lock the door. "Do not let her out. No matter what. I don't care how much noise she makes." She ordered the two dark haired snake shifter men who stood on either side of the door, eyes vacant as they listened to her orders. "No one goes in or out of that room until one of us comes to get her."

With a quick nod, the guards settled into position for the long haul.

Emmy headed back to the audience chamber, taking the twists and turns of the interconnected, concentric halls with ease.

"Hey! Ems! Wait up!" Mormo called from behind her and Empusa turned in time to see her compatriot jog down the hallway towards her, towering combat boots thudding with every step.

"You got Verrin's girlfriend?" Mormo asked, coming alongside her.

"Yes. Just finished locking her away." Emmy grinned. "She's actually a feisty little thing for a human."

Mormo's eyes with their dark kohl lining widened in mock surprise. "Are you telling me a human got the best of Empusa, greatest succubus ever to walk the earth and ruler of erections near and far?"

"Ha. Ha. Very funny." Emmy grinned and socked her friend in the arm. She plastered a smug look on her face and inspected the nails on her right hand, buffing them on her cotton T-shirt. "Although the rest is all true."

Mormo snorted out a laugh. "Yeah, yeah. We'll buy you a golden phallus so you can start your award shelf."

They rounded the arched doorway into the audience chamber and found Lamia hard at work, the computer desk she'd acquired set up with her laptop and thermos of tea. The blonde woman glanced up, giving them a cursory head tip in acknowledgement. "How did it go?"

"Got the girl," Empusa confirmed. She reached into the black leather jacket she wore and pulled out a red medallion on a gold chain. "This could use a recharge."

Lamia accepted the teleportation charm and set it on her desk to be recast later. "Any word on Verrin's arrival time?"

"No, but I left a demon shade behind that should deliver my demands nicely," Emmy said, heading over to her chair on the dais. "I can't wait to get this job done. I'm not even sure the money is worth the hassle anymore."

Mormo put a hand over her heart, the look on her face comically aghast. "Blasphemy! Don't say such things! You just might jinx us!"

Lamia sipped tea from her thermos casually and looked at her friends over the small lenses of her glasses. "Based on our current bank statement we are not lacking funds. We could actually take a hiatus and still be financially soluble."

Mormo stared at the blonde and blinked before turning back to Emmy. "I have no idea what she just said, but if I can't swim in money like Scrooge McDuck it's not enough."

Empusa couldn't help but laugh. "Is that really all you want?"

Mormo shrugged. "What can I say? I'm easy to please. As long as there's money to be made, veins to tap and pretty boys to be laid, I'm on Team Merc!"

"Well, there's a ringing endorsement for loyalty!" Emmy teased. She turned her attention to Lamia and grinned. "So we really are in the clear?"

"Yes," Lamia confirmed as she removed her gold-rimmed glasses and set them on the table beside her laptop. "With the funds from our current client, we have a sizable investment. I've split it up into multiple accounts worldwide for safe keeping."

Mormo grabbed a chair from the dais and dragged it across the stone floor until it was even with Lamia's desk before she threw herself into it. The fact that it made a horrible screeching noise the entire way didn't seem to faze her as much as it did her wincing audience. She assumed her usual sprawl of sitting sideways with one black leather clad leg tossed negligently over the arm of the chair. "I still don't think we should quit. I'm rather enjoying this mercenary gig."

Emmy sighed and looked heavenward as if the ceiling would have the patience she didn't contain. "We talked about this. We even voted. We're not going to quit yet. We're at the top, quitting now would be a waste of all the hard work we've put in. We also decided that we take another vote in a years time in case opinions differ by then."

Mormo gave a derisive snort and crossed her arms across her breast. Black nails with little gray tombstones painted on them tapped dangerously. "As if there's any better gig for us." She mumbled.

Lamia picked up her glasses and slipped them back on, going back to her computer and pointedly ignoring the discussion.

"That's true, not to mention playing mercenary is helping us amass your swimming pool's worth of cash." Emmy mused. "Hell, I'm not even sure we would know what else to do with ourselves. I'm not the type to retire quietly with a house full of cats and the Olympians certainly want nothing to do with us."

Mormo shot straight up in her seat, a brilliant look on her face. "I got it! We could open a blood bar!"

Empusa's groan synchronized with Lamia's and the two women burst into laughter at a disgruntled Mormo's expense.

***

Verrin stared at the smartphone in his hand and

cursed at the lack of bars. He shouldn't have been surprised that he was getting no signal but he'd been mildly hopeful when Merihem had handed him the device this afternoon that he might eventually have some luck. If this wasn't his only connection to Cassidy he would have thrown it into the brush he was so frustrated. He had annoyed Dantalion into taking him back to the hotel room they'd rented in Buenos Aires just so he could call her. Unfortunately, although he guessed it was to be expected, she hadn't answered his call and he'd ended up leaving her a message.

Releasing a deep sigh, he shoved the phone back into the pocket of his black military pants. He grabbed his black leather jacket off the branch he'd left it draped over and shrugged it on, making sure his weapons were all readily available to draw before turning back to the others.

They had spent the day preparing to storm Empusa's fortress and making sure everything was perfect for their rescue of Seir. Dantalion had portaled in the nymph volunteers Pithius had found to help tame Seir as well as enough weapons to properly outfit a small army. Verrin had been introduced to the bounty hunters, Iain and Solain, who had helped his brothers track down this hideout and would be launching the attack with them shortly.

As Verrin walked up, Iain gave him a cordial nod and handed him a bottle of water. "Ye ready for this?"

Verrin broke the seal on the bottle and took a hefty swig. He shrugged in answer and eyed the Lycan. "Can I ask you a question?"

Iain shrugged his indifference. "Aye, go ahead."

"Why does it seem like all Lycans are Scottish?"

Verrin asked seriously, remembering the highland Weres that starred in some of Cass's books.

Iain blinked at him for a moment before dropping his head back and letting out a riotous laugh. "Och, now that's a new one! Canna say I've heard that before!"

Verrin glanced away, trying to casually brush it off. "Just something I noticed."

"Well, I know for a fact not all Lycans are Scottish," Iain answered with a sly smile. "Although, to be fair, the Scottish ones are the most popular with the ladies."

Verrin snorted and took another drink of his water. "I wouldn't know. I've never been able to see past the swarm of women around me long enough to notice other guys."

That caused Iain another round of laughter and he slapped Verrin on the back, nearly knocking him over. "I like you, Incubus! The lot of you are a hell of a kick!"

Verrin grinned and gave him a little salute before taking another drink of his water bottle.

"Gather up!" Dantalion called, gesturing them all over to where he stood.

"Time to get our marching orders." Pithius intoned as he wandered past them toward their eldest brother.

Dantalion faced them and assumed his General pose, hands on hips, feet braced apart and looking every inch the commander he'd once been as he surveyed them and waited till they had all circled round. "So where are we at?"

"I donna think we'll have much trouble with the guards. By the info Solain gathered, they are all mortal." Iain said.

"Are any human?" Merihem asked.

"Not that we've seen. Snake shifters mostly. Nothing too dangerous." Dantalion assured.

"Do snake shifters bite?" Pithius questioned, joining them.

"In their snake forms, yes. My guess is that either Lamia or Mormo is in control of the thralls and has told them to stay human so they are easier to keep enthralled. Animal minds are different and their thoughts are harder to pin down." Solain put in. "If enough broke free I'm sure they would have fought to get control of their home back."

"What if we kill whichever chick is controlling the thralls? Would that release them or would they all just keel over?" Pithius asked and winced as a thought occurred to him. "Man, if they keel over, clean up on this little adventure is going to be a mess."

Merihem frowned at his sibling. "They will not die. If the controller relinquishes her hold on them, depending on how long they have been under her spell, they will either collapse or be highly disoriented. Easy enough to subdue."

"So is the plan to disarm the guards?" Iain asked as he twirled a bright green leaf between his fingers.

"Disarm if possible. If they pose a serious threat, do what you must." Dantalion turned to Pithius. "Do we have the women ready for Seir?"

"Yes. They're hanging out in the tent at the moment, but they know the drill. I personally made sure they were ready to service him as soon as we track him down." Pithius replied with a dirty grin.

With that settled, Dantalion started splitting them into groups. "Iain and Solain, you might as well stick together. Take out as many guards as you can while you track down your bounty and avoid Seir if you come across him."

The adopted brothers nodded.

"Pithius, you're in charge of the nymphs. Merihem, I want you to provide cover for Pithius and make sure he doesn't run into any trouble with the women." Dantalion continued, before turning on Verrin. "You're with me. We're going after Seir. The guard changes in an hour. We move out in forty minutes. Prepare yourselves."

With that, they broke up and Merihem pulled Dantalion aside to talk. Solain disappeared into the woods, no doubt watching over the fortress, while Iain sat down to sharpen a dagger he pulled from a sheath on his belt.

"Were you able to get a hold of her?" Pithius asked quietly as he stepped up beside Verrin.

"No." Verrin's reply was clipped and he refused to look at his brother.

"Ah hell... V, I'm sorry. I didn't mean to be such an asshole." Pithius rubbed a hand through his hair, messing it up. He stared at the ground and kicked a rock buried in the dirt. "I didn't think okay? If I had realized she was more than just the average summoner I wouldn't have stuffed my foot in my mouth. It just never occurred to me she might be more."

Verrin gave soft hum of acknowledgement but still wouldn't look at his brother.

Pithius was silent for a moment before he asked the question that had apparently been bugging him. "Do you think you can get her back?"

"I don't know." Verrin turned on his brother and glared daggers at the blond man. "And I won't know for sure unless she's willing to talk to me again and who the hell knows when that will be." With that Verrin stormed off, leaving Pithius behind.

He came up beside Merihem and Dantalion who were just finishing their conversation. Dantalion's hand casually stroked the pommel of the Roman spatha sword at his side, its long, straight blade glinting as he turned to Verrin. He opened his mouth to speak but shut it again when he saw the dark look on Verrin's face.

Merihem glanced between the two of them and sadness crossed his features. "We will do anything we can to help you, Verrin. She will come around."

Verrin sighed. "I really don't want to talk about it."

CHAPTER 23

Verrin glanced back over his shoulder as Pithius and Merihem guided the nymphs up a set of stairs and into a darkened room, tucking them down into a corner. Once everyone was safely inside the first floor room Dantalion, Verrin and the bounty hunters headed toward the archway across the room. Peeking out, Dantalion gestured the Sinclairs out and to the left. They crept out on silent feet and disappeared down the hallway, in search of their own target. Verrin came up behind Dantalion, ready to follow his brother's lead as they stepped out and went to the right. With any luck, they could avoid guards and not cause too much of a disturbance before they tracked down Seir.

Such was not their luck.

They had made it most of the way through the first level when a group of guards came around the corner. Immediately the five men drew weapons and came at them. Verrin and Dantalion jumped fully into the melee, leaving Meri and Thius to hang back and protect the women.

Verrin swung his fist and plowed it into one of the

guards jaws, knocking the man to the side. The next he reached out with his powers, draining the energy from him and leaving him to drop. Another came at him, but before he could pull the knife at his hip, the guard was missing his weapon hand. Dantalion swung his sword once more and ran the snake shifter through. The limp body fell at Verrin's feet and he stepped over it with haste.

"You didn't have to kill him." Verrin pointed out as he joined the warrior and eyed the defeated men on the floor.

"Any man who wields a weapon against me and mine courts their own death," Dantalion stated stoically and kept striding down the hallway. A servant rounded a corner up ahead and he just bared his teeth and snarled. "Hide."

Verrin snickered as the poor young woman's dark eyes rounded in terror and, dropping the stack of sheets she held, she turned tail and ran as if the hounds of hell were snapping at her heels.

As they strode side by side down the halls they checked every door they came across, startling servants and disarming – sometimes literally in Dantalion's case – guards as they went.

Verrin was just peeking into the kitchen, waving at the scared servants with a placating smile, when a scream echoed down the stone hallways. The feminine sound chilled the blood in his veins and he jerked around, looking down the hallway the noise had come from. "You don't think..."

"They wouldn't do it. If they let Seir loose they would have worse to deal with than us." Dantalion agreed.

At the far end of the hallway, Iain rushed by, hot on

the heels of a petite dark haired woman. Even as he watched the girl opened her mouth and a glass shattering shriek burst out. Iain was right behind her, hands reaching for her as they disappeared around a turn.

Verrin frowned and poked his head back into the kitchen. "Do any of you know where we would find either a dark haired man, an Incubus, or the red haired bitch?"

An older woman whose black hair was liberally streaked with silver and held a trembling young woman to her ample bosom looked up at him with tear-bright eyes. "Lady in central room." She admitted in broken English.

"And the man?" Verrin prompted her.

She shook her head and gave a little half-shrug.

"Okay. Thank you. Stay in here. Barricade the door when we leave." He ordered her, slipping back out of the room. There was silence for a few heartbeats, but he waited until he heard the kitchen staff dragging over furniture to block the entryway.

"Let's find Empusa. She can lead us to her hostage herself." Dantalion said, turning on his heel and stalking down the narrow corridor. They pushed open a small wooden door and exited into a much larger hallway.

***

Murmur sidled up to the end of the hall and glanced both ways down the adjoining passage. Just an empty hallway to the left and to the right two men standing guard at the door of the dungeon. Obviously, their post wasn't highly exciting as, even through the stoic look of a thrall, they both looked like they would rather be anywhere else.

Murmur withdrew behind the wall and straightened

his suit jacket and tugged his french cuffs down until they were perfect. It was time to do a little dirty work.

He rounded the corner casually and walked up to the two guards as if it were the most natural thing in the world. "Evening gentlemen."

The guards hardly blinked at him.

Murmur cocked an elegantly arched brow. "Empusa sent me down here to check on the merchandise so if you don't mind..." He gestured toward the door they stood on either side of and took a step forward.

The guards stepped in, blocking his entrance. "No admittance." They said in unison.

Murmur wanted to growl in frustration, but instead he stepped back and considered the situation. He sighed and gave them a sad smile. "As you wish."

With a swift gesture he put a hand up in front of each guard's face, palms flat. With a quick strike of his thoughts, he broke through the thrall that Mormo had on the guards, overpowering it. *You will walk away. Lock yourself in a room and sleep. This will all be over soon.* He directed them, implanting the thoughts in their minds. As he let go of their minds the men dropped to their knees, wide unblinking eyes showing their now silvery gaze. The compulsion would wear off in an hour or two and with it, the shimmer of his power would leave them.

Murmur looked down at the two men collapsed at his feet and sighed. "That was far too easy." He pushed open the door and stepped past them. He turned and pulled a keyring off the belt of one and then closed the door. Even as he descended the stairs he could hear them gathering themselves and quietly walking away.

Murmur came up to the cell Seir was being held

within and looked in on the poor man once again. His body was a ruined mess and in the silence, the Incubus's breath rattled ominously. If he wasn't the immortal child of an angel, Murmur would be seriously worried.

Might as well get comfortable.

He wandered down the aisle of cells until the darkness enshrouded him and settled his back against the wall to wait. Hopefully whoever Seir's rescuer was would show up promptly and Murmur could continue on with his plans. He really didn't have time to wait for someone's tardiness when he had so many things going on.

It turned out to be a false hope.

Murmur glanced at his watch for what felt like the millionth time and let out a soft growl of frustration. He was buried in the back of the dungeon, lost among the shadows, as he watched the stairs for Seir's liberator.

Unfortunately for Murmur's schedule, the poor soul was startlingly absent.

Murmur paced the short distance between the cells that lined both walls. This couldn't be happening. The person had to show up! Everything else had fallen into place perfectly. He racked his brain trying to figure out how he might have accidentally gotten in the way of someone freeing the demon. The guards were sleeping off his control somewhere, unable to stop anyone from interfering, and he'd done nothing but sit here quietly observing for what seemed like hours. No one had appeared.

The battle had started seven minutes ago by his watch and if the Incubus wasn't freed soon all his planning and hard-wrought successes would be for naught.

For his part, Seir was curled into a ball on the floor,

hands over his ears as if the sounds of the battle above them were too much on his damaged mind. Fine tremors ran through his battered body and Murmur feared that meant Sariel's son was almost too far gone.

God save the soul who opened that cell door.

The sounds of battle had started to fade into the distance and Murmur worried his bottom lip. He stopped and leaned heavily onto the bars of one of the cells. With his eyes closed, he tried to sink deep enough into his subconsciousness to see the vision again.

It was a struggle, but when he got it the vision had grown hazy as if it was fading away. Damn it! He had to fix this!

He focused hard, eyeing the hand in the vision as it toyed with the lock on Seir's cell. Another hand was gripping the bar beside the lock and with surprise Murmur recognized the watch on that wrist.

A gold Patek Phillipe.

Murmur's eyes flashed open and he looked down at his own left wrist, at the same watch from the vision circling it. With dawning horror, he looked to the cell that held Seir.

Fuckity fuck fuck!

How had this happened? Why in the world would he be the dumb ass stupid enough to unleash Seir on a fortress full of unsuspecting people?

Unless...

To make the other visions come true, this had to happen. Murmur had to release a madman to make everything else fall into place.

Gods damn it all to hell!

Taking a bracing breath, he strode down the aisle to

Seir's cell and looked in. The Incubus hadn't moved from his curled up position on the floor. Maybe he could just flip the lock and get the hell out of the way.

He withdrew the ring of keys he'd taken off the guard from his pocket and found the correct key, striding to the locked door. A fight with a crazed Incubus wouldn't kill him, but it wouldn't endear him to Sariel's children in the future either. Perhaps if he opened the lock quietly and then locked himself into one of the other cells Seir wouldn't bother with him. Besides, the poor boy was probably exhausted physically from the abuse. He may prove to be no danger whatsoever.

With these reassurances on a ticker tape running through his head, Murmur took a deep breath and stuck the key in the lock. A little jiggle and the old key was turning in the lock. At the final click, Murmur raised his eyes and looked into the cage.

Glowing blue-violet eyes stared back at him.

In the time he had taken to unlock the door, Seir had come up into a crouch on the other side. Murmur put his hands up in a placating gesture and took a calming tone. "It's okay. You're free now. Just stay calm and you -"

Seir's body slammed into the cell door, cutting off Murmur's words as the barred door knocked into him. Hurled back, his body crashed into the cell on the opposite side and he crumpled to the dirt floor.

The cell door swung wide and Seir was out, looking down at him with eyes feverishly bright in their malice. Murmur watched him, not wanting to move in case he drew violence from the unpredictable male. Seir glared, teeth bared in a silent snarl as he stared down.

Murmur barely breathed, watching the panting

breaths heave through Seir's chest. This particular tableau was one he had worried would come about. While Seir couldn't kill him he could do some rather serious damage that would take a while to heal. On his side, Murmur had no desire to beat a fellow Watcher's sons into unconsciousness.

They held position for what seem to be forever before Seir lunged forward, snapping his teeth with a bestial click inches from Murmur's nose before turning and racing for the stairs.

Murmur collapsed into the dirt, a lunatic chuckle rising in his throat. He lay there laughing as Seir disappeared into the fortress. That had gone better than he'd expected. Perhaps Seir had recognized him even through the lust haze. Then again, perhaps Seir just didn't see him as an appropriate sex partner and left him in search of better fare.

Lord save whatever woman that man came across in his current state.

With that thought, Murmur decided it was high time to take his leave. He got up, dusted himself off and followed Seir up the stairs at a leisurely pace. At the top, he listened carefully. Hearing fighting from the right, he decided to avoid the path of destruction that was Seir and went left.

CHAPTER 24

Breath held, the demon stayed quiet and still on the floor of his prison. He'd listened to the angel pace back and forth, murmuring to himself for a while now. The godly servant had seemed impatient at first and then transitioned into wary.

The demon's mind flitted around, uninterested in the angel. His body ached all over, his muscles twitching in their desire for action. His skin was heated and his pulse pounded in his ears. His cock was as solid as a lead pipe between his thighs and his balls swelled with seed.

He needed to sink himself inside a woman so badly his whole body throbbed with the need. Unfortunately, there wasn't a single female within reach so his abused body just lay there on the floor, reserving its energy.

The angel came closer and the demon

suppressed a twitch when he heard the sound of keys jingling. Would the haloed bastard actually release him? His sensitive hearing picked up everything, from the rustle of fabric to the shuffle of steps.

When the sound became the slide of flesh against pitted metal and the grind of lock tumblers, the heartbeat racing in his chest became a driving, incessant beat. Just as the lock slid open the demon rolled over, coming up on his hands and knees.

The darkness faded before his eyes and as soon as the angel had stepped back, the demon rushed the prison door. Crashing into it hard, he rammed it against his liberator, slamming the winged one into the bars of the opposite cell and dropping him to the floor.

Giving the stunned angel a warning snap of teeth not to follow him, the demon raced to the stairs and vaulted up them three at a time. When he breached the door at the top his body purred and he tipped his head back, nose up to test the air.

Women. This building held hundreds of scents but only a handful were recent and female.

All he needed was one.

One female body to pin beneath him and sate the aching lust that clenched his balls. One woman to ease the frantic pace of his thoughts as he buried himself in her slick heat. One pliant form he could force to orgasm over and over until his passions cooled.

Turning right, he ran down a stone hallway,

following the scent of two women. Skidding around the corner he came up in front of four men, glassy-eyed shifters with healing bite marks on their necks. The moment hung in the air as all five men stared at each other in surprise. Gathering himself, the one in the lead drew a machete from the sheath at his hip, brandishing it at the demon. "Stop right there!"

The demon hissed at him, baring straight white teeth and raising fingers hooked into claws. With the first wild slash of that blade, the demon lunged at the man, catching the base of the knife with a firm hand and effectively negating the blow. Gripping the guard, he wrenched the sword from the man's fingers and threw it down the hallway behind him.

The demon shot out his other hand, gripping the guard by the throat and lifting him off his feet. With a negligent toss, he threw the man into the stone wall head first to land with a sickening thud.

The others came at him with equal effectiveness. The demon tore through the men, disarming them and then taking them down one by one. Even as the last one turned tail and ran, the demon chased him down and tackled him, swinging punches at the man until all movement beneath him ceased.

The demon climbed to his feet and started back down the hall, following the female's scent.

His pace picked up as the halls seemed to lengthen. Every second he followed that tantalizing scent was one he sunk deeper into madness. He needed her now.

The feeling of the stone floor beneath his raw bare feet had disappeared. Likewise went the feeling of sweat stinging open wounds or the awkward jounce of his half hard cock against his thighs and belly as he ran.

The beast rounded another corner and paused. Four distinct female scents assailed him. Three of them had the tang of godly ones about them. Not angels certainly, but perhaps goddesses of some old pantheon or another.

It didn't matter.

The fourth smell, a human one, was closer.

He looked down the hallway to a door by two men. She was behind that. His prize lay just beyond those men.

His lips curled in an unconscious snarl.

Why were they waiting at her door? Were they her guards? Or were they awaiting her favours? The beast didn't appreciate competition. Whether they were guards or lovers those men were breathing their last.

The lust and rage became one in his chest, pounding through his veins with an audible beat. He stepped out and walked toward the men, arms held loosely at his sides in anticipation. The low rumbling growl that vibrated through him was the only advance warning they had before he was upon them.

They never drew their weapons.

The beast reached out, snapping the wrist of the man on the right as he reached for a matte black gun. The man howled while his companion took a backhanded slap to the face. Stunned, the second man stood there as if patiently waiting for the next blow.

The beast delivered.

A swift hit with a closed fist crushed the poor sod's nose, letting blood gush as hands came up to cover the injury. As the man bent over, the beast caught him by the forehead and slammed his skull back into the wall with a sickening crunch. Letting go, the body fell in a careless sprawl beside the door.

A glint of silver had the beast turning even as the knife flashed out and sliced across his arm. The barest hint of pain flared but was buried under the instant fury that tore through him like a blast furnace.

The other had died easily. This one he would play with.

The beast advanced, teeth bared in a vicious grin.

***

Cass groaned and rolled over, burrowing into her bed. She really should get up and take something for her headache. Pain was pounding in her temples and her face ached as if she was coming down with a sinus infection.

Crap, she hated being sick.

She rolled over and flung an arm out, sprawling across the bed. Her t-shirt caught around her and she opened her eyes, looking down to wrestle the fabric into a more comfortable position.

Cass blinked.

This wasn't her room.

The events of earlier came back in a rush, making her head ache even worse. The crazy woman had broken into her house and kidnapped her.

Lifting a hand, Cass gently probed her cheek and up around her left eye. The area hurt like hell and felt hot and swollen. With her luck, there was a good chance she was sporting a black eye. Dried brown flakes drifted down as her fingers brushed across her temple and into her hairline. Apparently, her head had taken the brunt of the redheaded harpy's abuse.

Sitting up, she looked around carefully. The walls were made of gray stone and there was a single lightbulb overhead that appeared to have its wires tacked to the stone ceiling. The bed was no more than a single mattress and an unadorned wooden head and footboard. A squat wooden dresser with a small covered tray on it rested against the wall beside a slit of a window. Across from the bed stood a large wooden door with thick iron brackets.

Cass climbed dizzily to her feet, using the foot board and wall as a brace until she made it over to the door. She gave the knob a tentative twist, hoping to ease the door open and peek out at whatever lay behind it. Lord knows what situation that crazy woman had dropped her into.

The knob wouldn't budge. Giving it a yank Cass pulled harder, thinking maybe it was stuck on the frame. With a few more pushes, pulls and curses Cass realized sadly that the door must have been locked from the outside.

Which would make sense if you'd kidnapped someone and were holding them prisoner.

Cass sighed and dropped her forehead against the door before she remembered how much her face ached. With a hiss she withdrew, turning to go over to the window instead. The window, if you could really call it that, was just a narrow six-inch vertical slit left between two massive blocks of stone in the wall. It felt kind of like those arrow slits you see in old European castles.

Glancing out the window she realized she must be on a second or third floor. The ground below was lit by large torches at random intervals, shedding light across the cleared grounds that slowly turned into a wild mix of fronds and vines. Jungle. She was in the freaking jungle.

Where the hell had that psycho woman taken her?

The sound of footsteps outside the door drew her attention and Cass whirled, the world tilting as her battered head spun for a moment, and dove toward the door. Coming up against it, she pounded the flat of her fist against the wood. "Hey! Let me out! Hello?"

The footsteps closed in and Cass quieted, listening intently until she realized whoever it was was moving away. "Hey!" She yelled, pounding again and rattling the knob. "Tell the red haired bitch I want to talk to her! Do you hear me?"

As the footsteps faded away Cass wound down, frustrated to be stuck here with no one listening to her. She turned, sitting on the stone floor with her back pressed against the wooden door. Her head throbbed with her pulse and she had to wonder if she had a concussion. As a librarian, she didn't get hurt often and had never suffered a head injury even as a child. She had nothing to compare this to.

She sat there, watching the small slice of sunlight move across the stone floor and enjoying her inner pity party, when a distant yell rent the air. Her breath froze in her lungs and she listened intently. Another scream followed by a nearby thud of something heavy hitting stone. Cass turned, getting to her knees and pressing her ear against the wooden door to hear better.

There seemed to be some sort of scuffle going on in the hallway. The sound of men yelling and fighting broke out, only quieting after numerous ominous thuds.

That was the sound of bodies hitting the floor, Cass's mind told her darkly.

Cass climbed to her feet and backed away from the door, putting the bed between her and whatever was in that hallway. She held her breath, hoping if she stayed as quiet as possible whatever was out there would walk right past her little room.

More footsteps in the hall, a single set, coming

closer. There was a soft noise, like something snuffling, and the footsteps stopped. The door knob rattled.

Cass's stomach clenched. Whatever was out there was right outside her door. What could she do? There was nowhere to go!

The door rattled again and then banged in its frame. She squeaked, terror getting the best of her, and ducked down behind the bed. She looked around for a weapon and her eyes settled on the covered silvered tray. It was the only thing small enough to wield in the room. She lunged for it, discarding the domed top in favour of the heavy metal tray. An assortment of crackers and cheese scattered across the floor as she dumped it, hefting its solid weight in her hands.

The door banged again as if something was running at it from the other side.

She tucked down, the tray clutched in trembling fingers, as her heart beat like a bird trying to escape in her chest.

There was an inhuman growl in the hallway and sudden silence. Cass was just starting to hope that whatever was out there was going away when a roar echoed off the stones all around her. She ducked her head down against the bed just as wood crackled and the door came flying into the room, hanging awkwardly from its bent hinges.

In horror, she watched as a huge figure filled the entry. The first thing she noticed was glowing blue-violet eyes and her heart stuttered in joy, thinking it might be Verrin.

The figure walked farther in and the bottom dropped out of her stomach. The man who entered bore a strong resemblance to Verrin, but it wasn't him. He had the same beautiful brown hair and patrician features, but his eyes were more purple than blue and had a wild light in them. He was completely nude and covered in cuts and bruises. His head was tilted back and he sniffed the air like an animal before glancing around. A low growl filled the room and those eerie eyes locked on her. He took a step forward, hands that were spotted in blood reaching for her.

CHAPTER 25

Merihem peeked around the corner, but couldn't see the fight he knew was ahead. The sounds of flesh hitting flesh were too obvious to miss. He turned back and gave Pithius a silent staying gesture, making sure he'd keep himself and the women in the room they had just secured.

Pithius nodded once and tucked himself back into the room, quietly closing the door.

Their path had been a careful one, moving the women from one cleared room to another. Thankfully with Dantalion and Verrin having gone before them most of the guards Merihem had come across were already felled. So far Meri had only had to crack one unfortunate soul on the back of the head and drag his unconscious body out of the way.

As Meri crept closer the noise of the fight died away and silence reigned once more. He kept his back to the wall, moving steadily onward until he reached the next corner. The rapier at his side brushed his thigh as he sidled up to another corner and cautiously sneaked a glance around it.

A handful of badly beaten bodies littered the stone floor, limbs twisted and faces distorted in fear and pain. Bile rose in his throat as the smell of death hit him and he willed himself not to gag. Meri breathed shallowly as he backtracked to the hallway he'd left Pithius in.

The sound of running footsteps coming his way had his heart rate spiking. It wouldn't do Pithius or Seir any good if he got caught here. Feeling along the wall, he watched the hallway ahead carefully until he felt the indent of a door. Pulling it open he slipped inside and carefully closed it again.

Merihem waited, breath held as he listened to a group of people run past. The footsteps thundered on and he let his breath out slowly. *I just have to make it back to Pithius and –* His thoughts were cut off by voices nearby. He turned, bracing his back against the door and stared across the room. The door he had come through was set in a deep archway and a few chairs littered a raised platform in front of him. Just out of sight the sound of female voices were engaged in conversation.

"We've got a breach!" A dark voice announced. "Someone's gotten past the guards."

"Could it be Verrin?" Another asked.

"Maybe. No one saw. Guards are out cold." The dark one responded.

"All right. Wrap it up ladies, we're getting out of here." That voice he recognized as belonging to Empusa. "Lamia, pack up here. Mormo, you're with me. Let's get the key and the blade. I'm not letting them out of my sight until we've been paid."

"What about the Incubus?" The dark one, probably

Mormo asked.

"We got some of his blood. I'd rather leave him than try to drag his crazy ass with us. If the client wants to bitch about the amount of blood she got, she can fetch another Incubus herself." Empusa reasoned, the tap of boot heels leading away. The thud of a door closing told him Mormo and Empusa had left.

That left Lamia with him.

He looked around the thick door frame and saw her. Lamia had her back to him as she stood at a small desk, unplugging a laptop from a portable battery. She curled the cord around her hand before tucking it into a black messenger bag she'd sat on the chair.

He couldn't have asked for a better opportunity.

Drawing the dagger from the sheath at his back, Merihem stepped out silently, making as little noise as possible until he was directly behind her. He surged up behind her, wrapping one arm around her waist and yanking her back against his body, the other coming up to hold the blade to her throat. "I suggest you be of ease, female. I would hate for my hand to slip."

The body in his arms stiffened and her hands, which had come up reflexively to pull him off, stopped in midair. "Who are you?" Her voice came out calm, not a waver of fear to be heard.

"Truly? Can you not hazard even a guess?" He cajoled over her shoulder.

"Incubus." She spat the word as if she found it distasteful.

"Congratulations. You got it in one." Meri praised snidely.

"Great. If you were going to slip me your dick as a

prize, you can keep it." Lamia sneered. "I'm not some common whore begging you to get her jollies."

Merihem couldn't help but chuckle darkly at that. "Oh no. You are anything but common, little Queen."

The body in his arms became impossibly still, as if she had ceased to draw breath. "You know nothing."

"That is where you are incorrect. I am thorough with my research. You were once a Libyan Queen of such beauty she attracted the eyes of Zeus himself. It is truly a shame that his wife found out about his little infatuation, Hera can be such a jealous person. I have heard it said that she destroyed your entire family for the insult after she cursed you to live forever as an immortal beast." Merihem countered.

"I'm surprised my story is still being circulated. I figured Hera would have that wiped from memory." Her delicate hand came up to adjust her glasses on her nose and his eyes caught on the little white crescents of her perfect french manicure. "It was bad PR after all."

Merihem couldn't help the smirk that tugged at his lips. "I will give you that. Now that we have taken care of the niceties, I have a few questions for you to answer."

"Your brother is in the dungeon."

Merihem paused. He hadn't expected her to just pop out with Seir's location like that. Although that hadn't been the answer he was looking for. "Actually I had already deduced that. My question was why did you take him?"

"The client requested it." She told him flippantly. "It's not my place to ask why."

Merihem growled at that. "Might I recommend that you start making it your business. The next man you wrong may not be so forgiving."

A hard laugh broke from her slender body. "Is this you being forgiving? Holding a knife to my throat?"

He leaned in closer, putting his mouth beside her ear. "You are still in possession of both your head and your dignity. Consider that a profound example of my forgiving nature."

"I hope you don't expect me to applaud you for your effort." She mocked. "Then again maybe you do deserve applause. It was rather easy to break your brother after all. I expected the same lack of control from you."

Merihem felt the rage that had been simmering just under the surface over his brother's capture rise and with it a desire to put this haughty queen in her place. Shifting his hold, he exchanged a firm hand for the knife at her throat, tucking the blade away. Wrapping his other arm around her waist, he lifted her lithe body up, taking two steps forward until they were in front of her desk.

He swept his arm out, clearing the top of the desk in one fell swoop. Lamia gave an undignified squeal as she watched her laptop crash to the floor with a bang and various other items scatter, a stylus rolling across the stone to rest at their feet.

"You bastard!" Her ladylike demeanor fled as she cursed him, the hiss in her voice becoming more pronounced in her anger. "What the hell do you think you're doing?"

He squeezed her throat just enough that it impeded her breathing and when her hands came up to pull at his hold, he caught both her wrists in his much larger hand. She writhed in his hold, trying to break free as he let go only long enough to turn her around and lay her across her desk, hands pinned above her head in his own. He pressed his weight down upon her, melding himself to her feminine curves and smothering her struggles.

"You and I are going to make a deal, snake." He growled in her face.

"Like hell! Get the fuck off me!" Lamia hissed back, her glare defiant as she bucked in an effort to dislodge him.

"Queen or not, you will listen to me," Merihem informed her menacingly. "We are going to make this deal. You will swear by it on your immortal soul before I let you leave this room."

Lamia eyed him suspiciously, the spiderweb thin scars around her eyes crinkling as she watched him, looking for all the world like she suspected this was all posturing. With a voice like smooth silk, she met his eyes. "You're not the only one who has done their research. I know about you, Merihem. Second son of the Angel Sariel. Always the studious one, more interested in knowledge than power or women. You're not cruel. You don't have it in you to harm a woman, enemy or not."

Merihem knew the deep forest colour of his eyes was brightening, their light shimmering across her fine features and golden hair, giving them the faintest green highlight. His mouth twisted into a lascivious grin and he moved one of his hands down to slip beneath her head. In a series of gentle tugs, he pulled out the gold pins that had secured her hair in a tight chignon, tossing them aside negligently. With her hair free, he burrowed his fingers into the shining mass and pull her head up until their lips almost met. "There are many ways to make a woman hurt that cause no bodily harm whatsoever." He promised darkly just before he ran his lightly stubbled cheek against her smooth one.

Lamia gasped as Meri released the full force of his Incubus gift on her. In a burst of power, he let his senses invade her nervous system, stroking against her nerve endings and making them thrum with pleasure. In mere heartbeats, she had gone from frustrated and angry to a state of heightened awareness that only hit a body seconds before an impending orgasm.

"Oh god!" Her voice had gone from outraged demands to plaintive whimpers. Her hips bucked beneath him, grinding her pelvis against his in search of relief. Her copper eyes darkened as she stared up at him in mixed lust and horror. "What..." Her words trailed off into a breathless pant.

Merihem smiled down at her, the desire pouring off her body awakening his own with a vengeance. He kept his own rising passion tamped down though, wanting to prove his point as succinctly as possible. With his power in control of her arousal, he watched the becoming flush colour her cheeks and felt her quickened breaths press her breasts beguilingly against his own solid chest.

"Did your sources not warn you of this?" Merihem wondered lazily as he nuzzled into the arc where neck and shoulder met. He lapped at her skin, tasting her, before he bit down slightly, drawing his teeth across her skin in a mimic of her own vampiric bite. His hips rocked into hers as she arched against him. Letting go of her hair, he dragged his hand down and cupped her left breast, stroking the still clothed flesh and circling the peak that tried to make itself known even through the layers of cloth.

"Pleasure," He informed her, breath tingling against her skin as he undid the top two buttons on her white dress shirt. "Is a double edged sword. Used correctly everyone gets rewarded." He brushed his lips across the cleavage he'd revealed and she gasped wantonly, all illusion of poise shattered beneath his onslaught.

His free hand traveled down, stroking the cloth that shielded her stomach and hips before slipping down to her thighs. He gathered her skirt up, letting it bunch around his wrist as he delved beneath to cup her mound in a strong hand. His warm fingers stroked ever so lightly over the warm, wet silk of her panties and her answering moan was pleading as her head thrashed. Her hips jerked against his hold, trying to get more of his touch.

"Used maliciously, it can cause nothing but anguish," Merihem advised her, pressing a finger solidly down over the soaked silk and against her entrance with the tease of possibility before withdrawing completely.

It wasn't easy for him to leave her. She was sprawled across her desk, breathing harshly with tears of frustration in her harvest moon eyes. He stood over her breathless form, erection straining his black slacks like a leashed hound. Meri's every nerve hummed with the desire to join with her, to push her body over the edge to bliss, but he needed to make a point. He knew that his actions were utterly mean but he needed to make sure she understood that he could have her under his power again in an instant.

Merihem had to give her props though. She might lay before him in a sexual daze, but she didn't beg him. Had she been a lesser woman she might have given in and thrown her pride away in a bid for more.

"You're a bastard." She spoke without moving, the curse she no doubt intended coming out more of a breathless sigh. Her eyes were closed as she fought to get her breathing under control once more.

Merihem tried to hide the smile that threatened to tip up his lips and shrugged nonchalantly. "That was just a taste."

She muttered something that sounded an awful lot like 'fucking Incubi' and managed to sit up, albeit a bit shakily. "So this deal. What the hell do you want?"

Merihem adopted his most business-like air, which he was sure was a failed effort considering the massive erection that was currently trying to force its way out of his pants, and answered. "I want your soul bound vow that you will leave my family alone and do your utmost to persuade your companions into doing the same,"

"Seriously?" Lamia choked out on a disbelieving snort. "You got all handsy just so you could warn me off your family?"

Merihem let a serene smile come through. "It assisted in getting my point across so yes."

She narrowed her eyes at him, dark gold eyebrows drawing down in a frown. "What do I get out of this deal?"

"I will grant you one favour. You may save it for a rainy day or..." He trailed off purposely, waiting for her to take the bait.

She rolled her eyes and sighed, obviously through with his bullshit. "Or what?"

Now that smile morphed into salacious, shit eating grin. "Or you may cash it in now and I will make you cum so hard you will be screaming my name to every god in heaven."

Lamia's beautiful face darkened into a scowl. "I don't need your fucking handouts! Get out of here!"

He raised an inquisitive brow. "Your vow?"

"I vow that I will leave your family in peace and try to convince my friends to do the same or my soul shall be yours in forfeit." She hissed out, her inner snake dragging over every S like the words were torn from her throat.

Merihem sketched a courtly bow to her in thanks, his green eyes dancing with mirth as he took her in once more. "I will graciously leave you alone to do what you see fit. Until we meet again, little Queen." With that, he turned on his heel and left.

***

"I don't like this." Mormo proclaimed as they jogged down the hallway, boots thudding on the gray stone floors. "We could just stay and fight."

Empusa sighed, resigned to having to explain why that was a bad idea. "Of course, we could fight and we would no doubt kick some ass. However, while we're fighting, that sneaky bastard Murmur will undoubtedly be taking the artifacts that we worked our asses off to get back to his owner. Sariel's brats just want their brother back. We can even use the girl if we need a bargaining chip. I would rather we keep the artifacts in our possession than fight with the brothers."

Mormo snickered darkly. "I can think of a few things I'd like to do with those brothers. Think they'd mind touching each other's dicks?"

Empusa looked over at her friend curiously as they came to a stop outside her bedroom. "I have no idea what you're talking about."

"Really?" Mormo gave her a patronizing look. "I'm

honestly disappointed in you."

Empusa shook her head and let herself into her room, not deigning to comment.

"So if you're having an orgy with five guys and only one girl," Mormo went on, following her in and shutting the door. "Dicks are going to touch. I mean, a girl can easily handle five cocks but you can't have that many moving parts in such close proximity without crossing the streams, you know? At some point, someone's gonna be banging nuts."

Empusa, who had wandered over and knelt beside her bed, stared at her friend over the bed with mock concern. "You know, I'm starting to think you're a sex addict. Maybe we can get you tested."

Mormo grinned fiendishly, flashing her fangs. "So says the girl who has to rescue her vibrators from under her bed before we evacuate."

"These are not my vibrators!" Empusa asserted as she drew out the aluminum briefcase she kept the artifacts in from beneath the bed. "I didn't have another safe place to store the artifacts. It's not like these temples are equipped with wall safes."

"Uh-huh, yeah, okay. Still not buying it." Mormo taunted, opening the door and gesturing her out. "Let's take your sex toys to safety."

Unwilling to bicker with her insane companion she headed out the door. They'd made it most of the way down the hall to get the girl out of her room when something odd drew their attention.

A line of ruby red left footprints marked someone's walk down the hallway as if the owner had stepped in a puddle of red paint on their trek. Blood. It was definitely blood considering Mormo's fangs had punched out and the vampire was sniffing as if she smelled fresh baked cookies.

"Snake shifter." Mormo whispered, letting her know the likely source of the blood. Someone had taken out one of their enthralled guards.

"Do you think it's one of the brothers or Murmur?" Emmy asked quietly, looking both ways down the hall. The brothers were a likely source, but Murmur was a wild card prone to betrayal.

"No idea." Mormo admitted, slipping out into the hallway and following the footprints slowly down the hall. As the corridor turned a corner a woman's gut wrenching scream pealed out, freezing everything.

Mormo and Empusa glanced at each other before warily peeking their heads around the corner. The footprints led straight to the broken down door of the room Emmy had tossed Verrin's woman into. Framed in the door's vacancy was the whip striped bare body of Seir.

"Shit!" Emmy cursed in a low whisper. "How the hell did he get out?"

"Uh, Em. We got more problems." Mormo announced hesitantly.

Empusa looked at her and followed Mormo's pointing black-nailed finger down the hall. At the other end, two towering dark haired male figures were running as fast their long legs would carry them towards Seir and his new target.

Dantalion and Verrin were about to run in on a really bad scene.

"Fuck this!" Mormo muttered, pulling Empusa back from the edge of the wall. "I vote we bounce."

"You're right. Let's go!" Emmy hissed, turning back down the hall and leaving the brothers to deal with their own mess.

A few more turns and they were striding into the audience chamber. As they stepped into the grand room Emmy felt her jaw drop as she came up short. "What the hell happened?"

Lamia looked up from where she was picking her laptop off the ground. The screen flickered weakly before going black. As she stood, her golden hair curled around her face, freed from the chignon it had been neatly tucked back in earlier. "I had a visitor." She answered calmly.

"Well, it obviously wasn't the maid service." Mormo snorted, taking stock of the mess by the desk and disheveled state of their friend.

"Was it Seir?" Emmy asked, reaching down to grab one of Lamia's burnished gold hairpins off the floor and holding it out to her.

Lamia shook her head, taking the pin and tucking it into her pocket. "One of the other brothers. I made him a deal."

"Sex and blood for leniency?" Mormo snickered.

Emmy shot her gothic friend a quelling look and focused back on Lamia. "What kind of deal?" She questioned, thinking of the angelic relics they had gathered for their client. If Lamia had promised those, they were about to do some serious double dealing.

"A hands-off policy. We don't touch his family and they won't touch us."

Mormo groaned. "Really? Hands off? Damn! I really wanted my hands on them."

"Drop it." Emmy hissed at Mormo under her

breath. Turning to Lamia she nodded. "Good deal. We can always find another Incubus. Let's just get out of here before Murmur finds out we lost half of what the client needed."

It was quick work to gather the little bit of essentials they wished to take and were ready to go in under five minutes. With a meager supply of water – and Mormo's apparently required flask of scotch - they headed out into the night.

If they moved swiftly they would be back in civilization by morning and far away from the angry angel whose client they had just ripped off. Not to mention the Incubi brothers who were going to be seriously pissed when they saw what had been done to their youngest brother.

They were about a half hour away from the fortress and Sariel's horrible children when a shadow moved to intercept them.

Out of the jungle's shadow, Murmur stepped in front of them. Silver wings glowed faintly in the inky darkness and the man himself looked thoroughly unfazed by the heat and humidity. He graced them with a serene smile but the light in his amethyst eyes was anything but angelic. "Hello, ladies. I do believe you have something my client requires."

CHAPTER 26

Cass jerked back, falling on her butt. A scream tore up her throat as she scrambled across the floor, trying to get away from him. The man growled low and leapt onto the bed, not letting a little thing like furniture stand between them.

She had to get free. She couldn't allow herself to be trapped in this room.

Stumbling to her feet, she tried to dive around him, hoping to reach the doorway and the only possible escape route. Just as she shot past the bed a hand buried in the back of her t-shirt, twisting the material and halting her flight. Her struggles only had the brute twisting harder until the collar tightened around her throat.

The beast yanked, pulling her backward to him as he climbed off the bed on the other side. She weighed her options briefly and went for the only one that seemed right. With the metal tray clutched in both hands, Cass whirled and slammed it into the side of his head with all her might. The impact vibrated up her arms but she held on tight, fingers white-knuckled on the curved edge.

Those glowing eyes narrowed dangerously on her as his teeth bared in a snarl.

"Let me go, you bastard!" Cass hauled back, ready to hit him again, when his fingers caught the tray mid-swing. She gripped it with all the strength she could muster, but he twisted her t-shirt, cutting off her air and tearing her away from it even as he pulled it with the other hand. Her fingers slipped, and with a frantic thud of her heart, she was torn away from her only weapon.

The clatter of the tray hitting the floor signaled her defeat.

The hold on her shirt loosened marginally and she dragged in a full breath, gasping even as she tried to push away from him. He caught one of her wrists, but she swung out, managing to box his ear on the left side. He growled and caught her other hand, maneuvering her until her arms were held behind her in his strong grip. She kicked at his shins, tried to knee him in the balls, but her flailing limbs seemed to have no effect on him. He pulled her in close, melding his body to hers until she could feel the massive erection that pressed against her.

"Let me go! What the fuck do you think you're doing? Get your hands off me!" She demanded, going wild in his arms. She stomped on his bare feet and writhed against his restricting hold. When he dipped his head forward, she rammed her head into his mouth, causing him to pull back with a curse and making her head spin.

Perhaps that had been a bad idea.

Those feverishly bright eyes flared with lustful anger and he shifted his hold so her wrists were captured in one big hand between them. With agile skill, he deftly spun her around and snaked his free arm around her waist, hauling her off her feet as he pressed her back to his broad chest. Cass shrieked, her legs kicking in midair as she tried to tug her hands out of his hold, but her struggles did little to faze the big man as he strode toward the bed.

Before she knew it he had pushed her to her knees at the bedside and forced her to bend over the bed until her top half was horizontal on the mattress.

No, no, no... This couldn't be happening. In this position, she couldn't escape. The bed frame dug into her hips with every grind of the stranger's eager erection into her fabric shielded backside.

The man growled low in her ear as he shifted her hands into a better position, pinning her crossed wrists to the bed above her head. The move brought his feverish body in full contact with hers. A whimper crossed her lips and she felt her eyes well with tears.

Oh god, how had she ever gotten into this mess?

Cass whimpered beneath him. She could hardly see. Her long hair had fallen across her face and with her hands captive beneath his strong grip she couldn't brush it aside. She shook her head, partly hoping to regain her vision and partly in denial of her present circumstance. What if she didn't get out of this? The man was so strong it would be nothing for him to kill her. God, who would tell her parents? What if she never saw Savvy again?

"Mine." His voice growled into her ear from behind.

The arm that held her wrists moved, coming closer to her face as he shifted. In a split second, she lashed out and sunk her teeth into the firm flesh of his forearm, biting until the tang of copper touched her tongue. The man yowled in pain, his grip on her wrists letting go to circle her throat and pull her up to her knees.

Her newly freed hands came up to tear at his grip on her neck, clawing at his hand and pulling for all she was worth. Her heart stuttered as she tried to drag in breaths and hot tears blurred her vision.

Where was Verrin? The redhead had said he should be coming. Would he not come because they had fought? What if he never knew she'd been taken? Would she be left here with this monster?

Did it really matter if he did come? Even if he did, it would be too late.

Cass choked on a sob. A thickly muscled thigh forced its way between hers and his hold loosened slightly as he became preoccupied. Her mouth opened and a wail of desperation tore up her throat. The feel of her attacker's hard cock rubbing against her through her thin pajama bottoms assured her her fate was sealed.

Help wasn't coming.

***

Something told Verrin he needed to help the woman who'd screamed. He knew it with a bone-deep certainty. Without a word to Dantalion, he took off running down the corridor. Skidding to a stop at a junction between halls, he looked both ways. Where had the scream come from?

Just as his brother came up behind him, another scream broke the air and Verrin whirled to the left, racing toward it.

They tore around a corner and Verrin narrowed his eyes at the jumbled pile of bodies that filled a section at the other end of their current hallway. As they closed in it was obvious that someone had torn through a group of snake shifters. Necks snapped, limbs at odd angles and splatters of blood everywhere. Bile rose in Verrin's throat. "You don't think..." He couldn't make himself say it.

"Seir." Dantalion nodded, examining the remains. "He must have gotten free."

A scuffling sound broke through the horror of the scene and Verrin was off again, following the noise toward an open door. Two guards lay outside it, tossed aside like unwanted dolls, their forms unmoving. The door itself was hanging awkwardly, barely attached to its bottom hinge with splinters of wood all around.

What the open door revealed was an image that would haunt him for the rest of his immortal life.

Cassidy, cheeks streaked with tears, was clutched to his youngest brother's body. His big hand collared her throat tightly and the edge of the bed hid their lower halves. Even as he watched, Seir's bare hips ground into hers from behind and Cass whimpered. When her brown eyes caught his, the sound of his name torn from her lips flipped a switch inside him.

"Get your hands off her!" He demanded as he burst into the room, violence plain on his usually jovial features.

Seir's head jerked up and those bright eyes didn't even blink. He emitted a low-level growl, acknowledging the challenge for his female, and tucked Cassidy behind him with a sweep of his arm as if he was protecting his property. The fact that she still wore her rumpled pajama bottoms was only a small consolation.

Lunging, he caught his youngest brother in the abdomen with a swift punch, taking the male down to the floor in front of Cass. He vaguely registered her startled cry but was too intent on bloodying his brother. Seir bared his teeth at him and dove forward as if he meant to rip Verrin's throat out, but Verrin buried a fist in his brother's face, tearing his knuckles apart as they slid across teeth.

Dantalion was yelling in the hallway, but Seir had his full attention. A punch slammed into his temple and the next thing he knew Seir was on top of him, a writhing, snarling thing. Hands clenched in his shirt and pulled him up only to slam his head back into the stone floor.

The world spun, but the sound of Cass's tears drove him. He swung, impacting flesh even as Seir laid into him. They pummelled each other in a frenzy, landing blows on any part of the other they could reach.

Suddenly Seir's weight on top of him lessened and Verrin blinked up to see Dantalion's arm around Seir's neck in a choke hold. Pithius was running into the room, out of breath, and waving what looked to be a scrap of blue silk.

Charging in, Pithius stuffed the fabric under Seir's nose and waved it with relish. "You smell that? Come on, you know exactly what that is."

Seir's body stiffened and his hands came up, trying to grasp the cloth, but Pithius yanked it out of his reach.

"Come on, how about you leave Verrin's girl alone, all right buddy? I got three beautiful ladies waiting right outside for you to give it to them nice and hard. Follow the nice wet panties to the pretty girls now." Pithius urged, stepping back and waving the panties in the air as if he was trying to coax a dog.

Seir stared longingly after Pithius's lure and Dantalion slowly eased his grip. Seir moved slowly toward the door before glancing back at Cass. Verrin growled low and struggled to sit up, putting himself between Cass's huddle form and his crazed sibling.

Obviously determining it was less painful to go after easier prey, Seir whirled and dove out the door following Pithius. Within a few seconds, the hallway was filled with feminine giggles and moans of delight. A male groan echoed down the hall moments later, proof that Seir had fallen for Thius's bait.

"V-Verrin..." Cass's voice was a shuddering whisper behind him and he whirled on his knees so he could face her. He wanted to touch her so bad, but she looked as if she'd fall apart at any moment. Her hair was disheveled and dried blood streaked down from her forehead and above her left eye. Tears ran down her cheeks and her brown eyes were dark with despair.

"Cass, honey, I – Gods, I want to hold you! Can I? Please just let me..." Verrin pleaded, hands up to show her he meant no harm.

Cass stayed huddled in the corner she'd been shoved into, eyeing him warily.

Verrin took a moment, breathing deep to get himself under control, before he tried again. "Cass, little one, please let me come to you. I was so scared when I saw he had you. I just need to make sure you're all right." He shuffled forward slowly on his knees until he knelt before her. With slow, gentle hands he reached out and gathered her close, cursing when she became a trembling bundle of sobs in his arms. He sat, clenching her to his chest as she cried, and petted her gorgeous hair. "Oh, baby, I got you. You're safe now. I got you."

"I thought you weren't coming!" She sobbed, head

buried in his chest. "I thought..."

"Always." He promised, burying his face into her hair and breathing deep as he held her. "I will always come for you."

***

The beast followed the scent that the blond man waved in his face, the cloth soaked in the cream of a willing woman. He plunged into the hallway and into the arms of three lovely women. Soft hands trail over his abused skin, pulling him into their clutches.

He went willingly, growling at the feel of fabric covering the flesh he wished to touch, shielding the orifices he wished to bury himself in. He tugged and tore and rended his way to his goals.

They landed in a writhing heap on the hallway floor, the beast and his sacrifices. Hands were everywhere. Rough fingers sunk into a warm, wet, willing channels. A harsh mouth met moist lower lips and delved inside to sample the sweet nectar created. Insistent cock plunged in to the hilt and froze in bliss before starting a frenzied pistoning.

The beast's growls turned into groans that were quickly outmatched by the cries and moans of the women beneath him. When one came, shuddering around his member, he didn't relent. He drove into her harder, letting her clasping sheath milk him as if determined to ring his seed from his flesh.

So close. Gods, he was so close!

His balls ached with the desire to cum, but his body refused, too long denied to fall prey to his desires now.

He howled in frustration and tore his cock from the woman beneath him. In a burst of speed, he had the woman whose core he'd just been devouring pinned on her knees in front of him, his larger body overshadowing hers. He grasped her hips and drove inside her tight sheath with one massive thrust, only stopping when her body had no more space he could fill. He pounded into her, dragging her mewling body down his cock in successive tugs.

His vision cleared enough so that he could see a woman standing over the vixen on her knees beneath him. He watched as slim fingers reached down and spread her nether lips, letting the delicious wetness inside beckon him. He watched as his own arm snaked out and caught the woman by the hips, pulling her in until he could consume her with his mouth. The beast groaned into her center, licking and sucking feverishly even as he pummelled his cock into the woman on her knees.

Hands gently cupped his sack and suddenly a warm, wet mouth was on him there, sucking on the flesh between his legs. He pulled himself away long enough to glance back at the other woman who had slid herself beneath his spread legs, licking and sucking at his flesh. With a potent moan, he let go of the woman straddling his face with one arm to reach back and sink his fingers into the sucking woman's core. She moaned against his sac and writhed beneath his touch.

And just like that, he worked the three women to a frantic climax, body straining to provide overwhelming stimulus to the vessels who would give him the essence of their pleasure.

A wet core strangled his shaft in clenching spasms

as the woman he pounded into cried out in bliss. He sucked hard on the clit in his mouth and quickened his fingers, driving the others on. He needed their pleasure, to be the creator of it.

Cries echoed in the hall around him as the trio of nymphs reached their pinnacle, shaking and writhing around him as they came.

The beast groaned out a plaintive sigh as the energy of their orgasms washed over him and his own peak gathered at the base of his spine until it tore out of him in great shuddering waves. More and more came until he felt like the torrent would never end and his body shook violently and jerked his shaft inside the woman beneath him.

As it tapered off he could hardly hold himself up. Muscles that felt as if they had never been loose finally slackened. His heart beat like a wild thing in his chest. Fingers of sated bliss raked his flesh, causing shivers to blossom across his skin.

His breath panted as his body weakened, the abuses of the last week adding up and dragging him down into unconsciousness. He ached and throbbed, sweat stinging cuts that now bled sluggishly after his frantic movements.

The beast's bulk listed to the side, the women's bodies tangled with his now weakened limbs. They sprawled across the stone floor, a panting, shivering mass of pleasured flesh.

The haze that had encompassed his vision slowly began to fade, leaving him staring at the dark ceiling far above him. The sound of voices trickled in over the sighs of the well-sated women. Some of those tones seemed vaguely familiar although he could hardly focus to place them.

His breath sawed in and out of his chest. He knew if he licked his lips he'd taste a woman's heavenly essence just as he knew it glistened on his fingers and spent cock. All around him, women dozed in spent exhaustion.

Seir stared at the ceiling and wondered how the hell he had gotten here.

CHAPTER 27

Verrin was pretty sure he couldn't remember a time in his long life when he had ever been so terrified. Rounding that doorway and seeing Cassidy clutched in his brother's grip, tears streaming down her face, had nearly stopped his heart in his chest. The fact that Seir could have killed her in a heartbeat just as he'd done to those guards in the hall hadn't escaped him. He'd been momentarily elated to just see that she was breathing.

Then the true horror of the scene had kicked in.

He was watching his youngest sibling caught in the midst of attacking the woman who held his heart. Knowing that his brother had chosen to quench his lusts with her had nearly driven him around the bend. Hell, he still wasn't sure how far Seir had gotten in his attack, but there was a good chance that he was still going to kill the insane bastard for touching her.

"I'm sorry," Cass hiccuped, the words hoarse and half choked by tears. "I -"

"Shh, little one. You have nothing to apologize for."

He soothed, rubbing her back as he rocked her gently in his arms. Her weight on his lap was a prize to him. Even the tears that stained her cheeks were blessings he had feared he might never see again.

Her head shook against his chest and she started again. "I got mad at you -"

"Because I was a jackass who should have told you the whole story. If I had just told you what was going on from the get-go we wouldn't have had a such a misunderstanding." Verrin's lips twitch with a sad smile. "My brother's idiocy certainly didn't help things."

She stiffened in his arms and kept her head down as she repeated him quietly. "Misunderstanding?"

Verrin couldn't help it. The joy of having this sweet, beautiful woman in his arms again was lighting him up from the inside out. He reached down and tilted her chin up to face him. "Cassidy O'Neill, I have so many feelings for you I don't even know how to comprehend them all."

She blinked at him and a watery smile started to break across her features. With a pathetic little laugh, she joked. "I hope they are mostly good feelings."

"They are pretty amazing!" He leaned in and pecked a kiss on her lips gently, afraid his touch on her battered face would hurt her. "But we can discuss all that later. I need to get you out of here. This place isn't safe."

Merihem came around the bed and held out a white bed sheet. "Take this. Wrap her up." He handed it off to Verrin and dropped his voice to a whisper. "She has had a trauma and shock is a possibility."

"Come on, little one." He sat her up straight in his lap and wrapped the sheet around her shoulders. She reached up to hold it closed and Verrin stiffened when he caught sight of the bruises forming on her wrists. He glanced up at her face and took in the damage there too. "Did anyone else touch you?" The words came out a harsh demand.

Cass clutched the sheet around her shoulders and shivered as his gentle fingers traced a bruise across her shoulder. "A red-headed woman. She called herself Emmy."

"Empusa," Verrin growled. "I'll make sure she pays for laying a hand on you." He promised her as he helped her to her feet.

"We will make sure she pays." Merihem reiterated. "No one harms one of our Ladies and gets away with it."

Cass gave a soft watery smile when Verrin hooked an arm around her shoulders and pulled her in front of him. He smirked as she gave a startled yelp when he swung her up into his arms. "Let's get you away from this place."

"Uh, look man, you might not want to bring her out this way," Pithius said, poking his head around the door jam. He glanced over his shoulder and turned back with a rather chagrined look on his face. "Our baby brother is doing things to those nymphs I wasn't sure were possible until I witnessed them for myself."

Verrin frowned, unwilling to subject Cass to the sight of a maddened Incubus in full rut.

"On the upside, my sexual bucket list has a hell of a lot more boxes to check off on it now." Pithius snickered from the hallway.

"I can send you both to her home. We'll wrap up here." Dantalion offered, stepping forward.

Verrin hesitated for a second, wanting revenge on Empusa for taking Cass, but cast the idea aside. Empusa was immortal. He had time to get his revenge. This was the only chance he would get to comfort Cassidy and assure her that she was more important than everything else to him. "Thanks, Dan." Verrin leaned his head down and put his lips close to Cass's ear. "All right little one, Dantalion is going to open a portal to take us home, but I have to warn you it's kind of a weird feeling. A combination of ice cubes running down your spine and feathers being brushed against your toes. Kind of chilly-itchy, if that makes sense. It's completely safe and a hell of a lot faster than any flight you can get commercially. Are you okay with that?"

Cass eyed Dantalion speculatively before giving him a small nod. "Yeah, we can try it."

"Okay, just tuck your face into my shoulder and I'll do the rest. You relax and we'll be home soon." Verrin purred in her ear and held her tight in his arms.

Dantalion stepped forward and waved a hand over the wall, a wave of distorted air spreading out from his hand until it was big enough to walk through. "Go ahead, I'll be right behind you."

Verrin nodded to his brother and stepped forward. He smiled down at Cass and whispered. "Take a deep breath and let it all out then close your eyes. I always find that helps."

Cass breathed deep and exhaled before squeezing her eyes shut and tucking her head into his chest.

Verrin took the single step through the portal that would take them both home.

***

280

Seir blinked at the rough-hewn ceiling above him and listened to the voices of his brothers. Their voices were low tones that went back and forth as they debated over something, but he was having enough trouble pinning down his own thoughts to focus on theirs.

He was weary with a bone-deep ache pounding in his body. Every breath strained muscles he hadn't realized he had. Part of him wanted to look down and check out what kind of damage his body was sporting and the other part of him was too exhausted to care. Even if his limbs were bent at odd angles and his skin flayed to the bone, he wasn't sure he could get up the gumption to worry about it.

Soft breaths surrounded him and he could just catch a shock of blonde hair swathing his right arm if he looked out of the corner of his eye. Instinctually he knew women surrounded him, women he'd recently taken.

His cock twitched.

He bit his lip, holding back a groan. Gods above, he wished his system would just lay off. The drive to take the women around him was rising again, but his body wasn't really up for the task. Even the blood slowly filling his cock seemed sluggish and resistant.

Maybe he could convince one of these beauties to ride him into oblivion.

"- do with him? I can't imagine Verrin is going to want him anywhere near his woman for a while."

That voice belonged to his brother Pithius and it felt closer somehow. Seir tried to focus on the nearby voices, hoping to hear what was going on. He had the oddest feeling they were talking about him.

"Verrin just needs some time to reassure himself that his Lady is well. Once he is secure in her safety and

281

affections, all will be well. I cannot see Verrin holding a grudge for something so out of his control."

That was definitely Merihem and his words struck Seir with worry. A ball of dread formed in his stomach and he strained to hear more.

"God lets hope so! Or else family get togethers are going to get plenty awkward." Pithius murmured.

Had he done something? It sounded as if they were worried Verrin would be mad at him and might hold a grudge over something he had done. Seir racked his mind, but his memory went from being taken by Empusa to this moment with only darkness and pain in between. He shook off the recollections and listened intently, trying to ignore his racing heart and needy erection.

" - place for him to rest. I doubt he'd want us to take him around his harem after what he just did to V's girl." Pithius pointed out.

"He could stay with me." Merihem offered.

"No. He shouldn't be in a highly populated area. I'll keep him until he's fit to be around humans again."

Dantalion was here? Lord, something must be seriously wrong if his brothers had hauled Dan out of the woods to help. And what did he mean 'fit to be around humans'? Had he done something to one?

Seir stared at the ceiling and tried desperately to recall what he might have done. All he got was painful blackness for the longest time. Right until he had felt a female body beneath his own.

But it was only a single body.

He screwed his eyes up as that stone of dread in his stomach sunk like the Titanic. Oh god. It had been a single woman, body trembling as she cried out, not in pleasure,

282

but seeking help.

He fought the pain to raise his head and take in his surroundings. Three women, nymphs by the look of them, were sprawled around him, limbs twined with his own. The lot of them looked as if they'd been thoroughly ravished. One's hips showed the slight bruising of fingerprints and the shoulder of another showed bite marks beneath her disheveled hair.

Obviously, he had torn through these women in a sexual frenzy unlike anything he'd ever experienced.

But it hadn't started here.

His horrified brain put the pieces together and he wanted to rail as he realized he had started with another woman, one whom he'd terrified and forced to submit to him. Gods, had he raped her? Had he irrevocably injured the woman his brothers seemed to believe was Verrin's?

Bile rose in his throat and Seir lurched, tugging himself away from the limbs on top of him so he could turn to the side and retch. He had to get out of here. Couldn't face his brothers right now.

He braced his hands on the cold stone floor and heaved his battered body up. Managing to get his knees beneath him, he used the wall for leverage to climb unsteadily to his feet. A quick glance over his shoulder assured him that his brothers were tucked just inside a room twenty feet away and the nymphs he'd used so thoroughly were undisturbed by his withdrawal.

With one hand against the wall for balance, he hurried along as fast as his ruined body would allow, choosing a direction at random when the hallway split into two. He kept going no matter how much every inch of his skin protested.

283

After countless turns, he stumbled across a group of fallen men. By the looks of them, they had stood against Dantalion. Poor fools. They hadn't stood a chance.

Glancing down at his own bare form, he shrugged off his disgust and began salvaging clothes from them. Boots from one, a shirt from another. Coming across an unconscious man he quietly apologized as he stripped the pants and socks from him, snagging his belt as well when he found the pants drooping on his hips.

His nudity covered, Seir continued along, knowing his brothers wouldn't be far behind.

If the hazy memories of his recent actions could be believed, Seir had been completely lost to the lustful designations of his dual nature. He had attacked at least four women, one of whom was Verrin's. It was pretty much guaranteed that his brother was going to be furious with him and Seir wouldn't blame him in the least.

Whatever Verrin wanted in recompense, Seir would offer, regardless what it might cost him.

The sound of his own name being called had him pushing his weakened body faster down the twisting hallways. He wasn't going back with his brothers. Couldn't face those strong males after having fallen into such dishonour.

His heart raced and he was starting to panic when a single door appeared in front of him. He hit it like a runaway train, barreling into the wooden portal. It flung open and he flew into a dark humid night. All around him the buzz of insects filled the air and the scent of green growing things and decaying plant matter.

"Seir! Wait!"

Seir glanced over his shoulder, staring down the

long hallway at Merihem's panicked face. Even as his sibling ran toward him, the pleading look in his eyes was clear.

"Seir! Wait! Talk to me!"

Seir took in Merihem's lean form as he raced forward, committing it to memory. He wasn't sure when he would see his brothers again and wanted to keep this image of Merihem fresh in his mind.

He wasn't sure when he would be able to face them again. He needed to regain his honour, needed to be able to face himself in a mirror, before he could stand in front of Verrin and the poor woman he had brutalized.

He was determined to apologize. Even if Verrin beat him bloody, Seir would beg at that woman's feet seeking her forgiveness.

With that decision made, Seir grabbed the solid wooden bar usually used to barricade the door from the inside and swung it closed. Jamming the bar into the ground, he wedged it against the wood to blockade the door before he spun away.

Seir raced for the edge of the jungle, uncaring of the pain as adrenalin mainlined into his system in his rush to escape. He dove in, branches and vines slapping at his skin. His feet slipped on the damp undergrowth, but he powered through, adamant that he not be caught.

The last thing he heard before the jungle swallowed him was his Merihem's plaintive call and the banging of his brother's fists on the blocked wooden door.

CHAPTER 28

"We're home."

Cass blinked and sucked in a shaky breath, inhaling Verrin's spicy masculine scent. The air around her which had been warm and humid moments ago was now chilled and smelled faintly of lemon wood polish. She looked around and couldn't stop the tears that came to her eyes when she saw they stood in the foyer of her own house.

The home around her was dark and silent.

All of a sudden all she wanted was to turn every light on in the big Victorian. She wanted to blast the old furnace until the chill was gone and bake until the smell of cooking food filled the rooms. She wanted her home to reflect the life she'd always had.

"Put me down," Cass mumbled, shoving ineffectually at Verrin's chest.

Verrin shook his head and started walking into the darkened living room. "Not just yet." He strode over to the sofa and sat her down carefully, reaching for a throw blanket to wrap around her.

286

Cass tried to get up, but Verrin placed a hand over her knee to halt her and sunk down into a crouch before her.

"Cass, baby, tell me what you need. I'm your servant. Anything you want is yours." Verrin told her, blue eyes meeting and holding hers in sincerity. "Just tell me what you need."

"Light," Cass admitted, glancing around the dark room. "I need the lights on."

"Consider it done," Verrin assured her with a smile. He patted her knee as he rose to his full towering height. "Sit tight." He reached over and flipped on the side table lamp before going back to the living room light switch.

Light blossomed all around the house as he methodically turned on all the switches, lighting up every square foot. Even the backyard and front porch were lit by their respective lights. She listened as his footsteps jogged up the stairs and knew he was treating the upstairs to the same.

Verrin came back down, but instead of coming straight to her, he stopped in the kitchen. Water ran and he rustled around for a minute before he came back over with a glass of water for her and a granola bar. "There, all set. I even put the kettle on so you can have tea or hot chocolate in a few minutes. Are you hungry? I can make food. Anything else can I do for you?"

Cass just stared at his handsome face with those blue eyes that were so earnest and couldn't help the sad smile that tugged at her lips. He was so good to her. Even when her requests were stupid he did them. No questions asked. This man had come to her rescue, beaten the hell out of his own brother, seen her a sobbing, broken down mess, and still stood here in front of her willingly. Hell, she'd sprayed him in the eyes with air freshener and he'd never even held that against her.

Cass launched herself off the sofa at him, wrapping her arms around his neck and letting him crush her in his embrace. She grinned and sniffled into his shoulder as he rocked her gently and rubbed her back with soothing strokes.

"It's okay. You're home. It's all over." Verrin crooned into her hair. "I promise nothing like this will happen again. I'll make sure of it. Everything will go back to normal. Once I'm gone I'll -"

She jerked her head back and stared at him carefully. Her voice was a deadpan as she parroted his words back. "Once you're gone?"

Verrin blinked, obviously caught off guard. "Well...yes. I can't imagine after all you've had to put up with, you want me to stick around. Our bond is broken now. You can continue as you always have, before I ended up in your life."

She narrowed her eyes at him. "And what will you be doing?"

Verrin looked away from her face for a moment. "I don't know yet."

Cass stayed silent, trying her hand at telepathically willing the information she wanted out of him.

He met her eyes and grimaced. When he spoke it was hesitant and he looked past her toward the patio doors as if afraid to watch her face. "I was going to stick around for while, make sure you were okay. Maybe get an apartment."

"An apartment?" She asked, puzzled.

"Well, yeah." Verrin sat back on his haunches and ran a battered hand through his tousled dark hair nervously. The look on his face was a little sheepish. "I checked. Mrs. Miriam said I'd need a fixed address before they would give me a library card."

"A library card?" Okay, she was really starting to feel like a parrot, but his words were so surprising they really didn't want to compute the first go round. Deciding she needed more information she went ahead and asked the question bothering her. "Why would you need a library card?"

Verrin looked her straight in the eye and gave her a shy little smile. Not his patented teasing grin or the charming bastard smile. Just a sweet, slightly embarrassed tilting of his lips that stole her breath. "Well, there is this really hot librarian who works there. She's a bit nerdy and has a pretty eccentric taste in music. She hates coffee for some ungodly reason and has addiction level issues with the written word, but I found she's really grown on me and I'm not sure I could live without seeing her smile every day."

Cass tried to hold back the feelings that were welling up inside her as she choked out a "Yeah?" that was as much a sob as it was a laugh.

"Yeah." He nodded, cupping her cheeks and leaning in until his next words brushed over her lips. "I was hoping I could convince her to give a reformed player like myself a chance and maybe get her to come out for coffee with me. Perhaps dinner some evening. I'm a really good cook, I'm sure I could win her over." He told her with a wink.

Cass couldn't help it. She giggled.

Verrin quirked an eyebrow at her, his smile wavering slightly. "Is that a good giggle or a this-man-is-such-an-idiot giggle?"

Cass tightened her hold on him until her cheek was pressed into his shoulder in a crushing hug. "You silly, amazing, gorgeous man. Of course it's a good giggle!"

"Phew!" He chuckled. "So you won't mind if I start stalking you at your work?"

"Nah, I think I might even like it." She withdrew until she could meet his smile with one of her own.

"I am *so* glad to hear that. Now I don't have to make that rather large donation to keep Miriam from outing me." Verrin admitted, grinning broadly. He hugged her tight and dropped little kisses on the top of her head. "All right, now that we have the good news out of the way, will you let me take care of you?"

Cass was just starting to nod when the front door flew open, its great bulk slamming into the wall and shaking the house.

"Cassidy! Cass is that you?" Savvy's voice rang out in the otherwise quiet house.

Cass gave Verrin a little smile as she pulled back, calling out for her friend. "In here Savvy."

The blonde woman tore into the living room and rounded the sofa just enough that she could see her friend wrapped in Verrin's arms before her knees seemed to give out and she dropped gracelessly to the floor. "Oh god Cass, you had me so scared!"

Cass took in her friend's appearance and smiled, reaching out to catch her shaking hands. Savvy's normally perfect makeup was nowhere to be seen, her eyes puffy and red-rimmed from crying. The jeans and RCMP hoodie she wore would never have left the closet on a regular day and her always smooth blond bob was disheveled with tufts going every which way. Her always put together friend was a wreck in her worried state. "Savvy, I'm sorry. I'm here, I'm okay. Everything's all right."

"You were crying and then I could hear someone else..." Savvy sobbed out, her relief and fear mixing. Her hands trembled. "I could hear you fighting and then nothing. It all just went quiet. I came over, but you were gone."

"Verrin came after me," Cass told her, trying to soothe her rumpled best friend. "How did you know I was back?"

"I had my brothers keep an eye on the place. I've been at the police station with Gray, but I made Grif promise to keep an eye on the house and call me if anything changed." Savvy explained wearily.

"How long was I gone?" Cass wondered aloud.

"Not long. The police wouldn't even let me file a missing persons report yet. You went missing Tuesday morning and it's like 2 am on Wednesday now." Savvy told her, wiping her eyes with her hands. "The police said you needed to be missing for 48 hours before they would look into it. That's when my brothers got involved. I should let them know you're safe. I left Gray at the station and Grif has been sitting across the street in his Jeep the whole evening."

"I'll do it." Verrin offered, giving Cass's forehead a quick peck before standing and heading for the front door. "Savvy, will you sit with her for a bit while I talk to your brother? I want to draw her a bath and make her some food too."

291

"Yeah, sure." Savvy nodded, climbing to her feet and sitting beside Cass. The two women hugged and just stayed that way, glad everything had worked out as Verrin left the room.

"Cassie, are you ever going to tell me what's really going on here?" Savvy spoke quietly once they were alone. "I know something has been up with you."

Cass thought about everything that had happened. God, had it really been only a week. It felt like a lifetime. Everything with Verrin had just happened so fast and then this, she just didn't know what to make of it. Giving herself a little shake, she met Savvy's eyes. "Yes, I will. I want to tell you all of it, but not tonight."

"Can you tell me something? I feel like I've been missing out on something major for days."

She hesitated a second, pulling at a loose thread on the throw. "A woman broke in and kidnapped me. She seemed to want something from Verrin. She took me and Verrin came to my rescue. Honestly, I'm not even sure all the details yet."

Savvy frowned. "Okay. Well, that's something I suppose."

Cass laughed even as her eyes teared up a bit. "Yeah. It is the craziest story ever."

"Promise you'll fill me in when you get all the details?" Savvy pressed.

"Pinkie swear," Cass smirked, sticking her little finger out. When Savvy curled hers around it, they both smiled before relaxing into the sofa.

CHAPTER 29

Three Weeks Later

Cassidy wiped her hands quickly on a dishtowel and hurried to the door when she heard a car pull up outside. It was less than a week to Christmas and this was their last girls night before the holidays officially rolled in.

Opening the big oak door she grinned widely at the sight that greeted her. Savvy was just coming around the side of her car, hands full of grocery bags, as she admired the Christmas lights that graced the edges of the Victorian-like gilding. Snow covered every unmoving surface in a blanket of fluffy white snow.

"This place looks awesome!" Savvy commented, carefully making her way up the few steps that led to the porch. "It's like your own winter wonderland."

"Thanks! I wanted to break with tradition a little." Cass grinned, reaching out to help with the bags as her friend came in. "White just seemed too plain."

"I love the blue, purple and green. It definitely stands out." Savvy praised, shrugging out of her coat and hanging it up. A wry chuckle broke from her as she bent over to unzip her cute low heeled ankle boots. "Makes me think I should put a little effort into my place. Maybe Gerard could use some Christmas lights and tinsel."

Cassidy snickered at the image of the sad little round cactus that was the only companion in Savvy's tiny apartment. "I don't think cacti count as Christmas trees."

"Then why do they have Christmas cacti?" Savvy questioned as she sauntered into the kitchen, putting her bags on the island. "Hey, where's your love slave?"

Cass rolled her eyes and started emptying groceries out of bags. "Verrin should be along soon. He said he had to stop somewhere before he came over."

"He does know I bring the food to these things, right?" Savvy asked, quirking a delicate brow as she scooted her butt up onto a stool. "I don't know if I can deal if he messes up our Friday night ritual."

Cass sighed and put a box of microwave popcorn beside the microwave. "As I promised you last weekend, he knows the deal. This is a trial run. If he screws up girls night, he gets voted off the Island."

Savvy gave an odd little snort. "Yeah right. You're too sweet on him and you know it. He'd have himself back in your good graces in no time."

Cass couldn't help a little blush, but she wouldn't deny it. Since her kidnapping at Empusa's hands and the subsequent attack of his younger brother upon her, Verrin had done anything and everything he could for her. From insisting that she allow his brother, Merihem, to look at her injuries to holding her hand and answering any question she'd asked, he had been an open book. He'd even sat beside her and helped explain everything to Savvy, including Verrin's status as Incubus, when Cass had thought the time was right.

Savvy had taken it surprisingly well. The freaking out had been minimal and consisted mostly of the 'you have got to be kidding me' sort. The blonde had railed at Verrin for getting her friend mixed up in his mess without telling her about it, but she soon simmered when she realized that Verrin was beating himself up about it more than she ever could.

For his part, Verrin had tried to do everything he could for her. He had given her space when she'd requested it and then been there, alert and comforting, for her late night phone calls when she woke up in a panic. He'd even helped her come up with a plausible reason for her injuries to explain her absence to her boss.

Last weekend he had given her time to enjoy girls night with Savvy before taking her out to the movies on Saturday. It had felt like an actual date with him picking her up at her house and going for dinner before seeing the latest superhero movie.

Dinner had been great but the movie she would have to watch again. Toward the end, Verrin had cautiously slipped his hand into hers and pulled it to his lips. He'd pressed a chaste kiss to every finger tip and that was when her concentration went to hell in a hand basket. She missed the movie's ending because she had been preoccupied thinking about the sex god sitting beside her.

Tuesday he'd showed up to take her out to get Christmas decorations, asking her to humour him as he'd never had the opportunity to really celebrate Christmas before. When he'd explained that he was born before the tradition and, while his brothers might get together, they'd never actually celebrated the holiday. She'd given in and he had bought hundreds of lights and even a cute snowman decoration for her front porch. In fact, anything she appeared interested in was thrown into the cart and she'd had to talk him down from more than a few expensive impulsive buys. When she'd come back from work Wednesday to see him on the roof stringing lights along the eaves, she'd called him down just to hug him.

A scuffling from the front of the house had both women looking at each other.

"It sounds like someone's at the door," Savvy stated the obvious, reaching for her purse and withdrawing a small black aerosol canister of deodorant spray. Ever since Cass had told her of her almost successful air freshener self-defence method, Savvy had started carrying one of the little cans. "I got your back."

Cass took a deep breath, thoroughly done with uninvited visitors, and hope to hell it was Verrin. Without a word, she swung open the door only to stop and stare.

Her doorway was entirely filled with the fresh green branches of a towering balsam fir.

"Hey, Cass! Surprise!" Verrin's head poked out from behind it and his smile was radiant. He noticed the blonde at her side and gave her a nod. "Oh good, Savvy's here too!"

The tree tipped precariously and both women put hands out to stop it, exclamations of worry cut off when Verrin seemed to balance it again.

"Oops. Hey, would one of you mind grabbing the stand from the back of my truck while I get this inside?" Verrin asked, trying to wedge the plump tree through the door without damaging either.

"I'll grab it!" Cass stepped aside to slide her feet into her sneakers and let Verrin and his burden pass. Savvy followed the tree, making sure nothing was knocked over in its wake.

Cass didn't bother with her coat when she stepped outside and made her way carefully across the driveway, avoiding the icy spots. Verrin's brand new black pickup truck was parked at the curb and she had to climb up onto the convenient tailgate step just so she could see in the back. Grabbing a bag that bulged with a plastic tree stand and another that overflowed with beaded garland and shimmering ornaments she hustled back into the warmth of the house.

Kicking off her shoes she followed her guests into the living room to watch Verrin try to find the perfect corner for the tree. Settling on the one between the window and the TV he managed to get it standing in no time.

Their evening was perfection. Relaxed and joyful as they decorated the tree while watching a marathon of Die Hard movies and munching on cookies and popcorn. With her house decorated for Christmas and her two favourite people in it, Cass couldn't have been happier.

When Savvy announced that she had an early morning ahead of her and had to leave, Verrin had looked at her speculatively. For the last few weeks, they had hardly ever been truly alone. They went out on dates or stayed in with Savvy but there was always a chaperone, a comfort level that Verrin seemed wary of breaching.

As Savvy got her shoes on and waved goodbye, Verrin followed her to the door, reaching for his own winter coat.

"Are you leaving?" Cass couldn't help asking from the kitchen archway.

Verrin paused, one arm in his black coat and stared at her. "I figured I should probably give you some space."

Cass glanced at the floor, using her bare toe to follow a seam in the hardwood. "And if I have had enough space?" She asked shyly.

Verrin's jacket hit in a pool of fabric and he was standing before her, big hands framing her face as he tilted her chin up so she'd meet his eyes. "Have you?" He asked, almost breathless in his excitement. "It's okay if you haven't. I'll do anything you need to feel good about this. I just -"

Cass's grin cut off his rambling. She pointed up, over their heads at the mistletoe Savvy had hung in the doorway, and giggled as Verrin's eyes widened. "You might want to take that as a sign!" She laughed, reaching up to tug his big body down toward hers.

"Oh, Cass..." The way he said her name was like a prayer and in an instant she was wrapped in his big arms, their lips meeting in a passion driven kiss. "By all the gods, I have never tasted a mouth as sweet as yours. You're perfect. I think I've been half in love with you from the very start."

Cass could feel happy tears welling up, but she just blinked them away, wrapping her arms around his neck and getting lost in the kiss and his roving hands.

"God, if you were mine -" Verrin mumbled against her throat as he trailed kisses down the column of her neck.

"I'm pretty sure I am yours, Verrin." She told him, catching his now shining azure eyes. "I think I've been half in love with you for weeks." She winked and saw the happiness take over his face.

The polite, watchful Verrin was gone, leaving with her fear and doubts. The man that was left was the cocky, loving man she couldn't resist giving her heart to.

"Only half in love?" He teased, hands slipping down to grab her butt and grind her into his straining erection. "I think you may have hit your head. Once you get reacquainted with my best feature you'll find your heart is entirely mine." He hefted her up, coaxing her limbs to wrap around his waist and neck tightly, so he could carry her up the stairs to her bedroom.

She couldn't help but laugh at this man who jogged up the stairs as if he'd been given the keys to the kingdom and couldn't wait to explore.

***

Seir slipped a pair of dark sunglasses on as he stepped out of the international arrivals lobby of Narita Airport and into the fading winter sunshine of Tokyo. With the sun setting, he'd need the lenses to keep his eyes hidden as they still bore a faint glow he couldn't seem to shed. He kept his head down and hiked the duffel bag holding his meager belongings higher on his shoulder, heading for one of the waiting taxis.

Since his time as Empusa's captive, he'd been having issues keeping his nature under control. His lust was running rampant, making even a casual association with a woman difficult. His eyes were still glowing like banked coals and would ignite into full glow any time a woman touched him. His cock was in a perpetual state of semi-erection and wearing jeans had become a test of endurance. Add to that the need to have a woman every day or his grasp on reality started to fade and he was in pretty rough shape.

He tossed his duffel into a taxi and slid in after it before directing the driver to a hotel nearby. He already had a room arranged and an appointment to keep. Dropping his head back on the headrest, Seir closed his eyes and tried to ignore the lust heating his blood.

The flight from California had been a long one, made doubly so because he'd had to crush his tall frame into an economy seat beside a single mom and her six year old daughter. If it hadn't been for the young child, he'd have lured the woman into the bathroom with him for some mile-high action. Instead, he'd spent the time cursing his luck and playing shark versus Barbie. The kid, Emma, had obviously seen too much Shark Week in her short life because she insisted on not only being the shark but also winning.

The burner phone in his jeans pocket buzzed and he drew it out, glancing at the notification on the display. New text message. He swiped it open and quickly read the text. I have arrived. The number was saved into the phone, but there was no name under the contact information. It was just a series of random digits that made up a tentative connection with another being.

Instead of replying, Seir slipped the phone back into his pocket. He could see the hotel's bulk looming through the front window as the driver turned onto the stretch of pavement that led under the portico. The taxi glided to a stop in front of the main doors and Seir tugged his wallet out of his back pocket to pull a few bills out and pay the driver. "Keep the change." He mumbled as he climbed out, slinging his bag onto his shoulder again.

The hotel lobby was bustling as he stepped through the double doors. Businessmen hurried across the marble floor, looking far too preoccupied to take in the splendor of their surroundings. A family walked toward the check-in desk, the mother's arms full of squirming toddler and the father loaded down with luggage like a pack mule. A redhead woman in a knee length pencil skirt and towering black heels gave him a warm smile as she headed into the car rental office tucked off to one side of the expansive room. His dick gave a desirous twitch, wanting him to follow the female, but he was on a strict no red heads diet.

Check in was quick and painless. He had his key card within moments and the clerk directed him to the eighth floor with a genuine smile. He thanked the young man and took the elevators up to the top floor, searching through the suite numbers until he found 807. A swipe of the key card and he was in.

The room was almost too extravagant by his standards. Seir had gotten used to a pretty cushy existence over the years at home in his villa, but this went beyond that. The marble floors from the lobby continued up here but now they had an inlaid gold and white marble trim that marked the perimeter of the room. The high white ceiling was sectioned into decorative square panels and the walls were a shimmering burnished gold. A white sofa and two chairs sat on a rug in front of a glassed-in fireplace, the furniture seeming far too delicate with its little wooden legs to hold his large frame. Floor to ceiling glass windows made up the far wall and he was sure that feature spread into the two bedrooms that branched off on either side of the common room.

The room was certainly an improvement from the dives he'd been living in for the past few weeks. Then again, he wasn't the one who'd picked it out.

The door to the bedroom on the left opened and his guest appeared, her delicate silk kimono almost see through on her willowy frame. She tucked a stray strand of her ebony hair behind her ear and leaned her shoulder on the door frame. "I trust your flight went well?"

"As well as can be expected," Seir answered, making sure the door was sufficiently locked behind him before he strode farther into the apartment. He dropped his duffel bag on the end of the couch and added his black leather jacket to it a moment later. "Thank you for meeting me here, Chiyo."

The woman smiled, her soft pink lips curving sweetly in her pale countenance. "It is my pleasure – or it soon will be." She gave a negligent shrug and came towards him. "I do not often leave my territory, but for you I will make an exception."

Seir caught her shoulders and pulled her into his body, carefully melding his solid length against her small form. He leaned down, catching her lips with his own in a lingering kiss. "I appreciate the sacrifice both you and the city of Nagano have made for my well being."

Her laugh was a tinkling sound, like wind through ice covered branches. "You are such a sweet talker, Seir-sama."

Seir growled playfully at her as he scooped her up into his arms. She circled his shoulders and giggled like a young girl as he stalked into the bedroom, using his foot to kick the door shut in their wake. He lifted her to stand on the end of the palatial mattress, her slight weight not making a dent in the bed spread. In this position she stood about a head taller than his six and a half foot height, giving him a perfect view of her compact body. Reaching out, he tugged at the belt of her kimono, loosening the silky fabric and brushing it off her slim shoulders.

Chiyo smiled down at him and stroked a hand through his hair until she cupped his jaw. "Is there a reason you asked for a secret encounter, Incubus? Who are you hiding from?"

Seir could feel a grim smile tug at the corner of his lips. "Lady of the Snow, you are ever observant." He leaned forward, pressing his lips between her breasts and kissing his way from one pale nipple to the other in an effort to distract her.

"That is not an answer, Seir-sama." Chiyo murmured softly.

"So very observant." Seir hedged, nuzzling her smooth flesh before sucking her nipple into his mouth. The moan she rewarded him with made his erection throb. Circling an arm around her hips, he took her down to the mattress, crawling up the length of her body as he went.

Hours later he stared at the ceiling in the darkened hotel room, Chiyo's slight body sprawled over his in exhaustion. Yuki Onna might be mythical wandering snow spirits, but they were not created to handle an Incubus any better than an average mortal woman. Multiple positions and multiple orgasms later and the Lady of the Snow was thoroughly worn out.

Seir stared at the paneled ceiling, wanting to close his eyes and drift off, yet that goal was unattainable.

Since his time in Empusa's tender care, he'd had

trouble sleeping. His mind was haunted, replaying images of himself performing terrible acts. Forcing a small woman down beneath him. Gutting the red headed bitch who'd held him captive. Stuffing his engorged member into a pliant female body over and over until he was sated. His hands tightening around the slender throat of a pixie-like woman with sharply pointed teeth.

He couldn't even tell what was reality and what was his tortured mind's nightmares.

Heaven above, was it any wonder he couldn't face his brothers. He was a mere shell of a man, utterly destroyed inside. The honour, the pride, even the trust, he'd once had in himself had all been carved out of him, pouring out with his blood to pool on that dungeon floor.

Giving up on sleep, Seir slid his body carefully out from beneath Chiyo's, covering her with the blanket even though her internal temperature tended to run much cooler than normal. He gathered up his clothes and eased out of the room, shutting the door behind him. Creeping over to the other bedroom, he used its bathroom to shower and dress before gathering his duffel bag and coat. He left the key card and the burner phone on the small coffee table and let himself out of the room.

If his brothers were looking for him they would eventually check in with Chiyo and it was doubtful she'd be able to keep the truth of their encounter hidden from them for long. It was better he take his leave of her. Unlike some Yuki Onna, Chiyo was a good woman. She had been while alive and was more so now that she was immortal. She would want to help him if she knew what was going on in his head and Seir couldn't have that.

Waiting for the elevator, he caught sight of the

shimmering glow of his blue-violet eyes in the metallic door and sighed. The remnants of his captivity were in no hurry to leave him be. He dug into his duffel for his sunglasses and slid them on just as the doors glided open.

ABOUT THE AUTHOR

Sarah Winters lives in Prince Edward Island, Canada. She has been writing since she was in elementary school and self-published her first book in 2017. Having always had an active imagination and an introvert personality, writing seemed the best career choice. She believes you can never have enough socks and always needs more bookshelves for her ever expanding library. She writes best on rainy days with a glass of iced tea beside her and her writer dog, Tails, at her feet.

For more information about Sarah Winters or her books visit www.SarahWinters.ca

Made in the USA
Columbia, SC
22 May 2017